IN GREEN PASTURES

✥ BOOK THREE ✥
MYSTERIOUS WAYS

A Frontier Novel by

Donna Westover Gallup

CLADACH
Publishing

Copyright © 2010 by Donna Westover Gallup
All rights reserved.
Published by CLADACH Publishing
P.O. Box 336144 Greeley, CO 80633
www.CLADACH.com

Cover Art: "Colorado Splendor" by Dan Young
View more of Mr. Young's work at www.danyoungstudio.com.

This is a work of fiction. Names, characters, places, and incidents either are the product of the author's imagination or are used fictitiously, and any resemblance to actual persons, living or dead, business establishments, events, or locations is entirely coincidental.

Library of Congress Cataloging-in-Publication Data:

Gallup, Donna Westover, 1958-
In green pastures : a frontier novel / by Donna Westover Gallup.
p. cm. -- (Mysterious ways ; bk. 3)
ISBN 978-0-9818929-1-7
1. Colorado--Fiction. I. Title.
PS3607.A4226I5 2010
813'.6--dc22
2009042798

ISBN-10: 0981892914
ISBN-13: 9780981892917
Printed in the United States of America

Praise for ROCK OF REFUGE (Mysterious Ways #2)

"[In this] follow-up to *White As Snow*, Charlie continues to learn about himself and his trust in God, getting hit with a bout of restlessness, leading him to ride towards Denver, where on his journey he learns about honor and trust. A deftly-written and excellently-researched novel. It's highly recommended to western fans everywhere and deserves a place on community library fiction shelves." ~ ***Midwest Book Review***

"*Rock of Refuge* is a good choice for high school students and adults. Male readers will especailly enjoy Charlie's adventures." ~ *Cari Young,* ***The Old Schoolhouse Magazine***

"A faith-strengthening novel for the entire family to enjoy together!" ~ *Kris Price, Sr. Editor,* ***HomesteadBlogger.com***

"Mixes Colorado history and the thrill of a western with a deeper story of faith." ~ *Erin Frustaci,* ***Fort Collins Now***

"A story of faith, love, and community prevailing in the tumultous Colorado Territory. A sensitive story of intergenerational love, respect, and surrender." ~ *Dr. Marc Johnson, Dean of the College of Agricultural Sciences, Colorado State University*

"Exciting, thought provoking, emotion stirring, historically and spiritually enlightening read.... I felt as if I were there on the cattle drive and sharing the campfire at the day's end. I was transported to the big city of Denver and felt [Charlie's] awe and wonder and uncertainty. I laughed and I cried as I traveled with Charlie on his journey towards adulthood both physically, emotionally and spiritually." ~ *Maurica C. Johnson*

"Wonderful books (*White As Snow* and *Rock of Refuge*). I couldn't put them down...." ~ *Marilyn Musgrave, former U. S. Congresswoman from Colorado*

"My 14-year-old son received *White As Snow* as a gift and he absolutely loved it and asked for the sequel. I purchased *Rock of Refuge* for him and now he is asking for the third! Bless you for writing such engaging, wholesome books. We can't wait for more!" ~ *Colleen Beckett*

"The Lord is my Shepherd
I shall not want.
He maketh me to lie down in green pastures,
He leadeth me beside still waters,
He restoreth my soul."

Psalm 23:1-3

*To my children
~ Michealle, Melissa, and Melanie
Reid, Ben, and Scott ~
the joy of my life.*

1872
Colorado Territory

1

CHARLIE PRESSED HIS FOREHEAD AGAINST the window pane and looked across the pasture. His gaze then followed the ridges of the foothills, covered with clumps of yellow flowers and puff balls.

He opened the door and a cool breeze rushed him. He watched, almost against his will, as hundreds of the fairy-winged seedlings lifted from the golden clusters and scurried on their way to new destinations. It was silly of him, but he envied them. He hated the sight of them, but he envied their freedom in being released to fly.

He walked out to the remains of his garden and kicked at a thick dandelion with the toe of his boot, releasing another small, round ball of seeds. "Go on," he muttered, watching as they, too, scattered on the breeze.

He got down on his knees. The soil was moist and cold. A slight chill ran up his spine. It was spring, but blankets of snow still skirted rock formations and hid in cold shadows of trees. Skyward, the mountain peaks were buried deep, not yet free from winter's cold grip. He shoved the hand hoe into the thawing ground and began to dig around endless weed roots. What a stubborn lot. He groaned.

I hope we get enough money out of Cousin Ralph's estate to buy one of those John Deere plows they have at the mercantile. Then I won't have to do this any more! He yanked at the weed, but the root had wormed itself deep into the soil and didn't budge.

Why don't wild roses and lavender bushes pop up like this every spring? At least they smell pretty. That thought brought Amelia to mind. He sat back on his heels and smiled. The bits of memory he had of her sea-green eyes, her auburn hair, and the way she smelled of sweet lavender was never far from the front of his thoughts. *I wonder what she's doing right now.*

Charlie stared into space and another tingle ran up his spine. *Maybe we'll hear from Judge Walker soon and Grandpa and I can go to Denver. Maybe it won't be long before I see her again.* He frowned. He probably wouldn't know what to say to her if he did see her again, but there was always hope that something would come to mind; something more than just a goofy, tongue tied version of "hello." He wanted to allow his mind to drift through his memories, but he forced his attention back to the garden and finished his tug-o-war with a large mass of leaves and roots piled in his gloved hand. Triumphantly he tossed the whole thing into the wheelbarrow. The sense of victory waned, though, as he took in what lay around him.

He crawled over the next clump of yellow weeds and plunged the hoe deep into the ground. He dug with one hand and pulled with the other. Dig, pull, dig, pull. The strength of the little buggers was maddening, but—

What was that? He cocked his head and listened. Nothing came back to him. He pulled a glove off and laid his palm flat against the ground. After a few seconds, the corners of his mouth started to curve upward. He felt the slight vibrations under his knees, like thunder beneath the earth, before he heard any noise.

The hoe slid from his fingers and fell to the earth with a soft thud. Before long, the echo of pounding hooves bounced off the hills above him. Someone was riding up hard and fast. Charlie remembered another rider pushing his horse so vigorously to get to the cabin—but that was a long time ago ... back in the winter of '64, when a giant of a mountain man named Jess, seemed to come out of nowhere to rescue Charlie and Grandpa. Charlie was just a boy then, and he and Grandpa were in an awful way. But Jess found them and stayed with them until he knew Charlie felt secure in his own faith and Grandpa was recovering from an illness, and back on his feet. Charlie never could figure out who Jess really was—a guardian angel? Jesus personified?—but for him, it didn't matter. He was just glad the big man had come into their lives ... and continued to, often at unexpected times.

He jumped up and brushed dirt from his pants then dropped his gloves to the ground. He lobbed his legs over the fence and headed to the front of the cabin. He raised a hand to shade his eyes and scan the prairie. A small cloud of dust floated across the grassland toward him. He studied it till he recognized the rider—Wilbur Tuttle.

Wilbur had been Charlie's best friend since they were little boys, but since Wilbur'd secured a job at the Pueblo post office his visits had been few and far between. Charlie waved happily.

As Wilbur got closer, he didn't appear to be slowing down. Charlie stared. The horse was practically at the cabin door before Wilbur pulled back on the reins and hollered, "Whoa."

The horse skidded to a stop. Dirt flew in all directions.

Charlie jumped aside. "I wondered if you were gonna ride on in," he said, wiping his face with the back of his sleeve.

Wilbur slid from the saddle and threw the reins on the hitching post. His lathered, exhausted horse rested its muzzle on the cross bar.

Charlie reached over and wiped a blotch of foam from the

gelding's face. "Where's the fire, Wilbur?" he teased, wiping his fingers on Wilbur's jacket.

Wilbur took his hat off and mopped sweat from his forehead. He put it back on with a tug and looked at his wet sleeve. "That's not funny, Charlie." His tone was sober.

Charlie frowned. "What? It's just—" Then it dawned on him that it wasn't what he had done, but what he had said that upset his friend. He searched Wilbur's face. "You're right, that wasn't funny. I shouldn't bring up such raw memories. After all, Mary Lou's funeral wasn't that long ago."

Wilbur's sister had died the previous year in the great Chicago fire. He shouldn't be so careless—of course those painful memories would still be fresh in his friend's mind.

Wilbur nodded but didn't pursue the subject. Fidgeting with a loose nail on the hitching post, he got right down to business. "I need to see your grandfather," he announced importantly. "Got a letter for 'im . . . from Denver."

Charlie's heart jumped into his throat. "About the settlement? Can I see it?"

Wilbur glanced at the cabin door and then at Charlie. "No. It's from that judge your grandpa met with last fall. It came in yesterday and the chief said I had to deliver it myself, straight to him and no one else."

Just then the door hinges squawked and a pale, wrinkled hand, with thin, gnarled fingers pushed the cabin door outward. Grandpa stepped out onto the stoop, his translucent features sharp in the bright afternoon sun.

"Did I hear you say you got somethin' for me, Wilbur?" Grandpa asked quietly, his voice quivering ever so slightly.

Wilbur circled the hitching post, nervously licking his lips, and pulled an envelope from his shirt pocket. "Yessiree, I do."

Charlie noticed both men's hands trembling as Grandpa reached for the letter. The old man stared at it for a second then muttered, "Can't see a darn thing without my glasses." Turning away, he pulled the door open and retreated into the shadows of the cabin.

"What do you reckon it's about?" asked Wilbur.

"Can't say," mumbled Charlie. He leaned sideways to watch Grandpa go inside. "How 'bout some water?"

Wilbur glanced at Charlie, then back at the closing door. "Sure," he muttered disappointedly. He yanked the reins from the hitching post and followed Charlie to the back of the cabin. His horse, still panting, lagged behind.

Charlie hauled the bucket up from the well's depths.

Ladling a drink and eyeing his friend, he asked nonchalantly, "So, what's new?"

Wilbur ignored him. He gulped noisily then dipped the ladle back for a second round. His horse was at the trough making just as much noise. Over in the corral, Charlie's horse, Star, rested his muzzle on the high bar and watched intently.

Charlie leaned against the well and waited. Wilbur looked tired. A salt stain encircled the rim of his hat. His face was sallow; his eyes were sunken and dark. His skin was already deeply tanned for this time of year. But what surprised Charlie were Wilbur's hands—bloodied and bruised. It was manual labor that left a man's hands like that, not working in a post office. He asked in a low voice, "How's the family, Wilbur? Everything all right?"

Wilbur tilted the ladle to his mouth, then wiped his face with the back of his sleeve. He avoided Charlie's eyes. "They're fine. Nothin' I can't handle," he muttered.

Charlie grasped his friend's arm.

Wilbur's eyes flashed anger, but Charlie held his gaze. "Talk to me, Wilbur."

Wilbur slowly set the ladle inside the bucket, never taking his eyes off Charlie.

"What's goin' on?"

Wilbur's face darkened; red blotches filled the hollows of his cheeks. "We're fine," he repeated firmly. He jerked his arm away and headed for his horse. "Everything's fine."

"I could help, if you'd tell me what's wrong."

Wilbur swung his leg up over his horse and plopped into the saddle. Adjusting his hat, he forced a smile. "You take care of your business here, Charlie. No tellin' what that letter said. And I'll take care of my business at home. Don't worry 'bout us, I know how to take care of my own family."

Charlie raised his eyebrows. "I'm sure you do, but—"

"Oh, I almost forgot. There's a letter for you." Charlie squinted up at his friend, not certain he'd heard him right, but Wilbur was digging a dirty white envelope out of his jacket pocket. Charlie reached for it, glancing at the return address: "Miss Amelia Taylor." Without another word, Wilbur whipped his horse around, clicked his tongue, and shot out onto the prairie. Charlie, fighting the urge to rip open the envelope right then and there, shoved it into the pocket of his jeans. He had more important things to think of first.

He watched Wilbur disappear over the hill. "You're not headin' back to Pueblo, that's for sure," he murmured. "You're headin' home. I'll have to find out what's goin' on, but in the meantime . . ." He looked back at the cabin. "I gotta see what ol' Judge Walker had to say to Grandpa."

2

AT THEIR SMALL KITCHEN TABLE GRANDPA sat crumpling a piece of paper in his fist. He was staring over the glasses resting on the tip of his nose, as if lost in thought.

Charlie pulled out a chair, swung it around and straddled it. Folding his arms across the back, he leaned in toward Grandpa. "Well, out with it. What'd the letter say?"

Grandpa scowled slightly, still staring into thin air.

"Grandpa, you all right?" Charlie waved a hand in front of the cloudy eyes.

The aged eyelids fluttered. "Mm, yeah. . . . I think."

"Well?! What is it?"

A smile slid across Grandpa's face, pushing blankets of wrinkles from his high cheekbones up to the corners of his eyes. "Here." He slid the letter over to Charlie. "Read it yerself."

Charlie smoothed the letter, then read aloud:

March 30, 1872

Mr. Stuart C. Smith
Pueblo, Colorado Territory

Dear Mr. Smith,
   Per our meeting last September, this letter is to confirm that the following transactions have been completed:
   The Deed to six hundred acres, house, barn, corrals, and all out buildings formerly owned by the late Ralph Smith, Saint Charles, Missouri has been signed and delivered to our office, and

is now officially and legally the property of Mr. Stuart Charles Smith and Mr. Charles Edward Smith of Pueblo, Colorado Territory.

All debts related to the late Mr. Ralph Smith have been paid in full by his estate. Total estate worth prior to Mr. Ralph Smith's death was recorded at $5,789,025.75. After debt pay-off, a balance of $5,246,100.14 has been deposited into the account of Mr. Stuart C. Smith and Mr. Charles E. Smith, Bank of Denver, Colorado Territory.

Upon receipt of these documents, a final Will and Testament has been drawn up by the office of Mr. Atkins, attorney for Mr. Stuart C. Smith and Mr. Charles E. Smith and is ready for signature.

Please come to Denver at your earliest convenience in order to sign your final will and speak with your accountant, Mr. Stanley Abel. No appointment is necessary.

At your service,
Timothy Atkins, Esquire

Charlie finished in a barely audible voice. He lifted his head and stared out the back door, beyond the dandelions, beyond the hills. Thunder had struck again.

The world became still and quiet, except for the pounding noise that filled his head.

Numbers and words tumbled around in his skull. A dull pain ached behind his eyes. The air felt suddenly so thick and stagnant he could hardly breathe. Even the animal chatter outside had grown silent. No cows mooed, no crows cawed, no eagles soared, nothing seemed to move.

A minute passed, validated by a muted *thunk* from the mantle clock. Charlie got up slowly, his chair scraping across the wood floor. The sound blotted out the noise in his head, but didn't help the ache behind his eyes.

He and Grandpa were millionaires! Quietly, he went out the back door, to the garden. *Was it just today that I was here last? Or a lifetime ago?* He knelt in the dandelions, scooped up a handful of dirt and let it sift between his fingers. He picked up the hand hoe and poked absently at the ground.

His mind raced. He thought of how strange Wilbur had acted. Wilbur might need his help; but Charlie wanted to go to Denver. The hoe slipped from his hand, and he got up and went to the barn, where he liked to do his thinking.

Alone in the cabin, Grandpa tucked the letter into his vest pocket. He wasn't sure what to think of it all, but one thing was certain: about an hour, come hail or high water, his grandson would want to eat, so he'd better get started on supper. He pushed himself up from the table and shuffled over to the cupboards. "Hope I can think straight," he mumbled as he pulled ingredients from the shelves. "Be a shame to ruin a good pot o' beans."

Time passed and finally he slid a pan of biscuits onto the table. He stood at the door and hollered, "Charlie!"

"Yessir," came the reply.

"Wash up, son, it'd be supper time."

"Comin'."

Grandpa had just put the fried rabbit and lima beans on the table when he heard the outhouse door slam. The second slam was followed by the squealing of the bucket being pulled up from the well. Then, shortly, Charlie was once again taking his seat at the small table.

Grandpa started to say the blessing a couple of times, but either lost his train of thought or fell asleep, Charlie couldn't tell which.

Finally the old man took a deep breath and said, "Thank

Mysterious Ways

you, Lord, for everythin'. Amen." He looked a bit sheepish as he handed Charlie the bowl of lima beans. Then he said quietly, "Mighty surprisin' letter, huh?"

Charlie put the bowl down and sat back in his chair. He ran his fingers through his hair and frowned at his plate. "I never knew this involved so much. I knew some debts had to be settled and there was an inheritance involved, along with some land near Saint Louie, but nothin' like this." He picked up his fork and pushed his beans around. "Yep, I guess I'm a bit numb."

"I know, boy," mumbled Grandpa. "I didn't know it myself until I read that letter. Judge Walker told me that Ralph did all right by hisself and that once the debts were settled, I'd be okay too, but I had no idea of the extent." Looking off in the distance, Grandpa murmured, "Five million dollars. How much money is that, really?"

"Grandpa, what are you gonna do with five million dollars and six hundred acres of land we've never seen?"

Grandpa glanced at Charlie then turned back to his food. Lifting his fork to his mouth, he smiled. "What else would I do, boy? Give 'em to you."

"Me? Why? I wouldn't know what to do with that much money, or land. What if I blow it all on foolishness?" Grandpa placed a feeble, yet firm hand on his arm. There was no doubt he meant business.

"Charlie, I'm going to tell you something."

Charlie stabbed his fork at his beans.

"I'm old, Charlie," began Grandpa.

Charlie sighed and rolled his eyes. "Stop right there, Grandpa. You're not old. You might be a mite tired and all, but you've got to—"

"Listen, boy!" commanded Grandpa. "The Lord has given me a good, full life, Charlie. I've seen lots during my seventy some years and I've been blessed more than a man deserves, but just as there is a beginning, there is an end, and I believe mine is overdue."

Charlie slumped in his chair.

"I know you don't wanna hear this, but you've got to. I can see—everybody can see—it's my time to go. And you need to move on with your own life." Grandpa spoke with authority.

Charlie swallowed hard.

"I know you feel safe here," continued Grandpa. "And you're used to me bein' around; but you saw a smidgen of the big world out there on your cattle drive, and you liked it."

Charlie cast his eyes downward. Grandpa placed a hand on his shoulder. "It's okay, son. There's explorin' to do, adventures to live."

The old man sat back and sighed. "I sure was surprised when all this nonsense with Ralph came up, and plenty annoyed about havin' to deal with it; but now I see it was a blessing from God. No matter when the good Lord calls me home, now I know you'll be taken care of, and I can go home in peace."

Charlie squirmed in his seat.

Grandpa ignored him. "So, we need to get ready and head on up to Denver soon as we can."

Charlie's eyes met his grandfather's. "We do?" he muttered.

"Like the letter says, I've got to go and finalize everythin'. I left instructions last time that if anythin' happened to me, everythin' was to go to you. But since I can make it back, I need to go, just to tie up the loose ends."

"I understand that, Grandpa." Charlie frowned. "But what

does all this have to do with me? I mean, of course I'll go with you. I want to go with you. But this is *your* business, isn't it?"

"No; it's your business. I need to go to sign some papers; you need to go because you need to meet certain folks. I wasn't kiddin' when I said I was leavin' all this to you, so I want you to meet the bull o' the woods, Judge Walker. But more important, you need to meet this Stanley Abel, your accountant. He'll help you oversee your finances. And Timothy Atkins. He'll be your attorney. He's the one who'll make sure no one tries to steal it all from you."

Charlie turned sideways in his chair. "You make it sound so final," he said irritably.

"'Tis," replied Grandpa softly.

The young man turned, sorrow and anger mixed in his eyes. "How can you say that?"

Grandpa shrugged. "I'm not well, son. Haven't been for a long time—and honestly, I never expected to live this long." He paused. He hadn't told Charlie of the deal he'd made with the Lord while suffering a heart attack the year before. "I need the rest, boy, and you need to go on with the life that God intends for you."

"I like this life," said Charlie, forgetting how that morning he had envied the dandelions their freedom.

"Not really."

Charlie met the old eyes with a scowl.

"This life won't be here much longer. That's the part you gotta accept. Me and this farm was only the beginning of your life, Charlie. God has somethin' else planned for the rest of it."

"It sounds like you're callin' it quits," said Charlie. "Once you've got things handled in Denver, you just gonna give up?"

In Green Pastures

"No. I'm not gonna give up, but I am gonna let go."

Charlie cleared his throat. He got up and walked over to the window, turning his back to his grandfather. "I can't imagine living without . . ." He gazed out the window, sighed heavily, and asked, "When will we be leavin'?"

"Just a few days," replied Grandpa. He rubbed his chest and laid his head in the other hand.

"Don't you think we should wait until the weather mellows out some?"

Grandpa pushed himself upright and closed his eyes. Patiently he waited for the pain to subside. "No," he finally said. "Don't have time. We need to do this, get it over with."

Charlie turned from the window and faced Grandpa; he had seen nothing. "Then the end of the week it is," he said quietly. *Then everything will start to change.*

3

SPRINGTIME IS CHANCEY IN COLORADO. A body never knows quite what to expect from the weather. One day could bring a snowfall so thick a mountain man could get lost in it, but the next day could be clear and warm. Fortunately, the day after Wilbur's visit looked to be pleasant enough to allow a trip to the Tuttle farm.

Charlie slid into the saddle and gave his horse the lead. Star tossed his head in approval and took off down the road. It seemed Charlie's watch had hardly ticked off a few minutes before they had traveled the seven miles to the Tuttle place and he was reining Star into the front yard.

Charlie was pulling his foot from the stirrup when he saw his friend, Phillip LeFaye sauntering over to him. He'd befriended the lean, fine-looking Frenchman last summer while driving the last herd of Hereford cattle from the Smith farm to Fort Collins. LeFaye was a soldier then, but had since been discharged. Now he was working as a hired hand on the Tuttles' farm.

"Good to see you, Charlie," he said in his tranquil accent.

"You too." Charlie smiled. "All well?"

"All is well." LeFaye glanced toward the farmhouse.

"Grandpa and I are going to Denver in a few days. Would you mind looking after the animals for us?"

"Of course. With pleasure." LeFaye glanced around again. "Your friend Wilbur seems tense this visit."

"Yeah, I noticed that yesterday." Charlie threw the reins

around the cross bar. "He stopped by the cabin to deliver some mail and—" Charlie remembered his letter. He thrust his hands into his jacket pockets. Nothing. He moved them to the pockets of his jeans. Nothing there either. What had he done with that letter? About to panic, he remembered that he'd slipped on a different pair of pants that morning. He breathed a sigh of relief. The letter was safe, back at the cabin. He silently reprimanded himself for being so absentminded. *But then again,* he thought, *I was preoccupied with the other one. After all, it's not like we have mail delivered every day.*

LeFaye was watching him as his face contorted with these thoughts. "Are you all right, my friend?" he asked cautiously.

Charlie grinned sheepishly. "Oh; sorry. I just remembered something—or, I mean I forgot something. Aw, never mind."

The cabin door jerked open. Both men turned to see Wilbur, who asked gruffly, "What are you doing here, Charlie? Did I forget to give you something yesterday?"

Charlie removed his hat and stepped up to his friend. "No. You didn't forget anything." He searched Wilbur's eyes. "I didn't know I needed a reason to come over here."

"You don't!" a female voice sounded from within the cabin. "Step aside, Wilbur and let 'im in."

Wilbur glared at Charlie and stepped aside. Mrs. Tuttle hurried to the door, the gathers of her gingham dress flowing behind her. She grabbed Charlie's cheeks in her plump fingers and drew his face down toward her own. Feeling his face grow warm, he bent and gave her a peck on the cheek.

She beamed. "How are you, Charlie?"

"I'm fine, ma'am," he said through lips puckered like a fish. "How are you?"

The twinkle in her eyes was just as vibrant, just as bright

Mysterious Ways

as it had always been. "Oh you silly child," she said merrily. Letting go of his face, she stood on her tiptoes and tousled his hair. "You and Phillip come in for some coffee and biscuits. Mr. Tuttle and I would love to chat with you a while. And you come join us too, Wilbur, if you can behave yourself."

Charlie smoothed his hair back down and answered, "Yes, ma'am," then nodded at LeFaye to follow him. "Coffee 'n biscuits sounds good."

Mr. Tuttle was already seated at the table, sipping a cup. Charlie motioned for him to stay there and greeted him with a warm handshake. LeFaye slid a chair close and they made themselves comfortable around the table. It saddened Charlie to see how Mr. Tuttle had aged since Mary Lou's death. He couldn't seem to get over the loss of his daughter.

"How are you, Mr. Tuttle?" he asked politely.

"As good as can be for now, I guess," said the old gentleman. "But Ma and I both are hopin' to be better real soon."

Charlie raised his eyebrows. "Really? What's goin' on?"

Mrs. Tuttle set cups of hot coffee in front of Charlie and LeFaye then took a seat at the table next to her husband. Wilbur didn't join them. He leaned against the doorframe and listened.

"Well, actually," replied Mrs. Tuttle with an edge of excitement in her voice, "we're gonna try some different scenery."

"What?" snapped Wilbur, pulling himself upright. "You're what? When? How? And when were you gonna let me know?"

"Calm down, son," said Mr. Tuttle. "Your ma and I were going to tell you this mornin'."

"Sure you were," he snorted.

Mrs. Tuttle carefully set her cup down on the table and slowly walked toward her son. "Don't talk to your pa that way," she scolded. "And we were plannin' to tell you. You just got home yesterday, Wilbur."

"I been workin' like a dog to pay—" Wilbur cut his words short and glanced at Charlie. "Never mind. But now you're sayin' you're goin' on holiday too. How on earth do you intend to pay for that? I'm doin' all—" Again he shot a glance at Charlie. This time, he shut up.

The Tuttles turned and searched each other's face for something. Charlie wasn't sure what. Then Mr. Tuttle spoke. "We're not goin' on vacation, son," he said slowly. "You've been workin' hard; we know that. We appreciate what you've done. We wouldn't go and do somethin' so frivolous as go on a holiday and leave you alone to pay for it."

Wilbur let out a heavy sigh.

"Your ma and I are actually leavin'. We're movin'. With hopes that I'll get better."

Wilbur's eyes widened and his mouth fell open.

Mrs. Tuttle looked her son in the eye and said softly, "It's for your pa. We need to go."

Wilbur's dark eyes darkened. "Where?"

"To live with your older brother. He and his family are willing to take us in and help me care for your pa."

"When?"

"As soon as we can. That's what we wanted to talk to you about. To see if you'd be willing to take over the farm. Or, if you wanted to come along, we could sell it."

"I ain't goin' with you," he spat. "But you might as well sell this place. I don't want nothin' to do with it."

Tears welled in the corners of his mother's eyes.

"That's enough, Wilbur," growled Mr. Tuttle. "There's no need—"

Mysterious Ways

"You don't know nothin' about what I need, Pa," snarled Wilbur. "And even if you did, you wouldn't care."

"Wilbur!" Mrs. Tuttle stepped away from her son. "Where is this comin' from? Why are you so angry about this?"

Wilbur's face turned crimson. Hot tears filled his eyes. "It's not just about this." He bit his bottom lip. "It's everything."

Mrs. Tuttle reached for him. "Son, sit and talk to us," she whispered. But Wilbur bristled at her touch and brushed her hand away. Turning quickly, he stomped out the door.

Mrs. Tuttle didn't move, but stared out into the yard. Fear replaced the twinkle in her eyes.

"He'll be all right, Ma," said Mr. Tuttle gently.

She turned and looked at Charlie, as if seeking his confirmation too.

"Come take a seat, Ma," encouraged Mr. Tuttle. Slowly she did and she remained quiet, as if in a trance.

"Can I get you anything, Mrs. Tuttle?" asked LeFaye.

She smiled wearily. "No, Phillip—thank you though."

Mr. Tuttle turned to Charlie. "So, what do you think about us leavin', Charlie?"

Charlie shrugged his shoulders. "I'd hate to see you go, but if it helps you get better, then I'm all for it. I mean, if you ever want to come back here, this ol' farm will be waitin'."

"But we're not sure—"

"I know. But this place should be the least of your worries right now. If you need to sell, we can help you do that later. Let's see how Mr. Tuttle does first."

The sound of horse's hooves pounded through the house as horse and rider dashed across the front yard. LeFaye jumped up and looked out the window. "It's Wilbur," he said, casting a glance back at the Tuttles.

Fear crossed Mrs. Tuttle's face again. Charlie leaned across the table to place his hand over hers. "Wilbur will be all right, ma'am. Let's take care of you and Mr. Tuttle first, and then we'll see about him."

"He's had to do so much since Mary Lou passed," she whispered. "I think he resents it."

"Maybe he does now," said Charlie. "But you know Wilbur; he'll snap out of it. And the Lord'll help 'im."

Mrs. Tuttle nodded. "I hope you're right, Charlie," she said quietly, her eyes focused somewhere out on the horizon.

Charlie pulled his chair closer to the table. "This is what we're gonna do right now," he said cheerfully. "Grandpa and I have to make a trip back to Denver to take care of some business. We'll be leaving in a few days. So, do you think you can be ready to go in a few days, too?"

Mrs. Tuttle looked startled. "Why so soon?"

Charlie cleared his throat. "We don't know if Wilbur will come back, Mrs. Tuttle," he said seriously. "But we can't wait for him to make up his mind. With Grandpa and I gone, there would only be LeFaye here to take care of both farms, and that just won't work. We've got to narrow things down all we can." Mrs. Tuttle glanced at her husband and they both nodded.

"LeFaye can stay with you and help you pack up," continued Charlie, "but once we put you on the stagecoach, he'll need to head over to our place and stay there till Grandpa and I get back. By that time, Wilbur might be settled down and hopefully, will know what he wants to do with the farm."

"Sounds good," said Mr. Tuttle, grabbing Charlie's hand and shaking it.

Charlie got up and went to the door. "I need to get back to Grandpa, but I'll come back for you in four days."

"Four days!" said Mrs. Tuttle, looking around the room and fluttering her hanky. "I better get to work. There's so much to do in four days." Charlie smiled, relieved to see the twinkle return to her eyes.

LeFaye rose from his chair. "I'll walk Charlie out," he said.

Outside, LeFaye inhaled deeply. "*Sacré bleu*," he said, shaking his arms. "I told you Wilbur was a bit tense this time!"

Charlie untied Star and swung himself up into the saddle. "He's angry." Leaning on the pommel, he looked down the road. "Really angry."

"Have you ever seen him like this before?"

Charlie shook his head. "No. Not even as a kid. Wilbur's always been pretty even tempered."

LeFaye looked up at his friend. "Well, remember him in your prayers, just as you remember me," he said with a smile.

"I will," said Charlie, as he gathered the reins in his fingers. "I'll pray. You watch him."

LeFaye's nodded. The Frenchman tugged his hat down onto his head. "I'll be watchful, Charlie."

That night after prayer, Charlie lay in his bed and listened. Grandpa snorted in his sleep and mumbled something incomprehensible. The fire warmed Charlie's face.

Outside, wind stirred and floated through barren trees and down mountainsides. A coyote serenaded her pups. Then another shrill voice rose from the darkness and joined the wild song. At times, the noise seemed close to the cabin, but then it fell back among the dark hills. Some animal was fighting for its life, out there in the night. The shrieking and howling lasted for some time. Then silence. The prey had apparently surrendered. Logs crackled in the fireplace. Charlie's eyes grew heavy.

4

SIX MUSCULAR HORSES PULLED A TRAVELworn stagecoach north. Its huge wheels bounced down the jutted road, sending a giant plume of dust skyward. Charlie and LeFaye watched it from where they stood on the boardwalk in front of the Pueblo Hotel.

Charlie waved his hat in the air one last time just in case either one of the elder Tuttles was looking back. He wanted them to know someone was there and sorry they were leaving. Wilbur had never come back home after hearing his parents were going to his brother's house; it was only Charlie and LeFaye who saw them off.

"Feel bad," Charlie mumbled, slapping dust off his hat.

LeFaye gathered the horses' reins and handed Star's to Charlie. "Why?"

"Well, the Tuttles always had some kinda shindig for anyone who was comin' or goin', but when it's their time to leave, there's only us to send them off."

"They understand, Charlie," assured LeFaye. "And if I know Mrs. Tuttle like I think I do, she'll hold you to owing her one next time she sees you."

Charlie broke into a wide grin. "I hope she does."

The Frenchman stepped onto the street, his horse behind him. Half turning he said, "I'll meet you in front of the saddlery when you've finished your business there. I shouldn't be in the post office long. Just want to get this box off for the Tuttles so it'll be there when they arrive."

"See you there," answered Charlie.

Charlie led Star a little farther down the street until he saw the familiar shingle: *S.C. Gallup Saddlery of Pueblo, est. 1869.*

Charlie stripped the saddle from Star's back and hauled it up the stairs to the saddlery. As he pushed the door open with his shoulder, a little bell hanging on the door frame announced his arrival.

He plopped the large saddle down on the counter. Resting an elbow on the seat, he looked around, catching his breath. Bridles, harnesses, and reins cascaded down the walls. In the corners, lariats and cowboy hats hung from wooden pegs. A glass counter held a display of leather gloves on the bottom shelf. On the top, silver spurs and bits glistened in a bar of sunlight.

But it was the back wall that held his attention. Against it were some of the finest saddles in the territory. He walked over to one and lifted a fender, studying the craftsmanship. The scent of tanned leather rushed him. He took a deep breath. *I could stay in here all day*, he thought.

A moment later, a blond, middle-aged man pushed through the curtains that separated the shop from the workroom, wiping his hands on a dirty apron. Seeing Charlie, he smiled. "Good to see you again, young Mr. Smith. How are things?"

"Just fine, Mr. Gallup," Charlie answered politely.

"Good then. Now what can I do for you?" Mr. Gallup eyed Star's saddle.

"Grandpa and I are headin' up to Denver in the next day or so, and I'd like for you to look this over, just to make sure everything is tight and as it should be."

Instinctively, Mr. Gallup flipped a corner of the saddle skirt over. "Yep, it's one of ours," he said, looking at the brand that had been burnt into the leather. "Most of 'em are. This one is one of the best we've ever made though. Your grandfather wanted it done just so. Very specific on his orders, if I remember correctly."

"That sounds like Grandpa," said Charlie.

"I'll take it back and give it a good once over. It shouldn't take long, but if you have business in town to take care of, feel free. I'll have it done by the time you get back."

"Thanks," said Charlie. "I'll run over to the general store. Be back in a while."

He'd just stepped out onto the boardwalk when LeFaye brought his horse up alongside. "Get down and come on," said Charlie. "My saddle'll take a few minutes, so I thought we'd go over to the mercantile and pick up a few things."

LeFaye tied his horse next to Star and the two walked up the street to the store. Its whitewashed walls glimmered in the sun. Inside, LeFaye quickly made his way over to the bookshelves. Books were a precious commodity and he bought one whenever he could afford it. He'd shared his dream with Charlie to one day own his own private library so he could read whenever it pleased him.

Charlie asked the clerk to bag a few sugar cubes for Star and Bessie and a handful of jerky for him and Grandpa. After that, he meandered around, trying to keep from attracting LeFaye's attention. Gradually, he made his way over to a counter where girly things like ribbons and silver grooming sets, scented soaps and trinkets were on display.

"May I help you, young man?" asked a pleasant, round woman.

Charlie was startled. "Uh, well," he stammered. Glancing over her shoulder, he caught sight of LeFaye peering at them from between a couple of books. Looking back at the woman he almost said 'no', but changed his mind. "Yes, ma'am," he said boldly, pointing to a basket full of hair ribbons. "I'd like a dozen of those ribbons right there. Two of each color if you don't mind."

The woman smiled and plunged her plump fingers into the basket. "For a special young lady?" she asked politely. "Or maybe a younger sister who's still in pigtails?"

Charlie smiled awkwardly. "For a friend," he said carefully. "A younger friend."

The woman drew up a handful of the silk strips and started to pick through them, pulling out the best of the lot. "I'll be over at the cash register," said Charlie. "Along with my sugar cubes." He felt like an idiot.

LeFaye walked up to the counter with a few books tucked under his arm. "Ribbons?" he snickered.

"None of your business," answered Charlie.

"But my friend, you forget that I've been in Denver, too," he teased. "Remember, Miller and I were with you when . . ."

The woman brought Charlie's order to the counter and handed it to the clerk.

"So what," Charlie muttered. He pretended to be interested in a jar of peppermint sticks. "I could be buying these to add to the Christmas tree this year. After all, Grandma's ribbons are old. I'd like to keep them as long as I can."

"Ah," said LeFaye. "New ribbons for the Christmas tree."

The cash register chinged. "That'll be one dollar," said the clerk. Charlie pulled a bill from his pocket and paid the man.

"I hope the Christmas tree appreciates the gift," teased LeFaye.

"I'm sure it will," said Charlie, taking his small bag from the clerk and stepping away from the counter.

LeFaye put his books down and asked the clerk to ring them up.

Charlie took a deep breath. Waiting for LeFaye, he walked over to the picture window and watched the meager bits of traffic go up and down Main Street. A man driving a team of Belgians pulled up in front of the school across the way. The instant the wagon stopped, a passel of children who were sitting in the buckboard behind him, scrambled to the tail and jumped out two by two. Screaming and pushing, they raced each other to the school house doors. Charlie smiled, thinking of his own childhood.

Suddenly he saw something that made him start. He stared down the street. LeFaye stepped up beside him, his new books wrapped neatly in brown paper. "Ready?"

"Almost," murmured Charlie, still staring out of the window.

Without another word, he turned quickly and walked out of the store onto the boardwalk.

Again, he looked down the dirt street. Handing LeFaye his bag, he motioned to a bench. "Have a seat, LeFaye," he said quietly. "I'll be back in a minute."

"Where are you—?"

"In a minute," he muttered.

Charlie walked briskly down the walkway. He passed several stores, without showing a hint of curiosity as to their wares—he stopped only when he reached the saloon. He glanced over his shoulder at a horse that was hitched to the post before pushing his way through the swinging doors.

The room reeked of alcohol. A thick haze of cigarette smoke hung in the air. Charlie looked around as his eyes adjusted to the darkness. Along the left wall, a bar ran from corner to corner. The bartender stood behind it, wiping glasses with a towel. His dark hair had been greased down, as well as his handlebar mustache. He acknowledged Charlie with a nod, but neither said a word. Charlie wasn't familiar with saloons, but he'd heard tales, and from them, he figured the bartender probably had a widow maker under that slab of wood. The reflection of the man's back was barely visible in the smudged mirror that hung on the wall behind him. Charlie's instincts told him there was a reason why that mirror hadn't been cleaned.

In the back of the room, a couple of men sat at a corner table playing poker. And in the front, three cowpokes were drinking and splitting cards. Face by face, he studied each man. It was the front table that caught his eye. Out of the three, Charlie was only interested in one.

"Bar Keep," barked a scraggly, old sidewinder from the back table, "bring me another snort of that 'oh-be-joyful'."

"It shouldn't be that hard a job," a bald, fat man at the front table was saying. "Tuttle here can sneak in through the back and break into the register while we're waitin' with the horses. Once he gets the money, we can take off and he'll be able to . . ." The man stopped abruptly and looked up.

"To what?" asked Charlie.

Surprised, the men snapped their heads up and stared at Charlie. One made the mistake of standing too quickly and reaching for his gun.

"I wouldn't do that," Wilbur warned him. But Charlie

had already pulled iron. His Smith & Wesson was pointed at the stranger's chest. It was his eyes, not his words that were coaxing the cowboy to slowly put his gun on the table.

"Sit down, Wilson," ordered Wilbur. "This is a friend of mine, Charlie Smith."

Wilbur stood up as a rattled Wilson slowly sat down. Charlie reached over and grabbed his gun.

Wilbur smiled nervously and hitched up his britches. "Charlie, this here almost dead man is Henry Wilson and the smarter one is Lem Calhoun." The men nodded. Their round eyes followed Charlie's hand as he holstered his gun.

"I don't mean to interrupt, Wilbur," Charlie said, keeping his eyes on the two others. "But would you mind stepping outside with me for a minute?"

Wilbur shrugged his shoulders. "Sure," he answered. Looking at his friends, he tossed a deck of cards into the center of the table. "Deal 'em, fair and square, or I'll have ol' Charlie come back in here and ream you." He snickered. Charlie walked outside. Wilbur followed, stumbling a little onto the boardwalk.

Turning sharply, Charlie grabbed Wilbur's arm. "What are you doin' in there?"

Wilbur stopped smiling. "Playin' cards, havin' some fun. Why? Can't I have some fun?"

"What's this about getting money from a register?"

"Aw, it's nothin'. Just drunk talk."

Charlie pulled his face away from his friend. "When did you start drinkin'?"

Wilbur tried to stand upright, but his feet wouldn't keep still. "Are you Charlie or are you my ma, dressed up like Charlie?"

"If I were your ma, you'd already be in a world of hurt."

Wilbur nodded his head and snorted. "That's true. She'll have my hide if she finds out about all this."

"She won't find out any time soon, Wilbur," scolded Charlie. "She's gone."

Wilbur looked like a whipped puppy. He grabbed a porch pole to steady himself. "Gone? What d' ya mean she's gone? What happened? I just saw her a few days ago and she was fine. You were there."

"Wilbur, you're drunk."

"Is that why she's gone?"

"I'm takin' you home, right now."

"I don't wanna go home."

LeFaye walked up leading his horse. "Need some help?"

Charlie looked relieved. "Would you mind helping me get him saddled up and on his way home while I finish my business here?" he asked.

"Not at all," said LeFaye. He looked at Wilbur in pity and disgust. "They told me over at the post office that he'd been fired. I took the liberty of gathering his . . . hmm, how do you say? Ah yes, his stuff from his former employer. Yours is still at the saddlery."

"Great! I'll catch up with you as soon as I'm done."

"By the looks of him, we won't be traveling fast, so we shouldn't get too far ahead of you."

Under noisy, but useless protest, the inebriated cowboy was heaved onto his horse. No one came out of the saloon to see what all the fuss was about. *Real friends they are*, thought Charlie. LeFaye mounted his ride and grabbed the reins to Wilbur's horse. "See you soon," he called to Charlie, tipping his hat.

Wilbur opened his mouth and sang loudly.

Camp town ladies sing this song,
Doo-da, doo-da,
Camp town racetrack's five miles long,
Oh, de doo-da day.

Charlie picked up a beautifully polished black saddle from Mr. Gallup. It looked just as taut and clean as when Grandpa first gave it to him. He strapped it on Star, then went over to the bank. He needed to have a long talk with the manager.

It was close to two o'clock when Charlie swung himself onto his horse and rode out of town. Star had been tied up too long and was ready to run. Charlie let him. He wanted to catch up with LeFaye and Wilbur. Somewhere up the road were his two closest friends. Wilbur was in a rotten state and LeFaye was in no mood to put up with him. He just hoped they hadn't stopped somewhere to duke it out.

5

THE NIGHT BEFORE THEY WERE TO LEAVE for Denver, Charlie paced anxiously in front of the fireplace, glancing at the gear that was piled at the front door.

Their saddlebags, bed rolls, and a couple of packs that Star would carry leaned against the wall. The only thing missing was Grandpa. It was getting late. He stepped out onto the back stoop and headed toward the barn. He could just make out the faint glow of a single lantern flickering against a dirty window.

The old barn was nearly hidden now by the grove of cottonwoods that stood between it and the road. A casual observer might have been able to make out its features if he knew where to look. But even to those who did know, it was just an old relic of yesteryear.

Even Grandpa said it looked old and worn. The lustrous red paint that once adorned its façade was gone. Merciless storms of snow, rain, ice, and time had left its windows cracked and blurred, blind to the colors of the prairie. Its doors groaned when disturbed. And the roof had started to sag. He once said its days of usefulness were all but over.

But to Charlie, the decrepit shed was alive. To him, it was like an ancient sentry, decaying with age, yet heroic. It had proven capable of holding back years of unruly overgrowth, tucking crawling foliage and climbing vines under its eaves to prevent them from advancing down upon the peaceful farm. He knew too, that the windswept building was still a place of refuge, a haven of sorts for a nesting raptor, a hungry field mouse, an injured squirrel, or any creature that needed to find sanctuary within its walls.

It was usually at the end of the day, when the sun melted behind the Rocky Mountains, that critters sought out its shelter. They could be heard scurrying between the walls, burrowing under blankets of hay, or flittering in the lofty rafters above until they felt safe. Then, when all was quiet and still, night would slip in and engulf the modest farm in its folds, allowing just a watery moon to provide a light in the thick darkness.

On those starless nights, when given permission by passing clouds, the golden orb was all that lit their world.

Charlie stepped over the threshold and took in his surroundings. Night often changed the familiar shapes of barrels, feedbags, and tools into strange and distorted forms. *How different things look in the dark*, he thought. Off to his right, he heard shuffling noises. Turning, he could barely make out the silhouette of his grandfather, who was squatting over a large, obscure figure. Charlie made his way over to the workbench and lit another lamp, then tip-toed noiselessly to the stall where Grandpa was working. Raising his lantern, he peered over the gate.

Grandpa was bending over a laboring heifer. Charlie pulled the gate open and tethered it to a nail then crept into the room. Eerie shadows, cast by the flames of the lamps, danced across the walls of the hay-strewn room, but Charlie's attention rested on the young cow that lay at his feet. Her breathing was fast and shallow. She was already exhausted, but he knew she still had a long way to go. He slid the handle of his lantern over a nail, knelt beside his grandfather, and gently rubbed her swollen belly.

"What's wrong with her, Grandpa? Why's she strainin' so hard?" he asked softly.

Grandpa winced. Squatting wasn't as easy as it used to be. "The calf's too big," he said, shifting his weight. "Bet it's a bull. Usually is when this happens."

"Will they be okay?"

The old man sighed. "We can only hope," he said wearily. "All I know is we got a long night ahead of us." He placed a hand on Charlie's shoulder and eased himself up. Nodding toward the barn doors, he glanced at Charlie. "Make sure we have plenty of hot water on hand. And we'll need soap, clean towels, lard, and more rope."

Charlie jumped up and grabbed his lantern. Grandpa hung his hat and started to roll up his sleeves. "Might want to make some sandwiches and bring in a bucket of fresh drinkin' water for us, too. We're gonna work up a mighty big appetite." Charlie was out of the stall and almost at the barn doors when Grandpa called, "Oh, and Charlie."

"What?" The heel of Charlie's boot caught a splotch of chicken manure and he slid across the wooden floor. With arms flailing, he tried to steady himself, but couldn't. Before dropping to one knee, he grabbed the edge of a barrel.

Grandpa flexed his jaw muscles to keep from laughing. "You've helped me deliver plenty of calves before, but tonight's gonna be a struggle for all of us and my indigestion is kickin' up, so I'm gonna leave most of this up to you. Make sure you bring whatever else you think you might need, 'cause once we start, we aren't leavin' till it's done."

Charlie pushed his hat back and stared at Grandpa. He'd never delivered a calf by himself.

In Green Pastures

"You'll do fine, son. Just go." He threw a quick glance down at the heifer, then back up at Charlie. The glow from the lanterns reflected in his faded eyes. "Now!" he cried. The cow moaned. Charlie lost the desire to argue. Darting past the barn doors, he vanished into the night.

An hour or so later, a large kettle of water hung over a blazing fire. Golden-red flames slapped at the pot's round belly. Inside, bubbles exploded on the water's surface, just below a cloud of steam. In the barn, a basket of sandwiches and a bucket of cold water sat on the workbench, and Charlie, sweating despite the cool air, was hunkered down behind the heifer, holding tightly to a rope. Attached to the other end of the rope were two small, protruding hooves.

Grandpa was sitting on a bale of hay behind Charlie's right shoulder. "Okay, now relax on the rope," he instructed.

"Boy, this young 'un is hardly budgin'," groaned Charlie. He wiped the sweat from his face with the back of his glove and cast a worried look at his grandfather.

"Actually, they're both doin' just fine," replied the old man. "And so are you. It's when his head is out that I'll start to worry, but we'll take care of that later, if we have to."

"We?" muttered Charlie.

Grandpa grinned. "Okay, *you*. I've been havin' trouble with—"

"Yeah, yeah, I know . . . with your indigestion." Charlie glanced at him. "Matter of fact, you've had a lot of that lately. Seems everything gives you stomach problems. Think you oughta go see the doc next time we're in town?"

Grandpa grunted and pointed to the cow. "Better grab that rope; she's gettin' ready to push again."

Charlie was ready. When Grandpa gave the signal, he

pulled. Not too harsh, not too gentle, but enough to help the young mother move the small body within her toward the soft light of the stall.

A couple of hours and several contractions later, Charlie could see a wet, pink nose, which was soon followed by a short snout, and then a pair of long, white eyelashes. "He's comin', Grandpa," Charlie said excitedly. "I can see his face. This should go pretty fast now, shouldn't it?"

"We'll see," replied Grandpa. His arms covered in lard, he bent low to the floor, ready to slide his hands around the calf's jaws. When he felt the contraction, he gently led the little head out into the light. Charlie changed course and pulled the calf's forefeet down towards his mother's hocks.

"Keep it steady, Charlie," Grandpa instructed calmly. "Pull too hard, we could hurt both of 'em real bad. Remember to work with the cow when she pushes. We still have to get past those hips, so follow her lead. And watch she don't kick the daylights outta ya."

The cow groaned and pushed again, but the calf didn't budge. Grandpa picked the lard can up with his slimy fingers and handed it to Charlie. "Lather up, quick!"

Charlie whipped off his gloves and threw them to the floor. Within seconds, his shirt landed on top of them. Goose bumps raced across his bare skin, but he didn't have time to worry about the cold. "Now what?" he asked, his jaw muscles flexing to steady his teeth.

"Turn him," ordered Grandpa. "Their hips are locked. That's what I was afraid of."

"How do I—"

"Just do it! A quarter circle," Grandpa gasped. Then he grimaced and grabbed his chest, but Charlie didn't notice.

Uncertain but focused, Charlie slowly slid his right hand beyond the calf's neck and alongside his ribs. The young man's eyes begged for direction as they searched his grandfather's face, but he soon felt what Grandpa meant. The calf's wide hips were stuck against his mother's narrow pelvis. The baby was locked in place. Charlie knew he had to work fast or either the calf would cut his mother's innards to shreds with his sharp rear hooves, or she would slowly strangle him with every contraction.

Charlie didn't waste a second. Carefully he pulled his right arm out and slid his left arm up under the calf and along its ribs until he could feel the hip bone again. He gently lifted the calf's hips with his left hand and held its front legs with his right. Slowly, he began to turn the calf. The heifer let out a deep moan, but Charlie kept turning until he felt the baby slide through the mother's pelvis and ease forward. After making sure the calf had righted itself, Charlie sat up and shoved his slimy hands into his gloves. *It can't be much longer now*, he thought.

Morning rushed across the prairie just as the cow gave her final push. Charlie gently guided the calf one last time. They'd worked through the night, but it suddenly seemed like the birth had happened in a flash. He stared at the beautiful, little white face and the rich cinnamon color of the tiny Hereford lying at his knees. He was always taken aback by the beauty of newborns.

He stroked the small cow. Then he saw the little fellow wasn't breathing. "Surely not," he whispered. He grabbed the fingertips of his gloves with his teeth and yanked them off. Reaching down, he drew back an eyelid with his thumb and touched the corner of the calf's eyeball. It blinked. To his relief, a large, brown eye rolled upward and looked at him.

"He's alive, Grandpa."

"Quick, Charlie, take a—"

"I got it," said Charlie, tossing a clean towel to his grandfather. "Rub his shoulders. He's gotta breathe!"

Grandpa glanced at his grandson. It was Charlie giving the orders now. Chuckling to himself, he grabbed the towel and started to rub.

It only took seconds, but it seemed like hours before the young bull finally blew his nose. Mucus flew across the floor. Charlie forced his fingers into the calf's mouth and opened it wide enough to swipe the inside with his towel. Then the little bull had had enough. He stood on his wobbly legs and ranted noisily for his mother.

The new mother recognized her baby's cry. She tossed her large head and kicked about, struggling to get to her feet. Charlie scrambled over to her before she hurt herself, then kneeling beside her, he whispered soothingly in her ear while he stroked her thick neck. When he thought she was calm enough to try again, he took her muzzle rope and carefully helped her up onto her quivering legs. He watched in awe as Grandpa introduced her to her new baby.

After a quick sniff, the cow started to clean her baby's face. Every stroke of her wide tongue pulled his eyelids up and exposed his round eyes. He soon tired of his first bath though, and became more interested in his first meal.

Grandpa and Charlie walked outside to the iron kettle and washed away the sweat and strain of the long night. "Amazing, isn't it?" said Grandpa, drying his arms with a towel.

"Yeah, it always is," answered Charlie, buttoning his shirt. "But I'm beat."

They went back into the barn to check on the new family again. "Always remember the little calf, Charlie," said Grandpa, gently rubbing the heifer between her eyes.

Charlie leaned against the stall rails. *Here comes a lesson.*

The grizzled old half-breed pulled a toothpick from his jacket pocket and slid it between his lips. Hanging an elbow over the rail, he got comfortable. "Charlie, these cows can teach you a good lesson about people."

Charlie hooked a boot heel onto a bottom rail. "People?"

Grandpa nodded. "Yep, people. See, God is a God of mercy, love, and grace, but He is also a God of character and integrity. He shapes us into who He wants us to be through the struggles He allows us to experience. Those struggles are intended to strengthen our character, which eventually should mirror His own. Sometimes during our times of struggle, God brings someone into our lives to help us, and that person is being shaped by God, too."

Charlie was watching the cow clean her calf again. "I know He certainly has sent help my way when I needed it most," he said thoughtfully. "If it weren't for Jess, we wouldn't have made it through that one Christmas back in '64. Miller and the Dobsons last year, who took you in when you got hurt. And then there's always been you, Grandpa."

Grandpa rolled the toothpick with his tongue. "And sometimes, you've been on the helpin' end, too, Charlie. You've been there for the Tuttles, for LeFaye, and for me."

Still watching the two animals, Charlie slowly nodded. "I see," he said softly. "It's like this young ma and her calf here. If we hadn't a' helped them, they both could've died. We need to help people just as much."

Grandpa nodded. "Yep, now you've got my meanin'.

Someone down the way may be in need of some kind of help, whether it be physical, spiritual, or emotional. No matter the need, no matter how messy the situation, or how long it might take, we have a responsibility to help those who are strugglin'. So just like this little mama and her baby boy, they'll be able to experience the beauty of somethin' new."

Charlie turned to his grandfather. "We've always done what we could do for folks, especially you, but we—"

"Are going to have so much more to offer pretty soon," interrupted Grandpa. "I'm just sayin' when that blessin' comes final, don't forget your responsibility to God and your fellow man. Make a difference."

"Yes, Grandpa. I'll remember."

The old man patted his grandson's shoulder. "Good." He smiled. "Now, I'm gonna go see to our other mama cows and make sure they're doin' okay. Why don't you go on inside and get some rest before we head out for Denver?"

Charlie shook his head. "How 'bout *I* go check on the other cows and *you* go get some rest." Grandpa chewed on his toothpick. "I'll give you a full report when I come in," Charlie assured him.

Yawning deeply, Grandpa mumbled, "Okay," and without further ado, he hobbled out of the barn toward the cabin in the cool brisk morning. Charlie turned his attention to the young family and saw them settle into the hay for a much needed nap.

When he turned to leave, a deep sense of satisfaction fell over him. He knew, for them at least, he'd made a big difference.

6

WIND BLEW IN HARD AND FAST, KICKING dirt into their faces. From the west, dark clouds drifted over the mountains dragging colder weather in with them. Charlie was faring all right, but he worried about Grandpa. The old man chilled fast, although he wouldn't admit it. Both men had tightened their slickers around their chests, but the wind cut through the fabric as if they wore no protection at all.

Charlie knew it would be useless to try to talk Grandpa into turning back, so he settled into the stiff saddle and pulled his wool scarf up around his neck. He kept a watchful eye on the darkening clouds. He didn't like what they were telling him. Grandpa motioned Charlie up alongside him.

"I think we better find some cover for the night," he shouted over the wind. "I believe we're close to the Dobson cabin. If so, they'll be right happy to take us in. Stay close."

They only had to lead their horses over a couple of ridges and along the dry riverbed when a cabin came into view. It was the first time Charlie had seen this place, where Grandpa said he recovered from his near fatal fall; something about it seemed strange to him.

A cold wind snuck up from behind and bit at them again. Charlie held onto his hat and kept Star moving. Strange or not, from where he sat, the cabin was a welcome sight.

As they got closer, Charlie noticed that Grandpa looked confused. His old eyes never left the cabin, looking at it like he was searching for something. When they reached the door,

Mysterious Ways

Grandpa hesitated for a second before sliding from the saddle. Charlie lit off his horse and walked up to the door. The cabin was empty.

Charlie glanced around the room. It was dark and cold. He pulled the scarf away from his face. "Where are they, Grandpa? Do you think they moved?"

Shaking his head, Grandpa limped swiftly around the cabin. He pulled his scarf down and said, "No, son; they didn't move. They weren't here."

Charlie took his hat off and scratched his head. "What do you mean? Is this the wrong place?"

"Nope. Right place, wrong time."

Charlie closed his eyes. Grandpa was talking in circles again. He was about to ask another question, but Grandpa cut him off abruptly. "Grab some firewood and let's get this place warmed up. Let's get the horses in here, too. Once they're taken care of, and we're settled in for the night, I'll explain."

A freezing rain met them head on when they stepped back outside. Charlie quickly gathered what wood he could find before his fingers went numb. Grandpa untied the horses and led them through the cabin to the back room. There was a barn nearby, but he wanted them all to be warm and safe... and close.

Charlie found a couple of rusty oil lamps in a cupboard. Lighting them, he set one down beside each bedroll. The two men hunkered down on the floor and got warm by a blazing fire. Grandpa pulled a few strips of jerky and a couple of biscuits out of his saddlebag and tossed them to Charlie.

The horses had been unsaddled and given a good rub down. In the dark room they contentedly chewed on oats and prairie grass. Every so often, swishing noises came from the shadows as they foraged the wooden floor with their large lips, lapping up the remnants. Charlie tugged at a bite of jerky.

"Take a look around, Charlie," said Grandpa, wiping biscuit crumbs from his mouth with the back of his hand. "Take a good look around."

Charlie glanced around the cabin and shrugged his shoulders. "It's dirty and looks old," he said. "Other than that, it's just a cabin."

"Anythin' strike you as strange?"

Charlie nodded. "I thought it was strange that the cabin was empty, but I noticed that when we came over the last ridge. No smoke comin' from the fireplace. No lights comin' from the windows. But I just figured the Dobsons had decided to move on."

Grandpa nodded. "You're half right, son. I think the Dobsons left after I did, too, but what gets me is my accident was just a few months ago. This place has been empty for years."

"What? You're not makin' any sense, Grandpa."

Sliding a finger across the floor, Grandpa gathered up a small heap of dust on the tip and held it up so Charlie could see. "It's been a while since this place has been cleaned, or at least as clean as I remember it. Orpha was a stickler for clean. And Gill never would have let the door sag so badly or the roof go without patchin'. He woulda had 'em both fixed before I left, especially with winter comin' on." Pointing to a dark corner with a crooked finger, he said, "Orpha wouldn't have allowed those thick cobwebs to gather up there either. And the windows wouldn't a' got so dirty.

"I agree that the Dobsons left after I did, but I don't think they actually lived here. They stayed here, for as long as I needed 'em, but when I left, they left. Then this old cabin returned to the way it was before any of us arrived. It turned back to the empty shell we see here before us. No, this cabin wouldn't have deteriorated this much in such a short time, Charlie. It's been awhile since this place has felt the touch of a human hand."

Charlie smiled. "So what you're sayin' is that the hands that touched this place a few months ago, when you were here, weren't human."

"Yep," replied Grandpa. "I'm convinced now that I was doctored by three angels, not just one. Micah wasn't the only one sent to me from Heaven. Thinkin' on it now . . ." Grandpa's voice fell to a whisper. "Gill and Orpha Dobson. Well, I'll be."

"What?" asked Charlie eagerly, the reflection of the fire dancing in his wide eyes.

Grandpa wrote the letters in the dusty floor as he spoke. Looking up at Charlie, he smiled and nodded. "I'm gettin' old, Charlie. I been readin' sign for a long time, but that one got right by me."

"But why would God pick us to be the ones to experience all of this, Grandpa? Why would He pick me to meet Jess and you to be doctored by angels? What's so special about us?"

"Why, there's nothin' special about us," answered the old man. His radiant smile unfolded below his high cheekbones. "God promises all of His children that He will take care of 'em and help 'em in their time of need. He didn't do anythin' for us that He wouldn't do for any of those that believe in Him. The only difference might be we were willin' to let Him."

Charlie blew out his lamp and laid back into his blankets. "I hope I'm always willin' to let Him," he whispered. Sleepiness swirled around his heavy eyelids.

"Keep your heart open to His Word, son, and you'll always hear what He has to say."

Charlie reached over and patted the old man's shoulder. "I will, Grandpa," he mumbled.

"I hope you do, too," murmured Grandpa. Staring into the fire, he continued. At first I thought I wouldn't have nothin' to leave you, Charlie. It seems now, that because of my cousin's kindness, all that's changed. But I had it wrong. I've always had somethin' to leave you.

"Somethin' more important than what's layin' in the bank in Denver. Somethin' that's worth more than all the gold on earth. That's to know Jesus. If I couldn't leave you anythin' else, Charlie, I would leave you my Bible and with it, Jesus Christ. Knowin' Him, havin' Him in your life will make you richer than anythin' on this earth can."

Outside, the howling wind threw sleet across the roof like a farmer throws feed to his chickens. Granules of ice ticked against the window panes. Inside, Grandpa and Charlie lay in their bedrolls and talked about Heaven, angels, and other spiritual matters.

"Do you remember when you first believed and knew you were saved, Charlie?"

"Yes, sir. It was Christmas, almost eight years ago, when Jess was with us."

"Will you tell me about it again?"

Charlie rolled over onto his back and put his hands behind his head. "Well, while you were laid up, Jess helped me around the farm and taught me about God's love. He taught me to read, too, so I could read the Bible on my own. Every day, he'd teach me somethin' new. I'd think about that and what you

Mysterious Ways

and Grandma taught me, like Adam and Eve, and about how we are born into sin because of Adam's disobedience by eatin' what God said was forbidden. It's because of one man, Adam, that we're sinners, and because of one man, Jesus, that we can be saved. Jesus' part was being crucified and risin' up from the grave on Easter morn to give us the way to Heaven. Our part is to ask Him to forgive us for our sin and trust Him to make our hearts right. All that with what Jess was sayin' made sense to me that day. And that's the day I believed."

A tear slid through the crevices on Grandpa's face. "Well, I'll be," he said, rubbing his eyes. "You did listen to all those Bible lessons your Grandma taught you as a young 'un."

"Yes, sir, I did," said Charlie smiling. "I'm not as hard headed as you think."

Grandpa chuckled softly and blew out his lamp. Carefully, he lowered himself down into his bedroll. "Well then, I can go to Heaven in peace," he said, pulling his blanket up to his chin. "When the good Lord calls me home, I can go knowing that we'll only be separated for a time."

"Just for a time," whispered Charlie.

"Lord," he began and his voice trembled slightly in the darkness, "thank you for your blessings." A blast of wind hit the cabin. It whistled around the corners, creaking through the wooden timbers and under the crippled door. Grandpa shuddered and pulled his blankets closer around him. "Especially for this cabin to keep us warm on such a cold night. Thank you for your salvation and the promises that govern our faith. Watch over your servants as we travel and help us to always do your will. In Jesus' name, amen."

"Amen."

In Green Pastures

The cold air followed them along the trail over the next couple of days, but to their relief, the wind and sleet stayed behind. That made traveling somewhat easier for Grandpa and Bessie. They were able to move faster and they made it to Colorado Springs with no trouble.

Resting at the top of a hill, Grandpa relaxed in his saddle and looked out across the valley below them. But Charlie stood up in the stirrups and tried to make sense of what he was seeing. To the west, he recognized Pikes Peak, but he had never before seen the new town that lay along the foothills. Just a few short months ago, a lone cabin stood in the shadow of the great mountain, but now there was a town; a whole town with streets, businesses, houses, and trees. It was as if an entire settlement had sprung up from the prairie overnight.

Grandpa whistled. "Lookie there," he said, resting on his saddle horn. "I guess ol' Mr. Dooley knew what he was talkin' about, huh?"

"I guess," answered Charlie. "I can't believe this is the same place."

"Isn't it amazin' what the railroad can do?"

As if in reply, a shrill whistle cracked the crisp afternoon air. A large puff of smoke followed it. Charlie watched it float above the treetops.

"There it is, Grandpa. There's the train."

Grandpa rubbed his chin. "Ya know," he said thoughtfully. "I didn't think about this earlier, but we could ride the train to Denver. We couldn't catch it from Pueblo 'cause it doesn't come down that far, but it obviously comes south as far as Colorado Springs now. And if it comes south, it's gotta go back north."

Charlie twisted in his saddle. "Can we? That would be

great! We wouldn't have to sleep on the ground, or eat jerky, or put up with the weather. And instead of makin' twenty miles a day . . ." He paused. "Wow," he muttered, turning back toward the train. "We'd be goin' thirty miles an hour." His brown eyes grew larger. "Good grief, Grandpa," he said slowly. "That means we'd get to Denver in about two or three hours instead of two or three days."

Grandpa beamed. "Sounds like good fun to me. Let's go."

Charlie was about to click to Star to run like the wind, but he stopped short and snatched Grandpa's sleeve. "Wait a minute," he said. "What about the horses? I forgot about the horses. It's not like we can tie them to the back of the train."

Grandpa laughed. "I'm sure they'll have a car to put livestock in, Charlie. We can't be the only passengers that ride horses." A monstrous hissing sounded in the distance. Clouds of steam billowed from the lungs of the iron horse. Its huffing grew louder, as if it were begging for permission to take off and run again.

Grandpa glanced at Charlie. His eyes gleamed with adventure. "Let's go," he yelled. He touched Bessie's ribs with his heels and off they went. Star jumped. Down the horses ran; down the hill into the new town, through the platted streets, and across to the new train depot.

To Charlie's relief, the horses were stowed safely in a boxcar near the back of the train. Before he left them, he made sure they had all they needed so Grandpa wouldn't fret about Bessie.

"Lot different than ridin' in a wagon," Grandpa said aloud, slowly stroking the leather seat with his gnarled fingers. "This is somethin' else."

Half way to Denver, the rocking motion of the train put

Grandpa to sleep, but Charlie stayed wide awake. He was fascinated by the scenery that glided past them. It was the same country he'd seen on the cattle drive, but this time he was able to really see it. He didn't have to keep his eyes on the ground for sign or on the cattle for strays. And although he couldn't smell the wild flowers or see much of the wildlife, he could see the colors of the wild prairie and watch bundles of dark clouds roll toward each other, threatening rain to end a brilliant day.

7

BY THE HUFFING LOCOMOTIVE GRANDPA and Charlie waited for their horses to be unloaded from the boxcar. It was late, but standing there on the boardwalk, it felt good to be in Denver. The dust and bland trail food were behind them.

Under a gas lamp's glow Grandpa found a bench on which to rest. "I might need a couple days to recover from this trip before we see Mr. Atkins. Me and Bessie are about dragged out. I want to be right as rain when we start talkin' about finances and such."

"That's fine, Grandpa," said Charlie. "We're in no hurry."

"Once we get the horses, I'd like to go to the hotel and get cleaned up. After that, if you'd take the horses to the livery, I'll go over to the judge's office and make our appointments. That a way, I can rest up before we take care of our business," said Grandpa.

"You sure you don't want me to go with you?"

"Naw," said Grandpa. "It won't take me long. When you're done with the horses, why don't you go on over to Dixie's and grab us a table. I'll meet you there when I'm done at the judge's office."

Charlie sighed heavily.

Grandpa smiled. "Don't be disappointed," he said, winking. "I'm sure she'd prefer to see you after you've cleaned up a bit, too."

Heat crept up Charlie's face. "Who?" he mumbled.

"Don't try to pull the wool over my eyes, boy," snickered Grandpa. "I might be old, but I ain't dead. You know I mean one girl in particular, but all of 'em in general. We need to be fine as cream gravy before we venture out into public."

"What are you talkin' about, Grandpa?" protested Charlie.

Grandpa smiled. "Okay," he whispered. "Play dumb."

Charlie shook his head. The horses were finally brought to them and they all left Union Station ready to eat and settle down for the night.

As they walked, Charlie noticed that Denver had changed some since he'd seen it last. More banks, more stores, more people, and more guns. The place was too crowded for him. To his relief, it didn't take long to find The Gold Rush Inn. He signed the register while Grandpa climbed the stairs to their room. After cleaning up and changing clothes, he went one way with the horses and Grandpa went the other to make his appointment with Mr. Atkins.

Amelia's eyes sparkled when Grandpa stepped into the lobby, but as he got closer, he thought he saw the sparkle dim. Her eyes were like mirrors that reflected his age. He knew he looked old and tired.

Standing up, she extended her hand. "Why, hello Mr. Smith," she said with a pleasant smile. "It's good to see you again."

"Good to see you too, Miss Amelia," he replied politely. "I'm here to set my appointments with Mr. Atkins and Mr. Abel, but, if we can, I'd like to go a couple days out so I can rest a bit before havin' to think so hard."

Amelia giggled and grabbed her black book. "You do remember that Mr. Atkins said you didn't have to make an appointment, don't you? I can just let him know you're

Mysterious Ways

in town and you can come in anytime."

Grandpa shook his head. "Naw, I'd rather make an appointment. Then I'll know they'll be ready to see me."

"Well then, how does Thursday sound Mr. Smith?"

"Thursday's fine. About what time?"

"Ten o'clock in the morning?"

"We'll be here."

"We?" asked the young woman.

"Me and my grandson, Charlie. I brought him with me this trip so he can meet Judge Walker, Mr. Atkins, and Mr. Abel, if that'd be okay?"

"Your grandson is with you?" She was blushing slightly.

Puzzled, Grandpa shuffled his feet. "Have you and Charlie met already?" he asked.

Amelia's expression froze. Without blinking, her fluid green eyes met Grandpa's stare. Quietly, she slid her appointment book closer and bent down to write. "Having your grandson with you is fine, Mr. Smith," she replied, ignoring his question. "I'll just make a note beside your appointment time to ensure that each person has a few minutes to meet with, um . . ."

"Charlie," said Grandpa. "His name is Charlie."

"Yes, Charlie," she repeated. Her gaze wandered aimlessly across her desk.

"Well, we'll see you Thursday, then," said Grandpa, absently turning his hat in his hands.

Amelia brought her eyes up to meet the old man's. "Take care of yourself, Mr. Smith," she said affectionately. "You look mighty tired."

"Ain't nothin' some hot grub and a good night's sleep won't take care of," he assured her, slipping his hat back on his head.

"So, if things are settled here, I'll be on my way. See you on Thursday."

"See you then, Mr. Smith."

Grandpa tipped his dusty hat and headed for the door, his thoughts on good food and a warm bed.

"Mr. Smith!" exclaimed Rebecca. "Where'd you come from?" Her eyes danced merrily as a smile slid across her face. She glanced at Charlie and blushed.

"Well, hello Becky," Grandpa answered. He put an arm around her shoulder and gave her a squeeze. "Ol' Charlie and I are up from Pueblo on business, so ya know we had to stop in here to see you folks, too. Couldn't come all the way up to Denver without stoppin' in at Dixie's."

Her eyes aglow, she smiled wider. "I'll let Grandma know you're here. She's in the back cookin'. Do you want me to take your order now or wait a bit?"

Grandpa looked across the table at Charlie then back at Rebecca. "I think we better order now before Charlie shrivels up and blows away." Charlie smirked. Rebecca giggled and drew her pad and pencil from a pocket in her pinafore. "I guess it'll be the usual then, huh?"

Grandpa winked at her and smiled, "You betcha it will be, girl. Now run along and get to it, and tell Dixie I'd like a cup of her coffee, too."

Rebecca scribbled on her notepad as she hurried toward the kitchen. She turned and smiled at them just before she disappeared behind the swinging door that led into the restaurant's kitchen.

Grandpa sat back in his chair and took a deep breath. "Mighty nice to be back here," he said with a slow exhale.

"This place is just as homey as ever."

Charlie looked around. It was homey, but packed. "She seems to be bringin' in a nice crowd since we were here last."

"That Becky's growin' up too," said Grandpa. "She's turnin' into a right nice lookin' young lady. Not wearin' pigtails no more, either."

Charlie, still looking around the dining room, nodded. "Didn't notice," he mumbled.

Just then the door of the kitchen swung open and Miss Dixie emerged holding a trayful of steaming mugs of coffee and some homemade cookies. She found their table and came over, smiling warmly as she placed the cups and cookies in front of them. She sat down next to Charlie, across from Grandpa. "It's so good to see you two again," she said blushing slightly. "But I do wish you would have given me fair warning so I could've tidied up a bit."

Grandpa, raising a cup to his lips, scanned the restaurant. "This place don't need tidying up, Dixie. Its looks great just like it is."

Miss Dixie cocked her head and smoothed her ruffled hair with thin delicate fingers. She smiled at the old gent. "You know exactly what I meant, Stuart Smith."

The cloudiness that had overshadowed his old eyes for so long seemed to melt away at the sound of her laughter. For a second, Charlie thought he saw a flicker of life, a blaze of fire, a sign of the young, robust man that once stood in the now withered body of Stuart Smith.

The three talked for a while, but Charlie soon fell quiet, listening instead to the warmth of Miss Dixie's southern drawl. How she pronounced her words. At times, it was almost like listening to LeFaye talk.

In Green Pastures

Rebecca let out "heh hem," and slid a tray of food in front of them. When she started to unload the plates, Charlie's attention was swept away from his grandfather and his charming female friend.

"Well, I'll let ya'll eat in peace, but I'll be back with dessert. Just take your time, though, and don't choke," Miss Dixie said, throwing a concerned glance at Charlie. "There's more where that came from."

Charlie nodded then bowed his head. He didn't mean to be rude, but he was hungry. Grandpa got the message and asked a simple, yet sincere blessing.

After minutes of delving into the heap of fried chicken and mashed potatoes and gravy, Charlie finally came up for air. Slathering butter across a biscuit, he eyed his grandfather. "Wonderin' how she's really doin'?" he asked before biting the biscuit in half.

Grandpa looked up from his plate. "What d' ya mean?"

Charlie finished chewing and swallowed before answering. "Well," he said, wiping his mouth with his napkin, "she looked well enough, but if she's this busy every day, I wonder how she's really doing. I mean, this would be a tough job for anybody to do only once a day, but if she does it two or three times a day, I'd think she'd be about ready to drop."

Grandpa sat in silence for a while, sipping from his coffee cup and staring out of the window. Finally, he set his cup down and looked over at Charlie. "Make me another promise, son," he said low.

Charlie stopped chewing. A knot of food held fast in his cheek, he looked over at his grandfather with wide eyes. Grandpa couldn't help but smile. "Silly boy," he chuckled. "Finish what you're eatin'."

Mysterious Ways

"Sorry," slurred Charlie. It took a few seconds for him to swallow, but when he got all his food down, Grandpa continued. "Make me a promise that you'll help her."

Charlie gasped and then coughed. "You want me to help her?" he said in confusion. "But why? I don't know how to cook! You been eatin' my cookin' for years and complainin' with every forkful. That's not gonna help her business none. I mean ... I don't even know how to—"

"Boil water," interrupted the old man. "I know, and cookin's not what I meant. So, if you'll just hobble your lip, I'll finish."

"Oh. Sorry," he mumbled.

"Once we get things straightened out with the office down the way, I want you to consider helpin' Dixie financially," Grandpa whispered.

"Ohhh," replied Charlie. He nodded slowly as Grandpa's words sunk in. Leaning low over the table, his eyes darted around the room, eventually stopping at his grandfather. "But why are we whisperin'?"

Grandpa smirked and rolled his eyes. "We'll talk about this later. In our room. Just eat up for now," he murmured.

"But—"

"Later!"

Rebecca appeared with a coffee pot and freshened their coffee. "You two ready for dessert?" she asked. "Grandma's made some delicious pies."

Grandpa sighed heavily and rubbed his stomach. He was about to answer, but she giggled and replied in his stead, "I know, Mr. Smith, you'll pass, 'cause you need to watch your figure, but what about you ... Charlie?"

Charlie pulled his greasy face away from the chicken leg he'd been attacking. With his cheeks laden with meat, he

In Green Pastures

threw a quick look at Rebecca, shook his head violently, then dove back down to finish the job.

It took a couple of seconds, but he finally realized Grandpa had thumped him on the head.

"Wha?" he asked, his cheeks bulging with food.

"You're blind as a bat, son."

Charlie reluctantly tossed the chicken leg to the pile of bones that were stacked on his plate. The meal was over. Grandpa was in a mood. Savoring the bites he had stored in his jaws, he chewed slowly, but finally had to swallow. He wiped his face and fingers with his napkin and sat back in his chair. "Why? What'd I miss?"

Grandpa stared at him, a look of hopelessness on his weathered face. Charlie squirmed in his chair. "Did I do somethin' wrong?" he asked.

Grandpa shook his head and chuckled. "No, son, ya didn't do nothin' wrong. Ya just missed how that girl was tryin' to get your attention, that's all."

Charlie sat up straight. "What girl?"

"Re-bec-ca," said Grandpa. "The young lady that takes our orders every time we come in here. The one that goes ga-ga over you every time she sees you."

Charlie started to laugh. "You mean that little girl with the pigtails and freckles, and—"

"Who turned twelve last fall, but will soon be thirteen, and is only five years younger than you, which is the same as your grandma was with me," chided Grandpa.

"I know Grandpa, but—"

"Just start payin' attention, son. That's all I'm sayin'. I'm sure God has a special girl for ya, but He shouldn't have to make her smack ya upside the head to cause you to be aware of her. And besides, you hurt her feelin's."

"I did what?"

Grandpa crooked a bushy eyebrow. "You goin' deaf, too? I said, you hurt her feelin's."

"How could I? I didn't do nothin'."

Grandpa grabbed his hat. Sliding it on his head, he glared at Charlie. His eyes formed into narrow slits. "Exactly!" he said stiffly.

"But?"

"Later!" he barked. Sliding his chair back, the wooden legs raked across the floor. But he couldn't stand. He grabbed his chest and leaned back. "Wretched indigestion," he muttered.

"You all right, Grandpa?" Charlie scurried around the table to the old man's side.

"I'm fine. Just got a bad case of heartburn, that's all." With some effort, he stood up straight and smoothed out his shirt. Pointing to the chicken he'd left on his plate, he chuckled softly. "This stuff's gonna be the death of me, for sure."

Charlie failed to see the humor in any of it. "Come on, Grandpa," he urged. "Let's get back to the hotel. You look tired." He took Grandpa's elbow and led him to the door. Pushing the door open with his shoulder, he turned and looked back before stepping out onto the boardwalk. What he saw made him look twice.

Rebecca was standing by the kitchen door. She didn't look twelve anymore. She looked older, much older. Her blond hair was no longer pulled back in tight pigtails, but fell gently over her shoulders. Her lips were pink and her eyes the lightest shade of blue Charlie had ever seen. Remnants of a few freckles splattered across her cheeks, but they too were almost hidden by the rose color of her skin. *She is growing up to be a right pretty little lady*, he thought.

Then he noticed the drop of water sliding down her cheek, sparkling in the light of the gas lamps. It was definitely a tear, but Charlie didn't know why she would be crying. Just as he was ready to turn back to Grandpa, she raised a small hand from her apron pocket and flicked her fingers in a subtle wave of good-bye. The corners of her mouth curled upward, until her weak smile met her tears, then both disappeared behind the kitchen door.

8

GREY DAWN ARRIVED. CHARLIE ROLLED to his side and pulled the quilt over his shoulder. The potbellied stove hissed a tune. He dreaded having to get out of his warm bed to feed it, but if he didn't, they'd be miserable when they got up to get dressed.

Grandpa, hidden among a mass of quilts and blankets, snored lightly. Charlie let his head sink deeper into his pillow. He would wait just a little longer.

Snowflakes swirled past the window. Charlie's eyes grew heavy. The hissing noise from the stove filled his head. But he couldn't fall asleep. He had to take care of Grandpa.

Making an effort, he tossed the covers aside and swung his feet to the floor. The cold bit at his bare toes. Goose bumps ran up his arms. He buttoned the top to his long johns and hobbled over to the stove. Quietly, he loaded its belly with wood. But despite his care, he still managed to wake Grandpa from his peaceful slumber.

Grandpa moaned and pulled himself up from his warm blankets. Yawning, he scratched his chest. "Lordy," he muttered, smacking his lips. "I feel like I been kicked by a mule."

Charlie grunted. "Me too, Grandpa. Whose silly idea was it to come up here this time of year?" The iron door of the stove clanged shut and he tottered back to bed.

"Yours."

Charlie threw a sock at him. Grandpa dodged it, then picked it up and inspected the seam. "How 'bout we do a little shoppin' today?" He stuck a finger through the toe. "We need us some new duds."

Charlie got up and retrieved his sock from Grandpa. "Well, I guess we can, but are new clothes somethin' we can afford right now?"

Grandpa looked at him like he was nuts.

"Oh, yeah," grinned Charlie. "I guess it is."

The old man shuffled over to the washbasin and splashed cold water against his whiskered chin. "Then shoppin' it is, right after breakfast," he said picking up his shaving soap and brush.

They ate in the hotel's dining room, which was grand with satin settees, silk linens, gold-tasseled drapes, and high-back chairs.

Grandpa nibbled a piece of toast while he read the Denver Post. He sipped his coffee. "Seems ol' Horace Greeley wants to give President Grant a run for 'is money this next election."

Charlie, working on a stack of flapjacks, grunted.

"Don't think Grant'll be that easy to beat, bein' the incumbent and all. They're both Republicans, too, so there'll need to be a run-off for the final candidate."

"Mmm."

"You know that small town to the southeast of Fort Collins was named for the same Greeley, don't you?"

"Ummm."

"Yep. He's a newspaper man from New York, I think. One day he wrote a few simple words in his column and changed the country."

"Reewy?" replied Charlie, his mouth full of flapjack.

Grandpa stared over his paper. "It would've been nicer to just grunt."

Charlie swallowed, half interested. "What'd he write?"

Grandpa lifted the paper again and read some more before answering. Finally, he lowered the paper and said, "Go west young man, go west!"

Charlie raised his eyebrows. "Is that all?"

"Well, that wasn't all he wrote in his column, but that's all it took for folks to get the message," said Grandpa. "And it worked too. Practically started the westward movement."

"So the folks out in Colorado just up and named a town after him because he suggested everybody move west?"

Grandpa folded the paper and set it on the table. "That's it." He tilted his head back and drained the last of the coffee from his cup.

"Geez," muttered Charlie. "We're gettin' too crowded out here already. If I'd had the chance, I'd—"

"Never you mind. I know there're several Indian nations that feel the same way you do, but it's done with. We just have to do our part to make it a good, safe place to live."

Charlie finished his coffee in a couple of gulps. "Guess you're right, Grandpa."

"Are you finally finished?"

Charlie chuckled. "Yep, let's go."

The two pulled on slickers and started down Larimer Street, checking store windows for the latest goods.

They stopped at The Golden Eagle Department Store where suits and dresses were displayed. Grandpa was getting tired, they figured this store was as good as any.

There was an overwhelming choice of suits in various colors and styles. With the help of a patient employee, Grandpa finally settled on a grey, double breasted three piece. Charlie chose a more debonair, two-button, black pin-stripe, and a black derby to go with it. His choice pleased Grandpa. He looked every bit of the young socialite his grandfather envisioned him to be.

The rest of the day was spent taking carriages around the city, exploring the sights. To Grandpa's delight, they happened upon a small college.

"Well, lookie here." He stared up at the grand entrance. "I think we should go in and pay these folks a visit."

"Why?"

"'Cause I know of a young man who needs some formal education."

Charlie shook his head. "Grandpa, I don't need to go to no more schools."

Grandpa clicked his tongue. "Right there!" he said, pointing a finger at his grandson. "That's the reason why you do. Did you hear yourself? 'I don't need to go to *no more* schools.' What kinda talk is that?"

Charlie rolled his eyes. "The kind I grew up with."

"I know. And that kinda talk was okay for me and the farm, but it isn't okay for the rest of your life."

"What do you mean?"

"I doubt you're gonna live on our little farm for the rest of your life. I believe you're gonna be someone special, so you gotta prepare yourself for whatever it is God's gonna ask you to do. And I'm sure He'll appreciate it if you don't massacre the English language while you're doin' it, either."

"You really think so, Grandpa?" asked the young man. "You really think God has a special plan for me?"

"Yes, son, I do. So, we're gonna go in there and talk about you comin' here for schoolin' next year!"

"How would I do that? I can't leave you on the farm alone."

Grandpa gazed at him tenderly. "We'll leave the little details to the Lord, Charlie."

The two men climbed the stairs to the school. Charlie stopped and read the inscription over the archway above the doors: "*University of Denver — 1864.*" He felt a tightening in the pit of his stomach. This wasn't a one-room schoolhouse in the back hills of Pueblo.

It seemed like Grandpa read his mind. The old man placed a hand on his elbow and led him to the entrance. "It's all right, son. Trust me. Let's see if we can get you signed up."

They stepped into the shadows of the main hall. The two big wooden doors closed behind them.

9

"CHARLIE, MY BOY, YOU'RE ONE HANDSOME fella." They studied their reflections in the mirror.

"Stop, Grandpa."

"Will not. I'm proud of you. Come from good stock, you do, and that's nothin' to be embarrassed about."

"I ain't . . . I mean *I'm not* embarrassed, Grandpa," said Charlie. "I'm just not used to compliments."

"Well, get used to 'em. You'll be gettin' more."

Charlie considered his image a moment longer. Almost nineteen, he stood six feet, two inches tall. His brown hair, which he'd combed neatly to the side, just touched his collar. His dark brown eyes looked out above the high cheekbones that he inherited from his grandfather. His dark skin was a testament not only to working a farm in the Colorado sun, but also to his Indian heritage. His new jacket fit his broad shoulders well. *Well*, he thought, *maybe a little handsome.*

Before turning from the mirror, he pulled on his coat and adjusted his bolo tie. He then slipped his hand into his pocket. The small paper bag that held the ribbons he had purchased in Pueblo was securely nestled in the corner.

"Still primpin' or are you ready to go?" teased Grandpa.

"Ready as I'll ever be. I wish I didn't have to go at all."

Grandpa opened the door. "Well, ya do; so let's go."

Walking down the street toward the judge's office, Grandpa's predictions started to come true. A few merchants stopped sweeping their walkways and stared, several ladies gazed lingeringly after Charlie, before blushing and turning back to the window display. One man even stopped loading his wagon and stared, a heavy bag of flour on his shoulder, as they strode up the boardwalk.

Charlie looked around nervously. "What's wrong with us?" he whispered. "Why is everyone staring?"

"There's nothin' wrong with us. Just keep your chin up and walk tall," replied Grandpa. "These folks just aren't used to seein' such fine lookin' specimens, that's all." Charlie's laughter eased his tension.

"Don't want people to think you're a snob, though Charlie," continued Grandpa. "Always treat folks with respect no matter how they're dressed. Treat folks as you want to be treated. It's okay to dress up once in a while, but don't put on airs. Most folks can tell crow bait from a thoroughbred any day of the week, no matter how pretty the saddle."

"Yes, sir," replied Charlie.

Rounding the corner, Grandpa touched Charlie's arm. "We're almost there." They soon stepped inside the lobby.

Charlie'd been in this room a few months earlier, but this time he noticed the elegant entry with its marble floor, the bright paintings and rugs, the leather chairs, and the grand fireplace on the far wall. There were textures and colors he'd never seen. He appreciated the aroma of the rich leather and the strength of the marble under his feet.

He was gazing at a painting of an elk herd when Amelia slipped into the room from the back chambers. Their eyes met and he smiled. She blushed ever so slightly. It seemed like forever ago since he'd looked into her sea green eyes or watched the sunlight shimmer in her auburn hair. She was still the most beautiful girl he had ever seen.

Grandpa was making the introductions when he realized no one was paying attention. Looking at Charlie, and then at Amelia, he smiled. "Well, I'll be," he teased.

"Did you say something, Grandpa?"

"Yep, I did," replied Grandpa. "I was sayin', remove your hat and allow me to introduce you to Miss Amelia Taylor."

Embarrassed, Charlie grabbed the hat from his head and tucked it under his arm.

"I beg your pardon, Miss Taylor," he replied, with a bow.

"It's all right," replied Amelia. "I lost my train of thought for a moment as well."

Grandpa grinned, watching Charlie fidget with his hat.

"Amelia, this is my grandson, Charles E. Smith, or better known to those who befriend him, Charlie, and Charlie, this here is Miss Amelia Taylor, the assistant to Judge Randolph P. Walker."

"Nice to make your acquaintance," said Amelia.

"The pleasure is mine, Miss Taylor," answered Charlie, his eyes gleaming.

"Well," she said, clasping her hands. "You two look handsome. And I trust you were able to get some rest. Today will be a full day of meetings."

"Thank you," said Grandpa. "Yes, we got plenty of rest."

"And you look quite lovely yourself," mumbled Charlie.

Amelia smiled sheepishly. "Thank you."

An awkward silence followed, then Grandpa said, "Well, who do we see first, Amelia?"

The young lady scurried to her desk. "Let me see, Mr. Smith. Ah, you are to see Mr. Atkins first. He will discuss your final will and testament, the deed, and all other pertinent information before you see Mr. Abel. Mr. Abel will then set up whatever you deem appropriate in the way of trusts or other financial accounts."

Charlie stepped up to the desk and cleared his throat. "Amelia, would you care to join us for lunch this afternoon?"

She looked up from her appointment book and nervously patted at her hair. "Well, I'd love to Charlie, but I have another engagement this afternoon. Could we meet for coffee sometime later today?"

The disappointment that had initially gripped Charlie slid away at her invitation for coffee. "That would be great! When should I pick you up?"

"Let's meet here around five thirty? We can go across the street to my friend's dress shop. She has a tea room there, too. If that meets with your approval?"

Charlie beamed. "Sounds wonderful."

"Good." She smiled back. "I'll see you at five-thirty."

Turning quickly, she walked back to the chamber doors. "If you'll excuse me, I'll see if Mr. Atkins is ready for you."

Charlie sat down on the edge of a big leather chair. Grandpa sank into another. He leaned his head back and chuckled. "Have the wind knocked out of you, boy?"

Charlie grinned. "Yes, sir, guess I did. I've seen some pretty girls in Pueblo, and even here in Denver, but she's different. Somehow I feel like I've known her a long time."

Grandpa laughed aloud. "Yep, you been bit. I had the same reaction the first time I saw your grandma. All I can say is you better hang on, son, 'cause when it comes to girls, it's gonna be a ride."

Charlie was about to unleash a million questions at his grandfather, when Amelia returned. Both men stood up. "Mr. Atkins will see you now," she announced in a profes-

In Green Pastures

sional tone, then turned toward the doors.

"Well, I guess we better follow her." Grandpa motioned to Charlie. "Don't think Mr. Atkins'll come out here."

Charlie put his feet into motion and followed Amelia through the back doors and up the stairs. They passed Judge Walker's chambers and several other doors. Finally, they reached one that read: "Mr. Timothy I. Atkins, Esquire."

Amelia knocked. "Misters Stuart and Charles Smith to see you, Mr. Atkins," she announced.

"Come in, come in," responded a cheerful voice.

Amelia opened the door for Grandpa and Charlie.

Mr. Atkins was a balding middle aged man with silver-streaked sideburns. His eyes looked sharp and clever but he had an easy smile. "Mr. Smith, it's good to see you again," he said as he motioned for his guests to be seated.

Charlie let Grandpa take the chair closest to the desk.

"And I assume this is your grandson, Charlie?"

"Yep, this is my boy."

Charlie gave a nod of acknowledgment and greeting. Mr. Atkins and Grandpa relaxed in their leather chairs, but Charlie sat on the edge of his and drummed his fingers across his knee.

The attorney reviewed the details of the situation, helping Charlie understand the probate process. Once the facts were stated and all questions answered, Mr. Atkins pulled out Grandpa's final will and testament.

"As you see here, Charlie, the first document is a temporary will drawn up per your grandfather's instructions prior to his knowledge of the full amount that would be left him. He chose you as his sole beneficiary, should anything happen to him before the matter was final. Now that Mr. Smith's debts have been settled, and we've completed the paperwork, a final will and testament has been drawn up and awaits your grandfather's signature. No major changes were made."

Mr. Atkins turned to Grandpa. "What you've expressed to me as your final wish is that Charlie will immediately inherit everything upon your death. That includes: the six hundred acres just outside Saint Louis, Missouri, actually located in the township of Saint Charles, Missouri, and the five million-plus dollar amount that has been deposited into your account at First Bank of Denver. It was not your desire to set up any type of trust fund or annuity. Correct?"

Grandpa nodded. "Yes, Mr. Atkins. I trust this young man with my life, so I can trust him with everything else."

Grandpa grinned, but Charlie couldn't smile back. This whole conversation seemed surreal. He objected to how Grandpa and Atkins were making plans for Grandpa's death and how his belongings should be divvied up. He wanted to put a stop to it right then and there, but out of respect, he kept his mouth shut.

Mr. Atkins continued. "Until the time of your death, Charlie is to receive a monthly allotment of one thousand dollars per month to pay for schooling, clothing, food, shelter, and anything else he deems essential to his well being. And this money is to be deposited into his bank account in the same bank previously mentioned. Correct?"

"That's correct Mr. Atkins. And we need to head over to the bank right after we leave here and open his account."

"Good," said Atkins. "And, sir, may I suggest that you consider adding young Mr. Smith to your account? With the final will, and him an established partner on your account, it will make the process much quicker should you unexpectedly pass."

"Why, sure," replied Grandpa. "I'll do that."

"And one final decree, Mr. Smith. It is your desire that the forty acre farm north of Pueblo, in the Colorado Territory, which includes a cabin, barn, several outbuildings, and all of their contents, as well as all of your personal worldly possessions, be left to your grandson. Is that correct?"

Grandpa confirmed it.

"Then if I may obtain your signature on this line." Atkins laid the document and a pen in front of Grandpa.

Grandpa signed name and date.

Charlie watched, feeling that Grandpa had just given himself permission to die.

Grandpa returned the pen, sat back in his seat, and took a deep breath. "Easiest money I ever gave away."

Atkins turned to Charlie. "Young man, this may be difficult for you to listen to, hearing us talk of death and such, but believe me, your grandfather is correct in preparing these documents. He is ensuring a secure future for you and your family to come, so please don't consider this a negative thing."

"But wills and such are for when you die. I'm not ready for him to even consider dying yet," said Charlie.

Grandpa sat back in his chair and crossed his legs. He was going to let the attorney handle this one.

"Mr. Smith," said Atkins, "you should draw up a will yourself in the very near future. Ideally, wills should be prepared before death is expected; then if it does occur unexpectedly, the living are not confronted with questions and probate issues, or in your case, your estate doesn't go to the Territory."

It was new information, and Charlie found himself becoming curious about these laws. He'd never given thought to such things before. He was in a different place in his life now, for sure; and nothing would ever be quite the same.

"A young man like you will be thinking about marriage soon. Before long you'll have your own heirs to consider."

Charlie blushed at that, but before he could think of an answer, Mr. Atkins was standing and thanking the men for their business. He assured them both that he was at their service, night or day, to answer their questions. With warm handshakes, they said good-bye.

Next stop was Mr. Abel's office down the hall. Charlie admired the mahogany walls, panelling, and marble floors again. Grandpa was quiet.

"Looks awfully official, don't it?" Grandpa pointed to Mr. Abel's name plate. "Takes brass for such fancy letters."

Charlie liked the brass name plates. He tried to imagine how his name would look: "Charles E. Smith, Esq."

When Grandpa softly knocked on the imposing door a strong voice answered, "Come in."

This office was littered with papers, tablets, and folders. Tucked in the corner, an adding machine spewed a long tab of numbers out of its mouth and onto the floor. Filing cabinets and bookshelves overflowed.

"Excuse my mess," apologized the accountant as he stood to shake hands. "I did clean up a bit, believe it or not." Looking around, he proudly said, "I can put my finger on any given document within a matter of seconds." With one long, thin finger he pushed up his glasses.

Grandpa nodded politely.

Mr. Abel cleared papers off of the guest chairs and beckoned Charlie and Grandpa to be comfortable.

While the accountant droned on, Charlie watched dust particles dart in and out of sun rays streaming in from the windows. This meeting wasn't as interesting. After two hours, Charlie felt as if his head was going to explode.

The meeting finally adjourned and they left the stuffy, papery room. In the hall, Charlie whispered to Grandpa, "How can anyone work in an office like that and do nothing but mess with numbers all day?"

Grandpa laughed. "I think you mean, how can anyone *work* with numbers all day in a *mess* like that office?"

Charlie laughed and nodded in agreement. Reaching the front lobby, he glanced around to see if Amelia was in sight, but her desk was empty.

"It's 1:30. She's probably out to lunch somewhere."

"You're right, Grandpa. She did say she had a previous engagement. I suggest we do the same. I'm starvin'."

"Me too. Let's go—"

"I know. Let's go get some chicken."

Grandpa laughed and patted his stomach, "Oh, I don't feel like havin' chicken right now, but thanks for the suggestion. I am hankerin' for her biscuits and coffee, though."

Shaking his head, Charlie pushed the massive front door and they stepped out in the cool air. They were done with meetings. The only thing left to do was set up Charlie's bank account and add him to Grandpa's account. They made quick work of that chore on their way to their favorite restaurant. The restaurant with the clean red and white checked tablecloths, the homey atmosphere, and the fried chicken that made a man's mouth water just thinking about it.

10

MISS DIXIE ENTERED THE DINING ROOM AS the two men hung their slickers on wall hooks. "My, my," she said, "don't you two look dashing!"

"Yes, we do!" Grandpa grinned. "Had to go see a friend this morning and thought we'd cut a swell, get gussied up."

Dixie giggled. "I hope she was worth it."

Grandpa chuckled and shook his head as he pulled a chair out from the closest table. "Not that kinda friend, Miss Dixie. Not for this old man—unless it's you, of course."

Mischief flickered in Dixie's eyes. "Why, Mr. Smith, are you flirting with me?"

Grandpa started to turn his hat in his hands, suddenly nervous. "May I have a . . . a . . . cup of coffee, please?"

Dixie threw her head back and laughed. "Of course," she said jovially. "I'll be right back."

Then Rebecca stood there blushing. "You two look awfully nice," she said. "Though cowboy clothes suit you better." She looked at Charlie.

He blurted, "I thought you'd . . . we'd—"

"I mean . . . I think jeans and boots make you both look . . ." she hesitated, but it was too late and she plunged on red-faced, ". . . manlier, if you don't mind me saying."

Charlie looked away.

Grandpa smiled. "Good thing these suits are only for special occasions then. We'll get back into our cowboy duds as soon as we're done eatin'."

Rebecca glanced at Charlie. "I didn't mean to—"

"Its okay, darlin'," Grandpa assured her. "We didn't take it too hard. Did we Charlie?" Charlie was pretending to read the menu. "Did we, Charlie?" Grandpa repeated so loud that folks at the next table turned to look.

Charlie glanced up at the girl. "Um, no, not at all," he said, forcing a smile. "Can we order now?"

Rebecca lowered her eyes. "I'll . . . I'll . . ." She turned and dashed into the kitchen.

"What'd you do that for?" snapped Grandpa.

"Do what?" Charlie frowned. "I'm hungry. I want to eat."

"Is food all you think about?"

"It is when I'm hungry."

"She was tryin' to pay you a compliment."

Charlie scowled. "Really? I couldn't tell."

"She was," said Miss Dixie, having just approached the table. "She thinks the world of you, Charlie. She may not know how to express it, but she does."

"See," chided Grandpa. "You need to start payin' attention, boy!"

"Listen, Grandpa, me and Mary Lou aren't gonna—"

"No, you're not!" the old man snapped. "Mary Lou's gone, Charlie. It's high time you came to terms with that fact."

"Did I call her *Mary Lou?*" Charlie asked, cocking his head and remembering the sister of his childhood friend, Wilbur. "I didn't mean to say that."

"Is that why you won't talk to her when you're here, Charlie?" asked Dixie. "Because she reminds you too much of a lost romance?"

"There wasn't any romance!"

"Then don't confuse Rebecca, or any other girl for that

matter, with someone from the past," Dixie cautioned. "Each is unique. For example, my Rebecca can call a wild turkey within ten yards then shoot him right in the eye, and that's with a black powder rifle mind you, but she—"

"She can?" the two men chimed in unison, staring wide eyed.

"Yes, she can. And she can catch blueberries in her mouth or take 'em and make the best pie this side of the Mississippi. She can swim like a fish and ride like the wind—but she still has feelings."

Charlie flinched. "I'm sorry," he moaned. "I didn't mean to hurt her feelin's." He threw his arms up in frustration. "I don't even know what I did."

"You forgot to treat her like you want to be treated," said Grandpa. "She is a person and deserves respect. Like we talked about this mornin'. Waitin' on tables is just a job."

Charlie sighed heavily. "Listen, I didn't mean to come across that way. I don't care that she waits on tables. Heck, I clean out barns. It's just that she's so young and I'm too—"

"Ah, her age," said Dixie, patting his arm. "I understand. Fret no more. Rebecca'll get over it. I'll get your food now."

Grandpa picked up his napkin and tucked a corner into his shirt. Charlie stared at the table. "Gonna eat?" asked Grandpa.

"Don't know."

"You better, 'cause once we get back to the hotel you're stuck with whatever they have."

Charlie didn't move. "Grandpa, I didn't love Mary Lou that way. Sometimes I barely knew she existed. So why do I keep callin' every girl by her name? Why do I think of her every time I'm near a girl?"

"I'd judge it's 'cause for so long, she was the only girl you

In Green Pastures

knew, so she's all you have to compare the others to."

"How do I stop doing that?"

Grandpa picked up his coffee cup. "By takin' the time to get to know other girls," he answered softly. "They're just people, Charlie. Nothin' to be scared of."

Charlie unfolded his napkin across his lap. Grandpa watched the traffic on the street and laughed softly. "Well, sometimes they can be scary. There was one time your Grandma got mad at me. She was a wisp of a woman, but when she got mad, wheeee. Scared the bejebees outta me."

Dixie brought a tray of food. "Okay, gentlemen, let's get you fed."

Charlie looked her in the eye. "Please tell Mar—I mean Rebecca—that I'm sorry . . ."

Setting the last plate down, she smiled warmly. "No, I won't. Only *you* can do that. I'll send her out when it's time for dessert." Surveying the table, she added, "If you need anything else, let me know. You two enjoy and I'll be back in a little while to check on you."

"She didn't give me time to finish," objected Charlie.

Grandpa spread butter on a biscuit. "Buck up, son. First time for everythin'. You said you're sorry; leave it at that."

Charlie pushed the mashed potatoes around on his plate, but soon, the aroma of the food started to play with his senses. It didn't take long before he was stuffing himself with chicken fried steak, peas and carrots, mashed potatoes and gravy, and homemade biscuits. His trouble with girls was no longer a concern, at least for the time being. It would be time for dessert soon enough.

11

BRIGHT SUN GLISTENED OFF STOREFRONT windows, but a cold wind blew through the town. Charlie wanted to get Grandpa back to the hotel, but he didn't want to exhaust him either, so he let Grandpa set their pace. When they finally reached the hotel doors, Grandpa pointed to the rocking chairs that lined the porch and quietly said, "I think I'll just sit in one of these rockers and rest a spell."

"Are you sure?" asked Charlie. "It's chilly out. Wouldn't you rather sit inside?"

"No," mumbled the old man. "I'd rather sit here, watch the horses go by, listen to the chatter, and relax a spell."

"Okay. I'll be back in a minute. Just gonna go upstairs and change into my um, manly cowboy clothes."

Grandpa nodded and grinned and slid into a chair. With his hands folded across his stomach, he took a couple deep breaths and relaxed.

A few minutes later, Charlie appeared on the porch. "Here, Grandpa. This oughta keep you warm." He wrapped a blanket around his grandfather's stooped shoulders.

Grandpa pulled the blanket tight. "Thank you, son. I'll be fine," he said softly. Closing his eyes, he laid his head back and began to gently rock back and forth.

The two sat in silence for a while. Finally, Grandpa looked over at Charlie. "Did you understand all the things that we went over today?"

"I believe I have a pretty good handle on it," answered

Charlie. "And if I have any questions, Mr. Atkins and Mr. Abel are there to answer them for me, night or day."

Grandpa chuckled. "Don't take that too lightly. You might find yourself needin' their help one day and it will be nice to know they're there for you."

"I don't take their sincerity lightly, Grandpa," said Charlie. "I just can't help but wonder if they're offering their services to me because I'm Charlie Smith, or because I'm young Mr. Charles E. Smith, with five million numbers behind my name."

"Probably a little of both," replied Grandpa. "But I trust 'em. And that says a lot."

"Yes, sir, it does," agreed Charlie. "If they've gained your trust, then I know I can follow with mine."

Grandpa closed his eyes and sighed. "And you did a right good job apologizin' to Becky, too."

"Hardest thing I ever did," admitted Charlie. "It's probably easier to wrestle a buffalo than to talk to one of them."

"Well, the secret to is to . . . ugh!" Grandpa jerked forward and grabbed his chest. The rocker tilted and he slid half way out of the chair, landing hard on one knee.

Charlie scrambled to his feet. "Grandpa, what is it?"

The old man couldn't catch his breath. His face went pale. Charlie grabbed his grandfather under the arms and held him up for a minute, then slowly helped him back onto the chair. As Charlie wrapped the blanket tightly around the thin shoulders again, Grandpa whispered something about indigestion and too much fried chicken, but Charlie knew better. When he was sure Grandpa was breathing, he ran inside the hotel to inquire about a doctor.

Within minutes, despite his protest, hotel employees had

helped Grandpa into the parlor and made sure he was lying comfortably on a sofa. The doctor was on his way. "Lordy," Grandpa mumbled breathlessly. "I don't know why everyone's fussin' over such a little thing."

Standing at the arm of the couch, Charlie looked down at the old man. "We'll let the doctor call it a little thing," he said firmly.

Grandpa stopped smiling.

The doctor came, a young man about thirty-seven years old, who walked with a distinct limp. Nodding to Charlie, he marched quickly over to the patient and pulled up a chair. He gave Grandpa a quick exam right there in the parlor. Charlie took a step back and waited patiently.

A few minutes later, the doctor folded his stethoscope and put it back into his bag. Turning to Charlie, he asked, "Can we get him up to his room?"

With the help of the hotel owner, Charlie carried Grandpa upstairs and laid him in his bed.

The doctor pulled a chair beside the bed and tended to his patient. Charlie sat on his bed and watched. He wanted to stay out of the doctor's way, but still be within arms reach if Grandpa needed him.

"Son, I'm going to ask you to wait downstairs while I give your grandfather a thorough exam."

"But, he won't care if I stay. I've lived with him since—"

"It's just my policy."

Charlie looked at Grandpa, hoping he'd interject and tell the doctor he could stay, but instead, the old man smiled and nodded weakly. "Go on, I'll be fine."

Charlie left with bent shoulders and bowed head, as the doctor said, "I'll call you when I'm done. No need to worry."

That's easy for you to say, Charlie thought.

After what seemed like an eternity, the doctor finally called him back in. Charlie took the stairs two at a time. The quiet room was lit by a single gas lamp. Shadows skipped across the floor, as he approached the bed. In the dimness Charlie could barely see his grandfather's form. Why was this so familiar? He felt he'd been here before. But when?

The young man looked into his grandfather's face. His body was almost lost under layers of blankets. He was barely breathing. Charlie threw the doctor a questioning look.

"He's sleeping," whispered the doctor.

"What happened, doc?"

"Well, looks like your grandfather had a serious heart attack. And what concerns me is this isn't the first one."

"Not his first heart attack?!"

The physician took Charlie by the elbow and motioned to the door. "Let's go down for a cup of coffee, shall we?"

Charlie glanced back. "I think I better stay."

"I gave him medicine to help him sleep. He'll be out for a while. It's all right."

Downstairs, over a cup of coffee the doctor explained how the heart pumps blood and what happens when the arteries get blocked. Charlie sat mesmerized. The doctor acknowledged that he was not certain what had caused Grandpa's heart attacks, but that his heart was very weak and, by the sound of its rhythm, was badly damaged.

Charlie fiddled with a salt shaker. He took several deep breaths to draw up courage, then asked, "What can we do?"

"There's nothing we can do. I'm sorry."

Tears welled in Charlie's eyes. He got up, walked to the window and stared out into the northern sky. He whispered,

"Lord, you mean to tell me I've got five million dollars and 640 acres of land and there is nothing I can do with it to help my Grandpa?" The silence pounded in his ears.

"I'm truly sorry," said the doctor. "If there was something that could be done, I'd tell you. But all we can do is keep him as warm and comfortable as possible."

Charlie turned to face him. "How long does he have?"

"I don't know; a day, a week. That's out of my hands."

Upstairs, in the dim light of the hotel room, Grandpa awoke from his medically induced slumber. He scanned the room for a moment, trying to remember where he was. Things didn't look familiar to him. He tried to sit up, but the weight on his chest held him down. Scared, he whispered in the darkness. "Charlie!"

"There's no need to be afraid, Grandpa," came a familiar voice from the foot of the bed. "It's me."

The old man lifted his head and searched the room, looking for his grandson in the shadows. The boy took a step forward. Even in the muted light, Grandpa recognized the angel who had saved him after his fall from his horse. With gnarled fingers, he beckoned him closer.

Micah walked up to the bedside and smiled.

"So, you'd be the one to come and take me home, huh?" Grandpa asked softly.

"Yes, Grandpa. I'm here to take you home," replied the young man.

"Will my Charlie be okay?"

"He'll be just fine, Grandpa. Our Lord is watching over him. He'll be just fine."

"Then I'm ready to go."

Micah laid a hand on Grandpa's chest. For a moment Grandpa wasn't certain what happened, but when Micah lifted it, he knew. He slowly stood to his feet. Micah pointed to Grandpa's hands. "Look," he said softly. Grandpa spread his palms out in front of him. He flipped them to the topside. His fingers were no longer gnarled and painful, but were long and strong. His knees no longer hurt, nor did his chest feel the heaviness that it had carried for so long. He felt his face. The skin was smooth and youthful. Turning slightly, he saw his worn, human shell lying among the blankets and quilts on his bed. He looked around the room through eyes that were clear and sharp. He turned to Micah and smiled.

"And Jesus?"

"He's waiting for you," replied Micah. "Just over there."

Grandpa's eyes followed to where the young man was pointing. Gently, the angel took Grandpa's hand and led him into a tunnel of light.

"Well, I'll go check on him one last time before I call it a night," said the doctor. Pushing himself up from his chair, he swallowed the last of his coffee.

Charlie held out his hand. "By the way, my name is Charlie Smith, and my grandpa is Stuart—Stuart Smith. Thank you for coming out tonight to take care of him."

The doctor shook Charlie's hand. "I figured as much. I'm Doc Taylor. Your grandfather came into my office months ago, but I didn't have the pleasure of making his acquaintance. He just left a small, empty bottle with my nurse. I refilled it for him, but he never got it."

Charlie remembered the brown bag that the hotel clerk tried to give him last fall. It contained a small bottle of laudanum; he refused to take it, not believing it belonged to Grandpa. Horrible thoughts filled his head. He asked, "Would that medicine have made any difference, doc?"

"I don't know if it would've or not, Charlie. He's an old man. It may have given him—"

Charlie bounded up the stairs; he'd heard enough.

Charlie rushed to Grandpa's side. Despite his apprehension, all appeared as it had earlier. Grandpa lay still. Doc Taylor came in and sat down in his chair beside the bed. He pulled the blankets back and held his stethoscope to Grandpa's chest, moving the instrument from point to point in silence. An uneasiness began to stir deep within Charlie. Slowly, the doctor sat back in his chair and pulled the ear tips of the stethoscope from his ears. He gazed at the old man, a look of compassion on his face.

"What is it, doctor?" whispered Charlie.

Without taking his gaze off the old man's face, the doctor softly replied, "He's gone."

"What? What do you mean he's gone?"

"He's gone, Charlie," repeated the doctor.

In the darkness, Charlie slowly moved closer to the bedside. He knelt on the floor beside his grandfather. Cautiously, he rested his head on the old chest and listened. There was nothing. No heartbeat, no breathing, just silence. He looked up into the old face. The wrinkles that had gathered in the corners of Grandpa's eyes didn't look so bad now. His lips, usually pursed in pain, looked relaxed, as if they were just forming a smile. Charlie half expected Grandpa to open his eyes and smile at him. But he knew those tired eyelids would never open again. The faded eyes behind them were now blind to the things of this earth. And those old ears would never hear the words, "I love you, Grandpa," no matter how many times he whispered them.

Tears streamed down his face. This wasn't like the time when he was ten years old and Grandpa had fallen deathly ill. There was no need to pray now. Nothing would bring him back. He was in Heaven—no longer in pain, no longer old. He was with Ma and Pa and Grandma. More importantly, he was with Jesus, the one who'd made all the difference in his life. "See ya later, Grandpa," Charlie whispered.

He knew he should be happy that Grandpa was at peace. He was, to a point. But deep down he felt as if his own heart had been ripped from his chest. He wanted to pray for comfort, but couldn't find the words. Dazed, he just groaned. Groans continued to rise from deep within his soul. Then they turned to sorrowful moans. He buried his face in his grandfather's side and sobbed with all the force of a broken heart. Loneliness started to overtake him. "What am I gonna do? How will I go on?"

Then Charlie felt strong arms embrace him and hold him close. In their warmth, he let go of the agony.

Jess rocked him back and forth, as a parent would a crying child, while the young man poured out his heart. Jess whispered, "And he loves you too, son. Always remember Charlie, that no one on this earth loved you more than your Grandpa. But no one in the universe loves you more than the Father."

Charlie buried his face in Jess's chest and cried. And unbeknownst to Charlie, Jess cried too.

12

CHARLIE AWAKENED TO THE THUMP OF RAINdrops against the window. He watched with heavy eyes as thin rivulets slithered down the glass. Streams of water cascaded from the roof and splashed on the muddy street below. He raised his head and looked at the bed on the other side of the room, hoping that the night before had just been a bad dream. But it wasn't. The bed had already been stripped of its blankets and sheets. Nothing remained except a cold grey and white striped mattress. His head fell back into his pillow and he closed his eyes. "Lord, help me through this," he whispered.

He dressed quickly, not wanting to spend any more time in that room than necessary. He checked the buttons on his slicker, gave his hat a good tug, then grabbed his saddlebags and slung them over his shoulder. Before closing the door, he turned and looked around the room one more time. It was the last place he'd seen Grandpa alive, but he didn't want this room to be a part of his memories. He wanted to remember Grandpa's smile, his wit, and the loving way he called him son. Sighing heavily, he turned away.

"Will you be checking out, sir?" asked the hotel clerk.

"Yeah, I am," muttered Charlie, stepping up to the desk. "I'll be headin' home today."

"I'm sorry to hear of your grandfather. Are there any arrangements with which we can help you?"

"Yeah," he said quietly. "A couple."

"Certainly, sir."

"Would you mind sending this box to the noted address, and then make sure that Misters Timothy Atkins and Stanley Abel get this letter? Their address is on the envelope."

"Absolutely, sir." The clerk handed him the forms to fill out, then the receipt. Charlie paid without uttering a word.

"God speed," said the clerk.

"Thanks," said Charlie. "I'll be seein' ya."

Turning, he walked out into the storm. He didn't care about the weather. He just wanted to go home, but first, he had to see to Amelia.

He stepped inside the lobby and removed his soaked hat, dripping water all over one of the judge's beautiful rugs, but he couldn't leave without explaining to Amelia why he hadn't kept his appointment with her the night before.

He glanced at her empty desk. "Where are you?" he muttered. He walked to the rear door that lead to the offices and was about to grab the handle when it opened. Amelia stepped through the door and met him face to face.

"Oh," she squealed, bringing her hand to her chest. "I didn't expect you, Charlie. You scared me half to death."

"Then I owe you two apologies," he said, bowing.

Amelia took his arm. "No, you don't owe me any."

"I didn't mean to stand you up last evening," he began, but Amelia stopped him with a hand on his arm.

She led him to the big leather chairs beside the fireplace. She sat down in one and motioned him to sit across from her. "I know, Charlie," she whispered. "I understand. Dr. Taylor is my father. He explained and . . ." She choked and paused a moment to regain her composure. "And I'm so sorry for your loss. He was such a special man. I wish I could've gotten to know him better."

"Thank you, Amelia, for your kindness," Charlie said.

"Can we have our tea sometime later this week?"

Charlie searched her eyes. "No," he said slowly. "I'm leaving this afternoon. I've got to get back to the farm."

"I see," she whispered. "Then would you mind if we spoke for a few minutes now?"

Charlie leaned slightly forward in his seat. "Is there something on your mind?" he asked anxiously.

Amelia nodded, blushing. "Yes. Please forgive me for bringing this up at such a time, but I need to talk to you."

"It's all right," Charlie assured her. "What is it?"

She lowered her eyes. "I've wanted to tell you this for such a long time, but now that I have the chance, I'm not really sure how to say it."

Charlie's heart was beating in his ears. "Just say it."

Amelia took a deep breath. "Okay." She focused on Charlie's collar. "I may be speaking out of turn, Charlie, but I believe I need to tell you that I'm spoken for." She slowly lifted her eyes until they met Charlie's stunned face.

"Well, he hasn't come right out and asked if he can court me yet, but I'm expecting that he will soon."

Charlie figured his face must've told her something because she suddenly stopped gushing and changed her tone. "I just don't want you to have false hope, or be led by feelings that I cannot reciprocate," she added carefully.

Charlie turned scarlet. What was Mary Lou's warning? Her words were jumbled in his head, but he remembered her saying something about losing at love.

"He recently graduated from West Point, in New York, and is now a lieutenant in the United States Army," Amelia was saying proudly. "He has been ordered to serve under the

In Green Pastures

command of General Custer. Have you heard of him? I've been told he's a wonderful commander. Energetic, charismatic; just the man to lead in the northern plains. The Lakota Indians are on the rise in that area for some reason, but I don't worry about John. I believe he's in the best of hands under Custer's care."

Charlie nodded mechanically.

"I would like to remain friends with you, Charlie. I hope I haven't discouraged that from happening."

Charlie stood to his feet. "Friends," he mumbled. "Yes, of course. We'll always be friends."

Amelia stood and gently took his arm. Together, they walked to the large mahogany doors. "Someday, when you have time, let's sit and talk," she said softly. "We haven't had a chance to talk about our lives, to share things, and I'd like to do that if we could." She looked up into his face. "I do want to be your friend, Charlie."

He started to turn his hat in his hands. Amelia giggled. "Your grandfather used to do that," she said affectionately.

Charlie's eyes dropped to his hands and he stopped.

She extended her hand. "Please stay in touch, Charlie." He looked at her hand for a second then took it in his own.

"I will." He gave her fingers a little squeeze. "Good-bye, my friend."

Darting across the street, he thought he heard someone call his name above the hammering rain, but he kept running. He didn't want to stop. He didn't want to make small talk; he wanted to make arrangements with Doc Taylor and head home, especially now. But the call came again.

"Charlie, wait a minute, please." This time, he couldn't avoid it. It was Dixie. Turning, he saw her swollen, red eyes and knew those weren't raindrops running down her face.

She clutched a cape tightly around her shoulders with one hand while trying to push a lock of hair out of her face with the other. "Charlie, are you all right?"

Rain poured down on them, flattening the rebellious tuft of hair to Dixie's face. He cinched his saddlebags over his shoulder again and nodded. Taking her elbow, he led her to the boardwalk, under the eaves. "I'm fine, Dixie. I had a fitful night, but I'm fine."

"Will you come see us before you leave? I believe Rebecca wants to share something with you."

Charlie cast an impatient glance down the street. "Thank you, ma'am," he said gently. "But I don't think so. I need to get home. I'm sure she'll understand."

Dixie smiled warmly and took his arm. "He meant the world to us. He was such a dear man."

"More than you know," agreed Charlie. "Thank you for everything, Dixie. You and Rebecca both. Tell her I said thank you, too."

Dixie tried to smile, but her chin wouldn't cooperate. "I will." She bit her lip. "Rebecca knew something was wrong when the two of you left the restaurant the other night. She said Stuart didn't look like he was feeling well. Like he was really sick, but she didn't know what to do."

Charlie nervously ground his heel into the wooden boardwalk. "Well," he said faintly, "according to Doc Taylor, there wasn't anything anyone could do. It was his time."

"And God knows best," she answered.

A clap of thunder unleashed a torrent of water. "Look," yelled Charlie over the drumming above their heads. "I've got to go. Get back inside before you get sick. You'll be hearing from me, Dixie. I don't know when, but you'll hear from me soon."

Dixie stood on her tiptoes and kissed his cheek. "Take care, Charlie. My prayers will be with you." She turned to run back across the street, but Charlie grabbed her arm.

"Miss Dixie," he yelled out. "I almost forgot. Would you do me a favor and give these to Rebecca? I've been cartin' them around and meant to give them to . . . well, I just hope she can use them."

He pulled a small worn sack from his saddlebag and handed it to her. She looked up at him in surprise.

"It's nothin'," he said shyly. "Just a few ribbons I bought for . . . well, just some ribbons I don't want to tote all the way back home."

"I'll be happy to give them to her." Dixie smiled. "I'm sure she'd be even more pleased if she received them directly from you, but she'll understand. Should I say they're a gift?"

He started to shake his head then stopped. Studying her face, he nodded. "Yeah, they're a gift from me. Tell her I thank her for all the kindness she showed my grandfather while he was here. He thought an awful lot of her."

"And you?" asked Dixie.

Charlie wished he could stop the burning in his cheeks. "And me too," he admitted. "Good bye, Dixie."

Charlie hurried to Doc Taylor's, who said, "Are you sure you won't wait a while, Charlie? The weather could get uglier."

"I'll just have to take my chances, doc. He only asked me to make him two promises, ever. One was to help a friend with finances and the other was to bury him on the hillside beside Grandma. I've already helped that friend like he asked and I'll fulfill his last wish as soon as I get home, so if you wouldn't mind getting him ready for burial, I'll get everything else ready for my trip."

Sighing, the doctor nodded. "He'll be ready this afternoon, Charlie. But I can't see making the trip all the way to Pueblo by wagon if you could catch a train, at least from here to Colorado Springs."

"I appreciate your concern," replied Charlie. "But I'll be fine. I'd rather do it this way. Now, if you'll excuse me, I've got to take care of a few things before I head home. I'll be back here around two o'clock. If you could, please have things ready for me by then."

The doctor reluctantly agreed and stood in the doorway watching as Charlie strode up the boardwalk toward the livery. On that bustling morning in Denver, wagons, carriages, single riders, and a few mule carts crowded the streets. Mud sloshed from one puddle to the next with every step or turn of a wheel. A cow plodded up the roadside, being poked and prodded from behind.

The rain let up; Charlie's spirits lifted. The task at hand was daunting, but not impossible—with God's help. He picked up his step, glancing occasionally at store windows.

Rounding the corner onto First Street, Charlie stopped in his tracks. Just a few feet from him stood none other than Trevor Cassidy. "Big T" Cassidy, a ruthless cowpuncher, and his accomplice McQueen, were the two cowboys who almost killed his friend LeFaye on the cattle drive the year before. Charlie felt a twinge of anger pulsate through his veins. Although Denver was growing by leaps and bounds, it wasn't big enough to prevent the two of them from encountering each other.

The cowpuncher was leaning against a porch post in front

of a saloon, smoking a cigarette and glaring at the jailhouse across the street. Charlie pulled his hat down over his eyes. He walked around to the other side of the post. Folding his arms, he leaned almost shoulder to shoulder with Big T. He hoped his casual demeanor gave passers-by the impression that sharing a post with this guy was as natural as the sun rising in the morning.

Cassidy didn't seem to notice him, or care if he did. He just smoked his cigarette and stared at the jailhouse. Finally, Charlie gave a quick jerk of his head and said in a low, heavy tone, "Who they got in the hoosegow?"

Cassidy shifted his feet and flicked the ashes from the end of his cigarette. Smoke streamed from his nostrils. "A bad hombre by the name of McQueen," he said coldly.

McQueen! Charlie's brain screamed. He forced every muscle in his body to stay poised. *McQueen here, in Denver! Why? Where was he going? What was Big T planning?* He closed his eyes and took a deep breath. Opening them slowly, he grunted, "Mm," as if not interested.

Cassidy tossed the cigarette butt to the middle of the road then stepped off the boardwalk onto the muddy street. Charlie's right hand moved to the inside of his slicker; his fingers found the gun he had tied to his right thigh. But Cassidy didn't turn around. With his back to Charlie Big T said, "And he told me, if I ever saw you again, Smith, to tell you he wants to see you one last time before he dies. So I reckon you should go over there sometime today, 'cause they're movin' him out early tomorrow mornin'."

Big T sauntered on down the street with his hard, white-knuckled fists balled at his sides.

13

THROUGH THE IRON BARS OF THE JAIL CELL Charlie studied the man's figure. Was it him? The deputy at the front desk said this cowboy was the only prisoner scheduled to be transported in the morning, so if Cassidy was telling the truth, it had to be McQueen.

The prisoner lay motionless with his eyes closed. His head rested against the hard brick wall. Thin, crooked hands lay across his sunken stomach. His stocking feet were crossed at the ankles. Was this the Irishman who had tried to kill Charlie last year?

For a moment, Charlie thought he was asleep, then he spoke. "I don't look like much now, do I?" said the man on the cot. He still hadn't opened his eyes.

Charlie carefully sat down on the only chair in the room and leaned his elbows on his knees. He didn't say anything, but kept an eye on the man until McQueen opened one eye and looked in his direction.

"I guess ye never taut I looked like much before, huh?"

Charlie remained motionless and silent. In a flash, McQueen was up—gritting his teeth, slobbering mad. This man who looked weak and tired moved with amazing quickness. Charlie almost fell from his chair, but he pushed himself against the back wall instead, dodging McQueen's hands as they grabbed at him from between the bars.

"If I were out thar I'd kill ye faster dan any bullet." McQueen's eyes bulged. He looked like a wild man. Watching

Charlie's expression, he burst into a fit of laughter. "Still ain't as cool as ye tink ye are, huh, pup?" he snorted.

"Listen, McQueen," said Charlie angrily. "I came in here 'cause I was told you wanted to see me. I'm here. Now what?"

"I wanted to tell ye dat I blame ye for dis, boy, and I curse ye for takin' me life from me. Live wid dat for de rest of yer life, preacher boy. Live wid knowin' dat it's 'cause of you dat I be a dayd man."

Charlie got up from his chair and looked the hardened man in the eye. "No, McQueen, it's not my fault. You did this to yourself. You killed a man in Texas and another in Missouri, then joined the army under a different name, thinkin' you could get away with murder, but you didn't. You were found out and now they have you. But you've always wanted to blame someone else for your messed up life. It's your ma's fault for not doin' this, or your pa's fault for doin' that. Now it's my fault for havin' faith in God and believin'."

The captive swung an arm out from the bars, missing Charlie's collar by inches. "If I'd grabbed ye, ye'd be dayd right now. Ye know dat, don't ye?" he growled.

Charlie didn't blink. "And I'd be with God. Where are you gonna be, McQueen, when your time comes?"

"Wid my dear ol' da," grunted the prisoner. "I'd be in de dirt, dat's where."

"Wouldn't you like to be sure? Wouldn't it be better to put your faith in God, then die and find out He isn't real, than to believe He isn't real, then die and find out He is?"

McQueen drilled into Charlie with his red eyes. "Dat be the same question yer friend asked me a few weeks ago."

"My friend?" Charlie frowned.

"De one ye sent to see me whilst I was still in de stockade

in Fort Collins. Ye know—big, stocky man. Beard. Let's see, what were 'is name, now? . . . Jake?" McQueen shook his head. "Naw, Josh."

Charlie whistled low. "Jess?"

McQueen smirked and pointed a crooked finger at the lad. "Yeah, dat be de man—Jess." He said the name with such malice Charlie took a step back. "I'll tell ye like I tolt him after I spit on his boots."

"Jess came to see you?"

"Listen, you—"

"He said he would, back on the trail, but I'd forgotten."

McQueen slowly walked up to the bars and stood face-to-face with Charlie. He wrapped each finger around the cold black bars with such deliberation his knuckles turned white. "Don't know what kinda prank ye were tryin' ta pull, but I hate ye both," he said through clenched teeth. "He acted like he were tryin' ta save my soul, too, but it didn't work. Ye self-righteous fools. I woulda kilt 'im wid my bare hands if I'd been able to."

"But he—"

"I don' care," snapped McQueen. "Get dat through yer head. I don' care."

Charlie looked helplessly at the prisoner. He doubted McQueen would have believed him anyway.

"Now, to answer yer questions. First, ye asked me where I'll be when my time comes, and I sayd, I'll be in the dirt wid my da," he snarled. "He'd be the first man I ever kilt and I wanna haunt 'im till the end o' time."

Charlie gasped.

"Dat's right, ye dumb pup. Ye see. I kilt my own da 'cause thar weren't a meaner man nor a bigger liar in de whole world dan him. I got sick o' him beatin' my ma, my brother, and me till we were almost dayd, so I kilt him before he kilt us. He often sayd he'd be a Christian and goin' ta 'eaven. If dat's true, I don't wanna go thar. But I can't believe dat thar is a God dat will take da likes o' us, so it'll just be dirt." The man scanned Charlie from the top of his head to the toes of his feet then spat on the ground. "Get outta here now!"

Charlie walked to the doorway, then stopped. Slowly, he turned and looked back at the defeated creature in the locked cage. "I won't carry your curse, McQueen, because I know I tried and you refused. But as long as the Lord lets you breathe, I'll pray you remember one thing."

Did Charlie catch a hint of longing in McQueen eyes, under the façade of harshness?

"Just remember what it says in John 3:16. That God loves you so much, He gave His only begotten son for you and if you believe in Him, He promises that you won't perish, but that you will have everlasting life."

McQueen turned his head, muttering something unintelligible.

"You may have to die on the gallows, McQueen. But you don't have to die forever. Remember that."

"Get out!" roared the Irishman.

"God paid your debt a long time ago."

"Get out, I sayd!"

14

THE WEEK ON THE TRAIL HAD BEEN ROUGH, rougher than Charlie had expected. Rain pummeled them every day. It soaked the ground, making sleeping in a bedroll difficult. He tried to wrap himself in a blanket and sleep on the wagon seat, but that was useless as well—it only made him stiff and sore. And having to get up in the middle of the night to change positions only made him more irritated than he had been before he tried to sleep.

But more than weather weighed on Charlie. Bessie, Grandpa's faithful mare, wasn't herself. She fought the bit. Maybe she thought Grandpa had been left behind and she wanted to go back and get him. Or she knew he was in the back of the wagon and wanted to walk beside him. Whichever, Charlie had a hard time controlling her head and, at times, his temper. He didn't want to blame her. Everything felt strange to him, too, but he needed her help to get home. On the other hand, Star pulled tirelessly, doing his share to keep them moving while Charlie coaxed Bessie.

At the shrill sound of a train whistle Charlie noticed puffs of smoke billowing above the treetops. He stopped the wagon and watched from atop a hill as the procession of cars clanked northward. Star tossed his head and snorted.

"I know, but you can't. You'd run Bessie into the ground and I can't let that happen." Bessie turned a big brown eyeball toward Charlie, as if to say she would do as she pleased. Then she lunged forward. That was all Star needed. The reins that Charlie held lax in his fingers slipped out of his hands. He scrambled to gather them up, but before he could regain control, the horses were off and running.

The wagon bounced across the harsh terrain. Charlie found himself thanking God for giving him the good sense to strap Grandpa's casket securely to the wagon. He could imagine it flying out and splintering on the ground.

"Stop, you two! Before someone gets hurt." But his orders went unheeded. The horses ran neck to neck. Bessie gave it all she had, keeping up with Star. Even when she began showing signs of fatigue, the old girl didn't let up. "You're as thickheaded as your owner was," Charlie hollered. "You're just like 'im, in fact. Won't stop till you die of a—"

The words caught in his throat. Finally able to shorten the reins, he pulled firmly. "Whoa, there," he shouted. "Whoa." Star threw his head back and fought the bit, but finally had to surrender. Bessie tried to keep running, pulling to go on, but she too, ultimately had to stop.

Charlie jumped from the wagon and ran around to Bessie. "Sorry, girl." He grabbed her harness and pulled her face to his. "I'm so sorry." Tears streamed down his cheeks. The old mare nuzzled his shirt while Star nibbled his ear.

They camped on a hill just above town. Star grazed a few feet from the fire, but Bessie stood at the back of the wagon, her chin resting on the lid of the casket. Hidden within the shadows of the great mountains rising behind them, Charlie watched the twinkling lights of the town below. He thought it ironic that hundreds of people slept in their beds just a few miles away, but there was no one to talk to or befriend him. Off in the distance, the lonesome sound of a train whistle pierced the stillness.

Mysterious Ways

He fell into his bedroll and searched the black sky. The night, cold and clear, held a brilliant display of stars overhead. "Hi, Grandpa," he whispered. "I'm sorry I wasn't there to say so long the other night." He flicked a tear from his face. "I hope you're havin' a grand ol' time, visiting with God and our family. You certainly deserve it. Don't worry 'bout me, I know I'm not alone. The Lord is with me."

He searched the sky until he found the North Star. "Thank you, Lord, for takin' care of us," he whispered. "It sure wasn't easy to hear Amelia say she just wants to be friends, but if you don't mind, I'm gonna let you worry about that right now. I'm just too tired. But when I do have the energy to think about it, will you show me what to do?"

It was close to the end of another day when the wagon jolted into the front yard. Charlie pulled the horses to a stop and let his head fall to his chest. Star pawed at the ground then bent his neck and nibbled the grass. Bessie stared ahead.

LeFaye stepped round the cabin. "You okay, Charlie?"

Charlie lifted his chin and peered out from under heavy eyelids. "I am now."

"You go on in. I'll take care of the horses."

Charlie didn't have to be told twice. He half jumped, half fell from the wagon seat and stumbled to the door. There he turned and saw LeFaye approaching the back of the buckboard. The Frenchman was removing his hat and pulling aside the blanket that covered the pine box. Slowly, he brushed his fingers across the lid. He was speaking in French under his breath, and his eyes were closed.

Finally, LeFaye returned to the front of the wagon and took hold of Star's harness. Neither horse resisted as he led them around the cabin to the barn.

Supper was quiet. Charlie appreciated LeFaye not pushing him to talk. Finally, as they were cleaning up, Charlie looked at his friend and asked, "So, what are your plans here on out?"

LeFaye shrugged. "Don't know. Haven't given it much thought. Why? Are you ready for me to move on?"

Charlie shook his head. "No, not at all. This is your home, too. I just don't want you to feel obligated to stay."

"I don't. But you're all the family I have, Charlie."

Charlie nodded. "You're all I have, too," he mumbled. "Guess we were destined to be brothers."

LeFaye said, "I've never had a brother. I'm a bit older; does that mean I can whip you?"

Charlie snickered. "You can try."

LeFaye grinned. "Maybe later."

Charlie pushed the back door open and threw the dish water out into the yard. "After I bury Grandpa and spend some time gettin' the place ready for winter, I'm thinkin' about headin' east for a bit."

LeFaye stopped drying the dish he was holding. "East? What's in the East?"

"Saint Louis." Charlie set the water bowl down and grabbed a cup. "More specific, Saint Charles. I might go and check on a parcel of land out that way."

"What for? You have land right here."

Charlie poured himself some coffee and sat down on the floor in front of the fireplace. "I know, but I haven't seen Missouri, and that's where I'm from after all, so I thought I'd venture out that way and take a look around."

LeFaye tossed his dish towel onto the counter. "If you don't mind, I'd rather stay here and work the farm. We're going to have a nice herd of young calves when the heifers are finished delivering. I'd like to see what we end up with."

"Okay." Charlie yawned, stretching out on the floor.

"Wilbur's been working his folks' place when he can, trying to raise crops to pay off debts. I'd like to help him."

"Yeah."

"Are you listening to me, Charlie?" LeFaye leaned over and looked at his friend. The soft glow of the fire fell across Charlie's face. His large brown eyes were closed. A snore floated upward. "Guess not," muttered the Frenchman.

The sun had not yet split the dark horizon when Charlie pushed the shovel into the hard ground next to the remains of his grandmother. Digging in the darkness, he couldn't grasp the fact that Grandpa was gone.

After daybreak he finished preparing Grandpa's grave. He leaned on the shovel and stared into the dark pit. *I'm so glad there is something more to life than just this,* he thought. *What would the purpose be if this were all it amounted to?*

LeFaye's voice broke the silence. "Come and get some breakfast. I'll help with the casket after we eat."

Charlie rested the shovel against the well, splashed water on his face then took a long drink before going inside. They ate in silence and left the dishes for later, hurrying back to the barn. When they went to retrieve the casket, Star greeted them with a loud cry. Prancing back and forth, his golden mane flew with every toss of his great head. Charlie slid the shovel into the tool bin, by-passed the wagon, and went straight to him. "What is it, boy?"

The gelding tossed his head and nudged Charlie in the chest with his nose.

LeFaye grabbed an apple from the workbench and started toward the stalls. "Charlie, come here!"

Charlie hurried over to LeFaye. Through the wooden slats, he could see Bessie. She was down. Without thinking twice, he jumped over the rails. "What is it ol' girl?" he whispered, kneeling at her head. Bessie rolled an eye at him. She grunted and pushed her nose into his hand.

"You're gonna go find him, aren't you?" Charlie asked, softly stroking her neck. She snorted again. "I understand, girl. And from what I hear, there's lots of pasture up there for the two of you to romp in. Just like in the old days."

LeFaye, standing outside of the stall, cleared his throat.

"Go on, Bessie," encouraged Charlie. "Go find him."

"Excuse me, Charlie," said LeFaye. "I've got to go back to the house for a minute."

Charlie smiled and nodded. "Go on, Phillip. We won't be ready to move Grandpa for a while yet."

LeFaye's footsteps grew fainter. Then they were gone, lost in the grass and carried by the wind. Charlie placed a hand on Bessie's ribs. Her heartbeats faded with each breath. Then, they were gone. Charlie kissed her muzzle.

"You were the best, ol' girl. He'll be happy to see you."

He lingered at the mare's side, caressing her neck and reminiscing. She was already at the farm when he arrived so many years ago. He used to watch Grandpa hitch her to the wagon or saddle her up for a ride. When they went hunting, she'd often carry both of them without objection. All his memories of the farm, or of Grandpa, included her.

He pulled himself up and retrieved the shovel from the tool bin. The family cemetery would hold another grave. There was nothing else he could do.

15

WORD OF GRANDPA'S DEATH SWEPT THE territory like brush fire. People came from all over to pay their respects and offer Charlie whatever help they could. He gratefully accepted the gifts of food. What he appreciated most was the stories about Grandpa. He had touched so many lives. Sitting around the table, out under the oaks, or standing at the foot of his grandparent's graves, he heard story after story about how Grandpa was a fair trader, an excellent hunter, and a wonderful friend.

One man told how, after he'd broken his leg in an accident, Stuart Smith provided food for his family an entire winter. Later, Grandpa wouldn't accept a penny in compensation. Another man had heard how Mr. Smith had traded two head of cattle for the use of a young farmer's plow. Smith claimed that his own plow needed repair and he couldn't afford to have it fixed right then, but several months later it came out that Smith's plow just had a loose handle. He knew the farmer was struggling but wouldn't accept the cattle unless he felt he earned them; so Grandpa made a trade, fair and square.

Charlie watched the faces of the visitors as they reminisced. Some laughed as they spoke; others bit their lip or stiffened their jaw to keep back tears. But each had known his grandfather, and their tales revealed their respect for him.

The mourners often traveled miles just to spend an hour with Charlie. They came to pay their respects, and to fill the root cellar with meats, preserves, pickles, and cheese.

In Green Pastures

A week or so later, LeFaye took the buckboard into Pueblo to get supplies, pulling out before sun up. Charlie was alone and, although he normally didn't have the luxury of taking a few days to rest, he didn't feel like doing much. He straightened up around the cabin, cleaned out the stalls, and filled the water trough. Nothing more.

After eating a simple lunch, he pushed his plate aside and laid his head on his outstretched arm. Guilt about not doing much around the farm began to plague him. *There's so much to do before winter, so many—*

He jerked upright. He hadn't intended to fall asleep. Late afternoon shadows were creeping across the farm as the sun started its western descent and the herd was moving up from the lower pasture. But what had awakened him?

He strained to hear. Only a raven's caw. No, whatever it was, was gone. He laid his head back down and was just about to doze off again when the noise floated to his ears once more. *I'm not dreamin'*, he thought. *But who? And where's it comin' from?*

Silently he pushed his chair back from the table and tiptoed to the fireplace. Very carefully, he pulled Big Blue, Grandpa's old rifle, down from its pegs above the mantle and moved noiselessly to the back window where he glanced out, just long enough to see if he could get a direction from the voice in the hills. Dark shadows were quickly blanketing the small farm, limiting his view in the muted landscape. But he could hear, and the strange sound was riding the wind.

Stepping out onto the stoop, Charlie paused. Whoever was out there was getting bolder or coming closer. He clearly heard a chant, and it was growing louder. Strings of unfamiliar words in what sounded like a native tongue rose above the trees in a mystic rhythm before floating out onto the prairie and being scattered by the wind.

Gripping his gun, he crouched low to the ground and followed the noise. He followed it beyond the barn, through the trees, and up the hill where—

Charlie froze in his tracks.

He was standing at the mouth of a small clearing. Although until now the ground had been lit by the light of a full moon, it was suddenly dark and foreboding. A cloud had covered the moon, and he couldn't make out much, but his eyes must be deceiving him. He squeezed the bridge of his nose, but the strange sight stayed on the hillside. The exotic chanting filled his head. He raised Big Blue to his shoulder. The cloud passed and the brilliant moon revealed a spectacular scene.

A bear! Charlie couldn't believe it. Lowering the gun, he squinted in hopes of seeing better, but nothing changed. Raising the gun back to his face, he couldn't deny it was a giant grizzly standing in the clearing—a mighty bear with its back to Charlie. Its massive head was turned upward. Its dagger-like claws shining in the moonlight. It was a strange, yet magnificent sight.

Charlie'd never heard of a chanting bear. There had to be an Indian hiding somewhere in the trees. He wasn't sure of the Indian's intent, coming onto his land with a giant grizzly, but he knew what a bear could do to a human when angered. As a boy he'd come face to face with a she grizzly. Now he kept the butt of the rifle against his cheek.

He slowly pulled the hammer back. The click echoed through the darkness. The Indian stopped chanting. The bear stopped moving. Charlie held his breath. Bears don't surrender willingly, but he wasn't going to lower his gun for curiosity's sake.

He had one shot with Big Blue. He wasn't sure why he had brought it instead of his own gun, but too late now.

"It is Eagle Eye's gun, but not Eagle Eye holding it," an ancient voice spoke out of the darkness.

Charlie steadied the gun on his shoulder. His looked wildly around the clearing and through the trees. The bear still hadn't moved. He set his sight.

"Who holds Eagle Eye's gun?" came the voice again.

Charlie lowered the rifle. "*Eagle Eye*," he whispered. "I've heard that name before. Where've I heard that name?"

"Is Ute name for white brother, Suet Smit."

"Ute?" repeated Charlie. Lifting his head, he squinted into the trees. He called, "Are you the Indian my grandpa talked to in Denver last fall?"

"I am."

"Step out so I can see you."

"You promise no shoot."

Charlie lowered the hammer and let the rifle slide to the ground. "I promise, but tell your bear not to move."

"Bear move."

"Why?"

"I am bear."

"What?"

The bear slowly rotated, not stopping until it faced Charlie. Hidden inside the golden pelt was an old Indian, the one Grandpa had talked to in Denver.

"Me Nakima," said the old man. "I know grandfather for many, many moons."

Amazed, Charlie answered, "He told me about you—how

you rescued him from the Cheyenne a long time ago."

Nakima pushed the bear's head off his own. "He repay debt by saving Nakima's life, too. We brothers."

Charlie nodded. "He told me about that, too." Tears rose to the surface; he swallowed them back. He wasn't going to show any sign of weakness in front of an Indian, especially in front of one wearing a grizzly hide. Yet, he missed his grandfather, and standing before him was a piece of Stuart Smith's history, a part of Grandpa's life that he knew very little about.

"I'm sorry you've come all this way to see him, Nakima, but Grandpa isn't—"

"Yes, he is," interrupted the old Indian. "He always here, young one. His spirit rides on wind. His voice speaks with eagle cry. Eagle Eye good man, brave man. He treat all men same. He learn from father, father learn from son. His heart, it beats in you. You are grandfather, Chalie Smit."

Charlie slid his hand over his heart and closed his eyes. In the silence, he felt the rhythmic beats inside his chest and considered Nakima's words. *His heart beats in me. I am Stuart Smith's grandson. I am Charles Edward Smith.* He was proud of his heritage, but not just because of Grandpa. Something else moved within him.

"I am Theodore Smith's son," he murmured. He opened his eyes and gazed at the old man. Nakima appeared to be as tired and as worn out as the man Charlie had buried a couple weeks earlier. "Thank you," he said. "I know what I need to do now."

Nakima nodded. "Then go," he said quietly.

"I will," replied Charlie. "But what are you doing here?"

"I do bear dance to honor Eagle Eye. He strong, courageous man. Mighty hunter like bear. I pray Great Spirit favor him."

"Will you show me? May I see this dance?"

"I come back tomorrow when the moon make full circle. It will be my last. Come, tomorrow."

Charlie smiled and nodded. "I'll meet you here tomorrow night, Nakima."

The old Indian moved so swiftly, Charlie almost didn't see him slip between the trees and disappear.

Somewhere in the hills, a wolf howled its ghostly song. Charlie shuddered and turned to leave. It was then when he realized where he was standing. Just inches to his left were his grandparent's graves. Nakima had been standing just beyond Grandpa's freshly dug burial site. "He's come to honor you, Grandpa," Charlie whispered hoarsely. Turning away, the young man wiped his eyes. Stars twinkled above and a cool wind blew through the trees.

The next day, Charlie tried to keep busy, but caught himself checking the position of the sun every few minutes. It seemed at one point that the giant ball got stuck in the sky, but finally, its radiant beams slid behind the mountains and traded places with another pale moon. Charlie strapped his gun around his waist and headed for the gravesites.

Just as he said, Nakima was once again standing on the other side of Grandpa's grave. Wrapped in the bear pelt, he stood waving his arms slowly and softly chanting his Indian song. Charlie sat on the ground and watched. As the darkness intensified, so did Nakima's voice. The faster his arms moved, the louder he chanted. Reaching a crescendo, he started to move his feet. To the younger man, it looked like the Indian was skipping, but staying in one place.

Mysterious Ways

Suddenly the old man lowered his voice to a raspy growl, arched his back, and like magic, the bear came to life. Charlie knew the real bear was dead, but watching the movements made by the man hidden within its hide seemed to awaken the animal. That unnerved him.

Nakima chanted louder until it was all Charlie could hear. The Indian chanted and the bear danced. Charlie didn't know the meaning of the bear dance, but he found it enthralling. The growling bear threw his front legs up toward the moon. He did this four times then came to an abrupt stop. The unexpected ending took Charlie by surprise. Thinking the Indian had heard something in the trees, he jumped up and drew his gun.

"That's all," said Nakima.

"Oh," muttered Charlie. "I thought—"

"You try?"

"Wh . . . Who, me?" said Charlie, holstering his weapon. "No, I don't think so. I'm not a great dancer, and as for the words, well, I don't even know what you're sayin'. I know a little Cherokee, and it's not Cherokee you're singin' in, so you can bet I'll get the words to this song wrong," he said laughing nervously.

But something about seeing Nakima standing in a bear skin on top of a grave with the moon beaming down on him made Charlie stop laughing.

"Dance go this way," the Indian said firmly. Slowly, he showed Charlie the steps. "Do four times then turn slow. That is all. Young one can do!"

Charlie nodded mechanically. "Okay." He took a deep breath. "I'll give it a try." He got up and stood beside the bear. At first, his attempts to follow Nakima's lead were clumsy and off beat, but before long, his feet were in perfect sync with those of the old man.

"Now bear move," instructed Nakima, and he showed Charlie the stride of a hunting bear. It took a little longer for Charlie to get his feet to move in a different pattern than the rest of his body, but when he finally did, he felt a connection between him and the old Indian. "Now arms," barked the teacher. Nakima threw the bear's front legs up towards the moon and started the motion that Charlie had witnessed earlier.

When they were finished, Nakima turned to him and nodded. "You make good bear," he said with a hint of a smile. "Eagle Eye be proud. Now we do words."

Charlie threw a hand up, "Now wait a minute, Nakima. I don't mind learnin' the dance, but it'll take me ages to learn the words, so I think I'll just leave those up to you, if you don't mind."

"No matter," grunted the old man. "I say Ute. You say Cherokee; English. No matter. Great Spirit make all words. Hear all words. Now, we do words!" he said decisively.

"Okay," muttered Charlie. "But I warned you."

The two started the bear dance again, slowly. Charlie watched Nakima. The ancient one seemed to fall into a trance, taking each step with grace.

Charlie closed his eyes and cleared his mind. He thought of nothing else, but the steps that he was taking, the emergence of the bear, and the howling of the words coming from the Indian beside him. Lost in the moment, he too began to chant. At first he chanted in his limited Cherokee, but soon moved into English. He understood what Nakima meant. It really didn't matter what tongue he sang in. He chanted in

English, and then back in Cherokee. With each step of the bear dance, words flowed from his heart, words of love and remembrance of his grandfather, words of peace and love for God.

High pitched, low pitched, Charlie soared with every word. *This should be a bird dance,* he thought. *Not a bear dance.* Then he realized he was the only one singing, and loudly at that. He stopped and opened one eye.

There was Nakima still standing awe-inspiringly on Grandpa's grave in the glow of the moonlight. He was staring at Charlie. Finally, he spoke. "Okay, Screaming Cat, you dance, I sing."

Charlie looked up incredulously. "Screaming Cat?"

Nakima looked down at him, eyes twinkling like the stars. "I call you Screaming Cat," he said. "It is Ute name for Chalie Smit."

Charlie smirked. "Great," he said with a smile. "My grandfather is Eagle Eye, strong and courageous and I'm Screaming Cat. Just great."

"Cat is strong and courageous," said Nakima encouragingly. Then he added, "Just not when singing." With that, he burst into laughter.

As Charlie strolled back to the cabin, he could still hear Nakima's laughter echoing off the hills.

16

A LAZY MOON HUNG IN THE DARKENING sky. Symphony music and perfume filled Charlie's senses. He looked into beautiful eyes, so close.

"I don't know how to waltz," he said, almost choking on his tongue.

The girl took a step closer. "That's all right. Neither do I, but we can pretend."

"I don't want to embarrass—"

"You won't, Charlie." She smiled up at him. "Let's try."

He couldn't resist the pull of her eyes. He stepped closer. His hands trembled as he took her right hand in his left hand and placed his right hand on her waist. Finding it hard to concentrate on the timing of the music, he led her in an awkward rendition of a waltz. They didn't exactly glide among the wagons and snickering horses. But at least they tried. And who cared what the horses thought?

She would utter "ouch" as he stepped on her foot, then she'd step on his and they'd laugh, all forgiven. They kept at it and got some steps right, and soon were swaying smoothly to the music.

Charlie felt that if he looked in her eyes again, though, the evening would come to an end. He felt he couldn't let her see what he was really thinking. The truth was, he was only doing this as a favor. All the other guys and gals had paired up, hadn't they?

But they were alone. And he'd *wanted* to ask her. Finally

he did raise his eyes from watching his feet, and he searched her face. She met his gaze.

He felt sick, dizzy. His heart beat so hard it hurt his ears. His heart was saying something, but he couldn't understand it.

And where'd his lungs go? He tried to step back and catch his breath. But she stiffened her fingers and wouldn't let him go.

He made the mistake of looking back into her face. A beautiful shade of pink. Eyes sparkling in the moonlight. Soft lips moving. Saying what?

He didn't remember her being so beautiful before. Sweat broke across his brow. "Air," he gasped, "I need air."

She stepped closer. Her face touched his cheek, her warm breath caressed his ear. "I love you, Charlie," she said. "I've loved you since the first time I saw you."

He felt like he'd been punched in the head. *What now? Take her in my arms? Answer her? Tell her how I really feel?*

He wanted to, but instead, he broke away and spun round on his heels. Ungentlemanly; but he had to breathe. Grabbing his knees, he took great gulps of air.

She ran to his side, and her silk purse banged against the back of his head. She cried, "Charlie, what's wrong?"

He rubbed his head, stood and struggled for composure. He straightened his jacket and ran his fingers through his hair. "Nothin'. I'm fine. I think it's time to take you home."

"But I don't want to go home. I want to stay here with you." She pouted.

"Look, Mary Lou, I'm not feelin' too good and—"
"Who?"
"What?"

Her eyes misted over. "Who is Mary Lou?"

"Mary Lou? Why do you ask?"

Her face darkened. Her eyes lost their sparkle. What was happening? . . . *Better get out of here.*

"Listen, Charlie." Her voice was shrill. "You didn't mention having a girl, but to call me by her name. Well, I never!" She turned away in a huff.

What to do now?! "Listen, I'm, well, I'm sorry." He stepped around her and started for the hotel. "Best come with me," he called over his shoulder. "Not good for a girl to be out here alone."

He kept walking then realized she wasn't following. He turned. She was standing in the middle of the street, her head down and her shoulders shaking. She looked small and alone.

"You're cold," he said.

She looked up and her eyes blazed. Her hair shone like flame in the moonlight. "I'm not cold. I'm crying. . . . You just think I'm a child, don't you?"

He froze in confusion.

She softened, then chewed her lower lip. She gathered up her skirt and ran up the street, away from the hotel, away from Charlie. She called back to him, "I'll never forgive you, Charlie Smith!"

Charlie yelled back, "Hey, what did I do?" But she disappeared into a dark building with the slam of a door.

"I swear, Grandpa," Charlie said. "You taught me how to wrestle a bull to the ground, but not how to handle the so-called gentler kind. Are they always like this?"

"'Fraid so."

Charlie whirled round expecting to see his grandfather, but saw nothing but the horses that had snickered.

Then another voice called from far away. "Charlie!"

"What?" he moaned. He rolled to his side and opened his drowsy eyes. There was LeFaye kneeling beside him.

"Wake up, Charlie. For pity's sake, wake up, man!"

"What? I just got to sleep. What are you wakin' me up for?"

"You were dreamin', my friend. I'm not sure who you were dreamin' about, but you need to figure that out yourself so you can tell her what you've been tellin' me most of the night. Then maybe both of us can get some sleep." He chuckled.

Charlie sat up and rubbed his face. "What're you talkin' about?"

"You kept sayin', 'I love you'," replied LeFaye wearily. "Like you were tryin' to convince someone."

Charlie fell back into his blankets. "Did I say her name?"

"Yep, you did. It was Amy. Or was it Lydia? Maybe it was Kay. Well, somethin' like that." LeFaye pulled on his jeans. He shrugged. "Don't ask me, Charlie. If you don't know who she is, I surely don't. Anyhow, it was just a dream. It's over. Forget it."

But days later Charlie was still mulling over the dream. He remembered the face of the girl, and he knew now who it was. But why would he dream about *that* girl, let alone say he loved her? She was just an acquaintance. And why did it bother him so much for her to say she hated him? It was just a dream.

17

LE FAYE THREW CHARLIE A PAIR OF WORK gloves. "You're leaving for Saint Louis in a few days?" he asked. "I'm beginning to think you don't enjoy my company."

Charlie chuckled at his friend's teasing and grabbed the hammer. "Quite the opposite." He pounded a nail into a shingle. "You've been a big help to me and I don't know how I'll ever repay you."

"Friends don't repay friends, except with more friendship," said LeFaye. "So we will be indebted to each other for the rest of our lives."

Charlie had his mouth full of nails. "Ah wite wi' me."

"How long do you plan on being out East?"

Charlie shrugged. "Dunno." He spit the last nail onto the palm of his glove. "Don't plan on being gone long. Just want to see the land Cousin Ralph left me, take care of some business, then come back here and settle down."

"Anyone out there expectin' you?"

Charlie hammered. "Well, they know I'm coming. Mr. Atkins was able to locate an aunt who lives near Saint Charles, and he sent word to her that I'll be in the vicinity, but I don't think she'll bother looking me up. I don't know her, so I don't expect she'll worry too much about me."

"Well, if you plan on settlin' down here soon, I should start looking for a place of my own."

Charlie stopped hammering at the barn roof and stared thoughtfully at his friend. "We'll see how God leads."

Mysterious Ways

It was mid-June when Charlie finished the pre-winter farm chores and felt it was time to head East. After some debate, he convinced LeFaye that he'd be all right travelling unaccompanied to Colorado Springs. It was hard to leave the farm again, and it felt a little lonely not to have Grandpa along on the trip—but he was on his own now, and he would have to get used to it.

At Colorado Springs, he and Star caught an eastbound Union Pacific train. It made a routine water stop at Fort Hayes, but didn't pick up more passengers until Kansas City. Charlie got out there and stretched his legs. He wouldn't have another chance until Saint Charles.

Looking around, he didn't see much difference between Denver and Kansas City, except that miners continued to flood Denver. Rounding a corner, he saw several mule trains lining up and getting ready to head west. Although it was the Union Pacific railway that brought hundreds of folks across the prairie each month, some people still crossed by covered wagon, desiring the freedom to choose their own direction, some that still hadn't been affected by nineteenth century progress. He thought it a little late in the season for mule trains to head out, but figured the group would hole up somewhere along the Snake or Platte River if they made it that far west before winter hit.

Before returning to his car, he stopped at the stock yards. Leaning against a corral, he watched through the thick cloud of dust as wranglers loaded cattle into boxcars. Thundering hooves pounded against the wooden ramps and train floors as the boisterous animals ran up the chutes in single file to be packed side-by-side in a sweltering car. The ground was trampled and muddy; the air smelled of sweat, urine, and manure. Above the moans of the cattle, shrill whistles echoed across the yards, accompanied every so often with shouts of "Move 'em up! Git on up 'ere, dogie."

The men looked tired, but determined to finish the ride. Their clothes, dusty and tattered, smelled of camp smoke. Their boots were worn and muddy. Their faces were taut and dark, but their eyes sparkled with life. Charlie guessed that even though some of those wranglers had probably driven herds through Colorado snows, Texas sandstorms, and Kansas twisters, to meet this train, they'd probably do it again in a heartbeat. He remembered the trials of his own cattle drive last summer, but he knew that was nothing compared to what these cowboys lived. It was a hard way to make a hundred dollars a month.

Climbing aboard the train again, he found his seat and made himself as comfortable as possible on the hard leather seat. Forward in the locomotive, the engineer pulled a lever and released puffs of steam. Charlie watched as passengers, old and new, boarded. Men grabbed women's hands and helped them up the steps into the car. Some women trailed children behind them, or carried them on their hips. The older children clambered up the stairs then ran from seat to seat, yelling, "Let's sit here, Ma! Can we? Can we sit here?" A few of the younger ones, in their rush to get on board, stumbled up the stairs, bruising a knee on the way.

"All aboard!" yelled the conductor as he strolled along the boardwalk beside the train.

Those passengers who had waited until the last minute to say their good-byes made their way onto the cars. *So many folks*, thought Charlie. *All going in different directions. It's amazing how far we've come.* A few minutes later, everyone had settled in their seats, with the exception of a few rowdy boys pulling the windows down so they could hear the train whistle.

"But ma," pouted one little fellow. "If the windows aren't down, I might not hear it, and then what'll I do? Tommy's heard one before, so I gotta."

"Hush, Joseph," whispered his mother. "When that whistle goes off, you, me, and everyone for ten miles around will hear it. As a matter of fact, we'll probably get sick of hearing it before we get to grandma's, so sit down and be still this very minute. I don't want to have to—"

"All aboard!" The conductor gave his final call and hopped onto the stairs, pulling the step stool up with him. The locomotive blew out steam as the giant wheels started to grind forward. Slowly, they pulled away from the station.

The engineer pulled the cord and the train's whistle blew long and shrill. The children squealed with delight. Charlie felt a familiar knot in the pit of stomach, just as he had the first time he and Grandpa caught the train from Colorado Springs to Denver. He couldn't help but smile.

As the train dashed through the rolling hills and across the silver rivers of Missouri, his thoughts drifted to the people he was going to meet while visiting Saint Charles. Some of them were even family. He'd never thought of them as family before because after all, they had never made an effort to meet him in all the time he lived with his grandparents. But all of that was beside the point. He wasn't going east to get to know them, but to see the acreage left to him by Cousin Ralph and to visit the cemetery where his parents were buried. That's all. After that, he was going back home, back to the cabin.

"Mind if I sit here?"

The voice was strong, but friendly and open. Charlie glanced up at a stranger, a few years older than himself, and ruggedly good-looking. His smile was warm, but his eyes hinted of mischief. Charlie liked the man right off.

"Don't mind at all," said Charlie, picking up his hat and sliding over so the stranger could sit down. Before taking his seat, the man turned to two others who were standing in the aisle a few seats away and ordered, "Sit close by and rest. Sleep if you can."

Charlie glanced back at them and, although he couldn't see their faces, one of them looked oddly familiar. He reminded Charlie of someone. But who?

The stranger slid down onto the leather bench beside Charlie and smiled at the two female passengers across from them. The younger woman quickly smiled back then turned away and looked out the window. The elder glared at him for an instant then went back to reading her book.

Apparently, the man didn't want conversation either. He folded his arms across his chest and pulled his hat down over his eyes as if wanting to sleep. Charlie wasn't in a talking mood anyway. He was content to turn his attention back to the landscape that was now racing by at a speed he could only guess.

He stared out the window in wonder. Most of his life, he'd only seen the prairie from his front door, but here he was sitting on a train, speeding across it, and it was beautiful. Lush rolling hills were dotted with green trees. The landscape wasn't as flat as the Colorado and Kansas prairies where a man could see for miles just by standing in the stirrups. Here, one could see a good distance, but before long, a hill or a rocky outcrop rose up to limit the view.

"Headin' home or goin' out on business?"

The question startled Charlie. At first he didn't realize it was the stranger who had asked it. He thought the man was asleep. But looking closer, he saw an eyelid flicker under the tilted cowboy hat.

"Business," answered Charlie. "How 'bout you?"

"Business," said the stranger, not changing his position. "We won't actually be goin' all the way to St. Charles."

"Mmm." Charlie turned back to the window.

"You a farmer?"

Charlie figured the stranger wasn't going to remove his hat, so he continued to look out the window. "Rancher," he answered. "You?"

"Farmer," said the cowboy. "Or we were before the war."

"Did you fight?"

"Naw, too young. But my older brother did. Came back too. One of the lucky ones I guess."

"I don't believe in luck," said Charlie.

The stranger snickered. "I s'pose you're a 'blessing' man?"

"Yep."

"Mmm."

"Do you believe in God?" asked Charlie.

"Absolutely!"

"Have you ever asked Him—"

"Enough, rancher." The cowboy's voice had lost whatever kindness Charlie thought it held initially. It now sounded cold and hollow. He'd heard that coldness before—from an Irishman locked in a Denver jail, waiting to die. Charlie threw a fleeting glance at the man sitting beside him. He looked too young to be a killer, but the war had turned many men into just that, regardless of whether they fought or not.

He'd be careful to watch this cowboy as the trip progressed. Signs like cold, steel eyes or the nervous twitch of his fingers were enough to convince Charlie that he'd have to stay alert around this hombre.

The man seemed content and didn't move, so Charlie turned his attention back to the window. They sat in silence. Outside, shadows grew long across the green grasslands. The rumbling and rocking of the car, mixed with the downward slope of the sun, put Charlie in a fog, but the growling in his stomach kept him from falling asleep. He stood up. The cowboy next to him slid his hat back and sat up in the seat.

"I'm gonna go to the dining car," said Charlie, flicking some dust off his hat. "Would you care to join me, Mr. . . . uh?" He saw the cowboy glance at the gun Charlie had hidden under his jacket. "I'm sorry, I don't think we actually exchanged names," said Charlie, extending his hand. "I'm Charlie Smith, from Pueblo, Colorado Territory."

The stranger stood up and tugged at his vest. He noticed Charlie's outstretched hand and smiled, as if he found it amusing, but he took it and squeezed it firmly. "Nice to make your acquaintance, Charlie. You can call me Tom. Tom Howard, from eastern Kansas. I could use some vittles."

"Good, then I'll follow you," said Charlie, pointing to the door behind Tom. "The dining car is that way."

As they went up the aisle, Tom tipped his hat at the ladies again. Then they passed Tom's two friends. Charlie tried to get a look at the man who seemed so familiar, but this cowboy slept with his hat over his face, too. Charlie studied the stranger walking in front of him instead.

Tom wasn't a tall man; he stood only about five feet, eleven inches. His hands were medium size, with long, slender fingers. His palms were calloused and blackened. He obviously used his guns and Charlie figured he used them well. The heels of his boots were worn down and the tops were dusty, as were his pants.

But the most telling piece was his wildrag, the scarf around his neck. Charlie could see he used it often. The knot was pulled tight and in the back of the stranger's neck. It had rolled around itself like a rope, except for the front. That part fluttered across Tom's chest like a bib on a baby. He remembered the cattle he'd watched being loaded into cattle cars during his walkabout in Kansas City. These guys have probably been workin' a Texas cattle drive, he thought. Been livin' hard and ridin' harder for a while. Bet he'll be glad when he can see the farm again.

A couple got up from a booth just as the two men entered the dining car. Tom slid across the seat and claimed the space before anyone else could grab it. Charlie slid in across from him and hung his hat on a hook. Tom kept his on his head.

"Here gentlemen," said a pretty young lady, "let me clean this table for you and then I'll take your order."

"Thank you," said Charlie.

"Mmm," hummed Tom. "Sure are a purty little thing. Too purty to be cleanin' tables in a dining car."

"Please, sir," whispered the waitress. "You're embarrassing me."

Tom laughed and grabbed her wrist. "Well, I don't mean to—"

"Enough, farmer," said Charlie low and even. The lady caught her breath and threw a look at Charlie. Tom looked at him too. His raised eyebrows exposed his hazel eyes. Charlie thought he caught a hint of curiosity in them. There was anger, too, but it disappeared before anyone went for their guns. Tom's smile wasn't friendly, but again as if he found Charlie entertaining.

Still holding Charlie's gaze, he let go of the young lady's wrist. "This time, Charlie Smith," he muttered. "No harm done, this time."

They shared sparse information about their families. Tom learned of Grandpa and Jess, while Charlie learned that Tom's ma still lived in northeastern Kansas on the family farm. After the war, he and his older brother ventured out and found excitement rounding up Union renegades and escaped prisoners of war. Recently they'd turned their attention to financial ventures.

After dinner, Charlie pulled money from his pocket and laid it on the table. Tom picked it up and handed it back to him. "No, sir," he said smiling. "This meal is on me."

"Well, no," replied Charlie. "I can pay for—"

"Listen friend." Tom held up a hand. "It ain't every day I offer to pay, but then again, it ain't every day I find a man I respect as much as I respect myself. Allow me."

Charlie took the bills from him and shoved them back into his pocket. "Well, thank you, Tom," he said, a little baffled. "Thank you much."

"My pleasure," replied Tom. "Now if you don't mind, I need to get back to my seat."

"I'll go with you that far," said Charlie. "My sleep room is a door over from where we were sitting."

As they left the diner, Tom was behind Charlie. He wasn't sure how it happened, but Charlie didn't like it at all. He had no doubt that Tom was sizing him up, just as he had sized up Tom earlier. *My jeans are worn, but clean. I'm wearin' 'em for comfort, not because I've been rounding up cows or renegades. My boots are too new. My bandana is tied around my neck with the knot in front, too fancy for a farmer.*

Tom's voice brought Charlie round. "Well, be seein' you later, Charlie."

Charlie turned, realizing he had passed Tom's seat. "Uh, yeah. I'll see you later." Charlie extended his hand again. Tom looked at it for a moment, as if waiting for something. Then, just as he was about to grasp it, the train lurched forward, almost throwing them both to the floor.

Women screamed. Children spilled from their seats onto the floor, which in turn, produced more screams. Men swore openly as they jumped up to help the women who were yelling at them to help the children. Steam billowed from the engine, immediately covering the windows in a dense fog. The big wheels of the locomotive locked and with great screeching and crashing, the iron horse strained to a stop.

Tom's partners got up from their seats and ran through the confusion to the back of the railcar. The familiar-looking one jumped from the train while the other remained on board and stood at the door.

Charlie found his balance and scrambled to assist the women who had been sitting across from him earlier. Their personal belongings had fallen from the shelf above them and had scattered across the floor.

"Are you all right, ma'am?" he asked the elderly lady as he gathered her toiletries from around their feet.

She didn't respond, but just stood there staring behind him, her eyes round and large.

"Ma'am?" Charlie stood to follow her stare and he found himself looking down the barrel of a six-shooter. Tom had regained his composure, too. He had not only pulled his faded bandana over his face, but he had pulled his gun.

"Told you I wasn't goin' all the way to Saint Charles," said the outlaw. "This is about as far as I go."

Charlie glanced over at the two wide-eyed women and slowly raised his hands in the air. The elderly woman's toiletries slid through his fingers and clanged back down to the train floor. "Smart man," said the voice behind the scarf. "Now hand me your gun."

Charlie shook his head. "Don't—"

"Stop!" the voice was harsh and deadly. "I'm no fool. Hand me your gun and sit back down."

Charlie glanced at the women again. If he went for it, one of them could get hurt. For their sakes, he wouldn't try to be a hero. Slowly, his left hand crossed his waist and he pulled the Smith & Wesson from the holster that was hidden beneath his jacket. Carefully, he handed it to the outlaw. Tom's cold, grey eyes looked up at him. In an instant, Charlie knew that had he tried anything, this man would have killed him without blinking an eye.

"Take care of it," said Charlie. "My grandpa gave that to me."

The grey eyes lingered on Charlie's face for a moment. "Let me see your hands," he said.

"What?"

"Your hands!" barked the stranger, waving his gun. "Show me your hands."

Charlie held his hands out.

"Turn 'em."

He flipped to palms up.

"Mmm," the outlaw grunted. "Just a poor ol' dirt farmer

like me. Had me goin' there for a minute, the way you're dressed and all, but I bet you don't have nothin' to call your own, but this ol' gun."

Charlie didn't blink.

The stranger pulled the gun's cylinder and dropped bullets into his dirty palm. Pocketing them, he handed the gun back to Charlie. "Today's your lucky day," he said, winking.

Turning to the women, he flashed his gun in their faces. "But not you two. You two have five seconds to give me your jewelry and your money. Now hurry!" Their hands shook so badly they couldn't find the tiny clasps that held the delicate jewels around their necks.

"For Pete's sake," growled the stranger. Leaning over he grabbed the necklace from around the younger woman's collar and gave it a good yank, ripping the chain from her delicate neck. Before they could react, he repeated his action and tore the necklace from the elderly woman. "Now the bags," he snapped. "Give me your purses."

The younger lady started to cry, but the older woman held her composure. "You brute," she scolded. "Does your ma know what you're doing to folks?"

The eyes behind the scarf lost their smile. He swore softly. "You leave my ma out of this," he warned.

"It figures that you—"

"Ma, be quiet," the younger woman fussed. "You're going to get us killed."

Just then a man appeared at the door. "Come on, Jesse!" he yelled. "We gotta go. That new guy hurt his leg bad."

Charlie's eyes locked with the outlaw's in one swift second. "Jesse?" he repeated softly. "Jesse James?"

"At your service," said the outlaw. "Meet my older brother,

Frank." He pointed his gun at the man standing in the doorway.

"Come on, Jesse!" yelled Frank.

"Frank," said Jesse, ignoring the urgency in his brother's voice, "this is Charlie Smith, from the Colorado Territory." Charlie and Frank looked at each other. "I was gonna try to recruit ol' Charlie here. I'd guess he's about as fast a draw as they come. But after havin' a fine meal with him, I concluded that he is truly one of the good guys. Like Pa was, Frank. A real good guy."

Charlie glanced at the older James brother then back at Jesse. "Don't do this, Jesse," he pleaded, rising slowly to his feet. "Don't run. God has a better plan for you than this."

The locomotive belched steam like a dragon awakening from its nap. The man who had been standing guard at the door disappeared. The passengers were growing restless and starting to mumble. Frank pulled his gun and aimed it at Charlie. "Jesse," he said through gritted teeth. "I'm countin' to three, and if you're not outta this train when I reach three, I'm shootin' this cowboy right between the eyes."

"Jesse, even if he shoots me, don't run," coaxed Charlie.

"One!"

The eyes behind the bandana smiled again. "I'll be seein' you, Mr. Charlie Smith."

Charlie grabbed Jesse's arm. "God has a plan, Jesse." He heard Frank cock the pistol.

"Two!"

"Too late, Charlie."

"No, it's never too late. God'll take you here and now."

Jesse glanced at his brother. "Three!"

A gun went off. Someone yelled, "Rush 'em." Women

screamed again. Babies wailed. Girls hid behind their mother's skirts while boys held tightly to their hats and crawled under the seats. All watched the skirmish with round eyes and open mouths as their fathers, husbands, and strangers rushed the trio.

Men tumbled out the door and onto the tracks. Gunshots rang in a thunderous chorus. Then sounds of running horses echoed through the canyon.

Charlie jumped off the train and ran down the tracks a few yards. A passenger, who was carrying several lanterns, yelled something about one of the gang members breaking a leg or being hit in the gun fire.

Charlie grabbed one of the lanterns from him and squatted on his heels. He could see dark spots of blood splattered across the rocks and rail ties, but those weren't what gripped his innards. Among the blood splatter were hoof prints; hundreds of them. But there was one set he knew. He squatted and studied them a little longer, finally understanding why that one man seemed so familiar to him.

The man that rode this horse was one of his dearest friends. He'd ridden with him, worked with him, laughed and cried with him. He should be home, working the farm.

"All aboard," shouted the conductor. "We've got to get this train moving again, gentlemen. Got a schedule to keep!"

Looking down the tracks into the darkness, Charlie sighed heavily. The James Gang was gone, and although a bit rankled, he was thankful to be alive to tell about it.

18

UNDAUNTED BY THE POUNDING STORM, the train sped through the darkness down the tracks toward Saint Charles. Outside, the landscape had been swallowed up in a murkiness so thick it choked out any hope of sunlight. Inside, the car was almost as dim, lit only by a single gas lamp.

Wind rattled the windows. Cold sheets of rain battered the car's flat surfaces. Children pressed their faces against foggy panes, chasing rivulets with tiny fingers.

They drew near to the bustling city of Saint Louis, but Charlie couldn't see beyond the darkened window. His mind was on the night before, puzzling over the presence of the familiar gunman in the hold-up gang.

"Saint Charles station, ten minutes out," bellowed the conductor.

Mothers packed up their knitting and gently shook sleeping children. Small heads appeared as children sat up in their seats, rubbing sleepy eyes.

Skirts rustled; voices rose. Women pulled jackets and toys from cluttered compartments while men grabbed hats and stuffed newspapers into attaché cases. Children wrestled with their wraps as the train's wheels ground to a stop.

Charlie put on his hat and slicker and gathered his belongings. Gazing out the window, he wondered what he'd find here. He'd meet people, some who even shared his last name; beyond that he didn't know what to expect.

Stepping off the train onto the gangplank, he took a quick

look around. Saint Charles looked peaceful—formal compared to Pueblo, but homey enough to be inviting.

As passengers disembarked, umbrellas burst open up and down the boardwalk like morning glories on a trellis. People scurried to greet waiting family or friends. Those who had neither hat nor umbrella used their folded newspapers to cover their heads as they darted through traffic to get to whatever appointment was awaiting them. Everyone seemed to be talking about the hold-up.

Charlie's attention was drawn to four boys, whose folks had stopped to talk to another couple. He watched as the boys took advantage of their parent's being distracted. They stole down the boardwalk, throwing quick glances over their shoulders. Charlie soon saw what had drawn the boys away—at the bend of the road, two very large, very inviting mud puddles.

Star hadn't yet been unloaded from the train so Charlie went to the station house for shelter from the rain. A few people looked up when he entered the waiting area. But he was only greeted by looks that were silent commands to close the door and make it fast.

Several people were huddled close to the wood burning stove, whispering to each other, while others sat or slept on the long benches. One woman comforted a sleepy toddler. Charlie found a seat on the end of a bench and leaning his head against the wall, closed his eyes. The crying child started to scream. All he could do was wait for Star, and for the rain to stop, so they could go and scope out the land.

He woke early the next morning to the tinkling sound of rain hitting the hotel window. There were a couple of places he had to visit, despite the weather. He ate a quick breakfast then asked the clerk for directions to the county seat.

Once there, a smiling lady helped him find what he was looking for: specific land documents and directions to the cemetery where his parents were buried. With the information tucked safely in his vest pocket, he mounted Star and rode the mile out of town with a renewed sense of purpose.

The relentless rain spilled from the rim of his hat and down his collar. The clothes under his slicker were soaked, but he didn't care. It had taken him almost sixteen years to get back to this spot, and he wasn't going to let a little water, from the sky or from his eyes, discourage him.

As he knelt, water pooled around his knees. Charlie leaned forward and ran his fingers across the face of the cold granite stone. Absently he traced each deeply carved letter with his finger: T-H-E-O-D-O-R-E. Here lay the earthly remains of his father, the man he couldn't remember. And beside him lay his mother, the woman he never knew. But they were his parents and he loved them.

A gust of wind pushed the rain into Charlie's face. He pulled his slicker tight around his chest and held it closed while he laid a couple of limp roses on his mother's grave. Star, standing behind him, whinnied and stomped the ground, unhappy with the thunder rolling in the distance.

He couldn't make out her name at first. It was blurred and he had to blink a couple of times before the letters came clear. Moving his lips, he read silently. *Anne Smith*. She had died in childbirth. Grandpa told him she died giving birth to him. *How ironic that while giving life to me, she lost her own.* Leaning forward he touched her stone, tracing the year of her death, his birth.

He thought it was the water in his eyes again, but after

blinking several more times, he realized that what he saw wasn't because of the rain. He brushed at the stone, just to make sure. The date was wrong. *I wasn't born in 1855, I was born in 1853. How could someone make such a mistake?* Anger washed over him like a splash of rain, then was gone.

Reading her name again, he gently stroked the headstone. "It doesn't matter, does it, Ma? You and I know the truth." Standing, he wiped his face with his soaked gloves and patted the headstones one last time.

Wind gusted at him again. This time it almost took his hat, but he caught it and held it tight to his head as he trudged back through the mud to his horse. Thunder rumbled through the dark clouds, but Star didn't seem to be paying much attention to it now. He was watching something off in the distance.

His golden tail swished back and forth. His ears rolled forward. Charlie recognized the signals and peered through the downpour to see what had distracted his horse. He caught a glimpse of something dark running through a nearby clump of trees, but lost sight of it when he threw his arm up to hide his face from a blast of rain. Star nickered. He'd heard something. Charlie heard it too. It was the unmistakable sound of a running horse.

Someone was leaving the area, and awfully fast. He mounted quickly. In a leap, he and Star were off, but they saw no one until they reached the Saint Charles Hotel. Whoever it was had disappeared into the storm.

19

THE STRANGER AT CHARLIE'S HOTEL ROOM door introduced himself as Charlie's cousin Ryan Smith. He said that his mother, Charlie's Aunt Rose, had demanded that he come into town and rescue Charlie from the dreadful hotel. Charlie was a Smith, she said, and there was no sense in a Smith resorting to shelter in a run-down hotel, when the ranch was at his disposal. Charlie didn't consider the hotel run down, but he didn't argue. He accepted the invitation.

Ryan was an older man, charming in his demeanor and immaculate in his attire. His brown hair showed a hint of grey at the temples and, Charlie noticed, every strand was in place. Charlie figured he was about the age his pa would have been if he were alive. Although Ryan wasn't an overly handsome man, Charlie imagined he didn't have many problems making the society pages of the local paper. Charlie assumed he was, after all, wealthy and educated; a good catch for any socialite. But despite Ryan's charisma, Charlie felt a bit uneasy. Charlie sensed something ruthless underneath the façade of a proper gentleman. Charlie had no reason for it; he'd just met Ryan. But something about the man didn't sit right.

Charlie's uneasiness grew as the two rode away from town. It wasn't what Ryan said that unsettled Charlie, but what he didn't say. Ryan was very communicative on the area's history, but very evasive on family matters. In fact, when Charlie asked how well Ryan had known his pa, Ryan ignored the question altogether.

"Now, this region," said Ryan, fanning his hand out over the landscape, "is known as the Femme Osage District in Saint Charles. Daniel Boone settled in these parts around 1799. At that point in time, Missouri wasn't even part of the United States."

"Hmm," sighed Charlie.

"Our little town also had the honor of hosting Lewis and Clark. Clark met up with Lewis here in Saint Charles back in 1804 before the two set out on their expedition to the Pacific Ocean. It was the last civilized American town they were in for two and a half years."

"Really?"

"Yes, really. We're quite proud of our little town and its place in American history. See that tree over yonder?"

Charlie spotted the massive oak and nodded.

"That's Boone's Judgment Tree. Daniel Boone was appointed as the syndic, better known as the judge and jury, as well as the commandant of the District. Under that tree is where he held court. It is said he was a fair judge; but many a man swung from the branches of that tree if he deemed it necessary. Glad I wasn't around back then," he added with a chuckle.

Charlie glanced sharply at the older man. "Do they still use the tree?"

Ryan laughed. "No! Or at least I've not heard of it being used."

"Interesting," murmured Charlie.

"We're a bit more civilized than that now, thank goodness."

The two talked more about history until Ryan pointed to a lane up ahead of them. From what Charlie could see, stone walls, loaded with blooming wisteria vines, ran parallel to the road. Above, a canopy made from the boughs of ancient walnut trees provided a cool retreat from the hot noonday sun. He assumed somewhere at the end of the lane was a barn, and he imagined it to be as grand as the house that loomed in front of him.

"Here we are," Ryan said jovially, leading his horse into a canter. Charlie followed and before long, they reined in their horses in front of an enormous red brick house. Denver had some nice looking places, but he'd never seen anything like this one.

A grand staircase rose to an impressive porch, which ran from corner to corner across the face of the house. Huge potted ferns hung between the white columns that supported the tiled roof. The roof, with its odd slants and curves, gave the house an air of mystery. The magnificent turrets and dormers hinted at secret rooms, dark nooks, hidden cupboards, and other places an overactive imagination might create.

Grandpa's cabin back home had three small windows. This place had at least twenty. And they all seemed to blink down at Charlie as he stared up at them. He thought it odd, too, that instead of a fence around the front yard, there was a small one around the house's roof. And at each corner, an ugly little winged creature scowled down at him.

"They're called gargoyles," said Ryan.

Charlie pulled his attention away from the house to his cousin. "What?"

"Gargoyles," repeated Ryan. "During the Dark Ages, gargoyles were believed to keep evil spirits away, protecting the buildings and their inhabitants."

"I see." Charlie looked at the hideous little beasts again. "They're ugly enough to scare away something."

Ryan chuckled. "Well, they seem to work. Haven't seen any evil spirits here lately."

"Good." Charlie smiled half-heartedly. "I'll sleep better knowing they're doing their job."

Ryan dismounted. "Shall we go in and meet your aunt?"

Charlie slid off his horse. Before he could slip the reins over Star's head, his hands were met by dark, smooth fingers. Charlie looked into the sparkling brown eyes of a short, plump black man with a smile that revealed white teeth. Charlie instantly smiled back. "Aw'l take 'im fo ya, sah. Put 'im up in da barn wid Missah Smif's hoss."

Charlie let go the reins. "Thank you. I'd appreciate it."

Ryan said, "Charlie, this is our stable manager, Mister Jonathan Holland. Jonathan, this is my long lost cousin, Charlie Smith."

Charlie and Jonathan shook hands. "Ya says yer a loss cousin?" asked Jonathan politely.

Charlie laughed. "I live in Colorado. Out West. Didn't realize I had family here until a few weeks ago, so I thought I'd pay them a visit."

"Ya don't say," whispered the man. "I knowd yo pa?"

"Oh no, I doubt if you knew him," Ryan answered quickly. "We don't have time to talk about that right now, Jonathan. Mother is expecting us, so we better get in there."

Jonathan nodded. The sparkle in his eyes dimmed slightly. "Aw'l give da hosses some extra oats afta I rubs 'em down, if dat be awright wid' ya, sahs?"

Charlie nodded.

"Yes, yes," muttered Ryan. "That will be fine. Now, come along Charlie. Mother is waiting."

Charlie turned to Jonathan. "Thank you again. I'll be

out after dinner to check on Star."

"Yessuh. You do dat, an' we bofe be glad ta see ya."

Ryan turned, halfway up the steps. "Charlie, come—please."

Charlie gave a quick nod to Jonathan then hopped up the steps three at a time until he was beside his cousin. Turning, he saw Jonathan leading the horses further down the pretty lane.

Ryan's voice brought him back. "Don't let Jonathan become a nuisance," he was saying. "He's a hard worker, but he sometimes talks too much."

Charlie grunted, still watching Jonathan and the horses walking down the lane.

"Shall we?" said Ryan as he waved his hand toward the door.

"After you," said Charlie, feeling slightly on his guard but not knowing why.

20

CHARLIE REMOVED HIS HAT AND STEPPED inside the splendid foyer. It reminded him of the lobby at Judge Walker's office with its richly colored paintings and rugs. The wooden floors were polished to a high gloss. Across from the front door was another grand staircase, its intricately detailed banister beckoning the visitor up to the second story. Ryan tossed his hat onto a round table that stood in the center of the foyer and walked into the huge living room. Charlie followed him, but held onto his hat.

Sitting in state in a wing backed chair, like a queen on her throne, was a plump, elderly woman. Long, silver ringlets cascaded down one shoulder, held in place by a diamond-studded comb. Her face, though friendly enough, looked artificial. He wasn't accustomed to seeing women wear color on their faces. He had to force himself not to stare at her blue eyelids, red lips, and the almost perfectly round circles of pink on her cheeks.

The smell of perfume filled the room. Charlie felt nauseous. Ryan walked over to the lady, his heavy footsteps hammering the wooden floor. Bending low, he took her hand in his and gave her a peck on a pink cheek. "Hello, Mother," he said softly.

"Hello, dear," she said in a southern drawl. "Please mind your boots."

"The floors are fine, Mother," he replied a little sharply. "If not, we have a maid to look after them, remember?"

The old woman glanced at Charlie and then at her son.

"Of course I remembah. I'm not daft."

Ryan cleared his throat. "Mother, this is Charlie Smith, Theodore's son."

Charlie bent and kissed his aunt's hand, but as he did he thought he saw her smile fade from the red lips at the sound of his father's name. He brushed the thought away. "I'm happy to make your acquaintance, Aunt Rose," he said. "Thank you for allowing me to stay in your beautiful home."

Some natural color came back into her face. She flicked her wrist and a silk fan opened in her hand. "Well, you're welcome, Chahlie." She smiled, waving the fan in front of her face. "I mean, of course. You're a Smith, so consider this your home away from home. We're delighted to have you."

An awkward silence followed. Aunt Rose searched her son's face. Fumbling with her fan, she finally said, "Ryan, take Chahlie upstairs to the guest room. Make sure he has what he needs, then come back down and tend to your mothah, won't you?"

Ryan bowed slightly to her then motioned toward the stairs and spoke to Charlie. "After you."

The guest room was so big Charlie imagined he could fit the entire cabin in it. And the walnut furniture was quite exquisite, probably in the family for generations. The giant four-poster bed had interesting carvings, delicate linens and a down filled mattress so soft he wondered whether he could sleep on it. He walked to the other side of the bed and searched the faces of former Smiths whose portraits adorned the papered walls. In a marble fireplace, a fire burned bright and welcoming.

Just off of the bedroom was a washroom, and to his delight, it had a bathtub. It wasn't a small tin tub like he and

Grandpa used; it was long and white. He could stretch his legs out in this one. Four claw feet held the tub up off the floor and to his surprise, knobs protruded from the wall. He sat on the side of the tub and played with them.

Turning one that had the word *hot* stamped in red across one of its white fingers, he was again surprised to see water pour from the faucet. He stuck his hand underneath the flow then yanked it back. "Yeow," he yelped. "I was wonderin' why the knob read 'hot'," he muttered, turning the knob again to stop the flow. He couldn't believe that water actually ran through the house and emptied into the tub just by turning a couple of knobs.

Leaving the bathroom and crossing the room, he pulled open a set of French doors and stepped out onto a small balcony. A well manicured flower garden lay below. In the middle of a beautiful rose bed, he caught sight of a large statute of a little girl. She was watering a stone pot of granite flowers with a little bucket. Real water streamed from the bucket and slid down the stone flowers, disappearing into the earthen pot that sat at her feet.

He closed his eyes and listened to the water as it trickled across her flowers. The scent of roses filled his nostrils. It was a beautiful home. And although he didn't plan to stay long, he was glad he had come with Ryan.

He emptied his carpetbag and saddle bag; stacking his clothes in the armoire. After that, he took a bath, if for no other reason than to further investigate the knobs.

Later at the dinner table Charlie felt awkward in his cowboy duds. Aunt Rose and Ryan had both changed into more elegant dinner clothes. All he had were jeans and work shirts. They were clean, and they would have to do.

"Thank you for dinner, Aunt Rose," he said, dabbing his mouth with his napkin. "It was delicious."

"You ah very welcome, my dear boy. I'll mention your compliment to Rachel, our maid and chief cook."

"Please do. Now, if it's all right with you, I'd like to go out and check on my horse before turnin' in for the night."

Rose waved her hand. "Of course, Charlie. You may be excused," she said. "Howevah, we do lock our doors at night, so you may want to obtain a key from the board in the kitchen before going out. You should find it hanging beside the back door."

Charlie thanked her again then slipped out of the dining room. It had been a pleasant meal, but the room was beginning to feel stuffy. The ever lingering scent of Aunt Rose's perfume was choking him. He was looking forward to getting out to the barn and enjoying the familiar odors of hay, leather and manure.

Swinging open the kitchen door, he poked his head in. No one was in sight, but just as Aunt Rose said, there was a wooden slat of keys hanging by the back door. More keys than he'd ever seen at one time—keys to the sheds, the basement, the old slave quarters, and the cabinet under the stairs. *Why keep so many things locked up? Why do they need keys to everything anyway? City folk do strange things.*

He spied a nail with three keys hanging on it, and above it, the word *House*. He slid this key into his pocket and stepped outside.

Cool, fresh air filled his lungs. He headed down the dark lane, looking forward to spending time with Star.

21

VISITING STAR EVERY NIGHT AFTER DINNER became routine. It was apparent to Charlie that Star wasn't comfortable in his new surroundings and appreciated his companionship. They spent most of their afternoons together walking around the ranch or scoping out the land across the river. And Charlie always stole a couple of minutes after dinner to say good-night to his friend.

One night, after his visit in the barn, he came in out of a thunderstorm, locked the back door and tip-toed across the kitchen as he always did. It wasn't until he reached the staircase that he remembered the key still in his pocket. He usually hung it up in the kitchen before going to bed, but looking back down the long, dark hallway, he decided it could wait until morning. Sitting on the bottom stair, he started to pull at a boot. Then he heard whisperings.

At first he wasn't sure he'd heard anything at all. But he stopped pulling and listened. At first, it sounded like a soft *sh* or *ch* sound. That's all he could make out; then nothing. Probably just the water boiler, he thought. He got the boot off and started on the other; then he heard it again. This time, it was a little louder. *"Ch- ah- lie. Ch-ah-lie."*

Though barely audible, he heard his name clear as day. He glanced around the room. Where did the whisper come from? Turning slightly, he looked over his shoulder and up the staircase. It was as dark as midnight up there.

"Chahlie. I'm here, Chahlie."

There it was again. He strained to hear while he scanned the darkness. Lightning flashed, filling the room with light for a brief moment, but he saw nothing amiss.

He heard a footstep. A boot hit a wooden board on the porch outside. Someone was out there, just on the other side of the door. Then a roll of thunder drowned out all sound.

Charlie stepped to the side and out of sight just as a bolt of lightning flashed again. His eyes immediately went to the front window. In it, a distorted, grotesque figure stared back at him. *What was that?* Charlie blinked hard. Another flash of lightning lit the room again. The creepy form was still there in the window, swaying back and forth.

It was as if one of those ugly little gargoyles had come to life and was trying to tell him something. He stepped toward the window. Lightning flashed again. This time the window was empty. The grotesque figure was gone.

Looking out the window, he searched the pitch darkness, but could only see streaks of blinding light. If someone were out there, the pounding rain would wipe out their tracks. But he had heard the footstep.

He backed away from the window and moved gingerly about the room, not wanting to knock over any of Aunt Rose's many knick-knacks.

Somewhere beyond the foyer, a floorboard squeaked and he knew he wasn't alone. *Can they see me?* he wondered. *Do they know I'm here?* Slowly he turned his head so he could see down the hall. Vaguely he made out a dark figure coming up the hallway from the kitchen toward him. Charlie took a step backward and slid silently behind a high-backed chair. Hopefully, whoever was there wouldn't light a lamp, and lightning wouldn't illuminate the room.

Two figures were in the living room now.

"Do you see 'im, boss?"

Charlie didn't recognize the voice.

"Shh! No. Must've gone up to his room."

Charlie caught his breath. That voice he recognized.

"Prob'ly cryin' like a little girl," the first voice added.

"Doubt it, Lonnie. He's better than that. We gotta be careful around this one. He don't fool easily."

"Um."

"I want you to keep an eye on old Jonathan, too. If he starts talkin' too much, you might have to shut him up."

"Jonathan? He wouldn't blab, boss."

The voice slid from between gritted teeth. "I said, he talks too much, and if he becomes a nuisance, he'll have to be silenced. Understand?"

Lonnie must have nodded in reply because Charlie didn't hear an answer.

"And as for this Charlie Smith, I want him outta here as soon as possible. The ranch, the land, everything that Ralph owned is *mine* and no upstart is gonna take it from me."

Charlie's foot had fallen asleep and he had been distracted for a moment while rubbing it, but Ryan's words immediately recaptured his attention. Rolling his eyes, he looked up at the ceiling. *Why me?* he asked silently.

"He's the nuisance," hissed Lonnie. "I thought if I killed the old man back on the trail months ago, all this nonsense would stop. Thought he was dead when his horse landed on 'im, but somehow, the old geezer made it out of that one."

What? Grandpa? His head started to buzz. *How? Why would . . . ? But I thought Big T . . . ?* Questions flooded his brain. He almost stood up to demand answers, but decided it was best to stay where he was for now.

"Yes, yes," said Ryan impatiently. "And it wasn't until I went to contest the will that I learned of Charlie and that his grandfather had already passed everything on to him."

"He doesn't know about the goings on this side of the Missouri, does he?" asked Lonnie anxiously. "So he doesn't know about . . . you know, the others either?"

"No!" snapped Ryan. "And he better never learn about any of it or I'll kill you with my own hands, understand?"

Silence. After what seemed like hours, the two men left the room. One went upstairs and the other back down the hallway to the kitchen. He hoped the man named Lonnie had continued on through the back door and down the path that led to the bunkhouse where the ranch hands slept.

When he felt it was safe, Charlie slumped back against the wall and let out a heavy sigh. He was numb all over, and not just because he'd been crouched behind a chair too long. *What were they talking about? Why would they try to scare me away from here? And Grandpa! It was Lonnie who shot at Grandpa a few months ago when he was coming back from Denver. Why? Why would this man want to kill Grandpa? And who did they mean by 'the others'? Was it Lonnie who whispered my name? But that voice had come from inside.*

The hard floor and the pin-prickles in his feet reminded him that he wouldn't be solving any mysteries tonight. It was late. He slowly stood up and limped across the room to the banister. Leaning over to pick up his boots, he heard a board creak at the top of the stairs. He couldn't hide this time. He was in full view of whoever was looking down at him.

"Wondered if you'd come and get those." It was Ryan.

"Yeah," said Charlie, feigning innocence. "I didn't mean to

leave 'em down here clutterin' up the place, but that storm got me riled and I forgot about 'em till now."

"Ah, yes," replied Ryan. His tone held a hint of doubt.

Charlie managed to climb the stairs without grimacing, holding in the groans that his sleeping feet produced. "By the way, has anyone ever mentioned seein' things at the windows during thunderstorms—you know, spooky stuff?"

Amusement flickered in Ryan's eyes. "Do you think this big, old house is a haunted mansion, cousin?"

"Um, it might be," answered Charlie, faking a nervous laugh. "Whatever I saw at that window earlier scared me half to death. It was there one minute, gone the next. Guess I ate too much fried okra and now its playin' tricks with my imagination. Sorry if my movin' around woke ya."

"No, you didn't wake me." Ryan said it so coldly, Charlie thought he saw his breath. "I wasn't asleep. It's rather unusual that you didn't make a racket on your way down the stairs, as they can get a little annoying with their creaking and groaning. But you didn't make a sound at all."

Charlie continued to climb the stairs, paying close attention to where the weak boards were in each step. "I guess that's what happens when I'm too tired to care," said Charlie, pretending to yawn. "Just missed the noisy ones, I guess."

"Hmm," muttered his cousin. "Makes me wonder if you were really downstairs this whole time."

Charlie reached the landing and stepped around his cousin. He wasn't going to take the bait. Instead, he gave a quick shake of his head and kept walking down the hall toward his room. "Good night, Ryan. See ya in the mornin'."

Charlie could feel Ryan's stare at his back. It was a relief to get to his room and shut the door.

22

THE BLADE OF FIRST LIGHT CUT A THIN, red gash across the horizon. Slowly, the night's dark sky began to peel back, spilling a brilliant dawn across the ranch. Charlie watched the sunrise from his bedroom window as he tucked his shirt into his jeans. He wasn't sure if any of his relatives were up this early, but he was ready to start the day. His original plan to stay at the ranch for a week had changed. He had more business to take care of than he had known at first.

Coming down the stairs from his room, he was hit by the aroma of robust coffee and quickened his steps. As he neared the kitchen door, he heard Jonathan chatting quietly with a female. Although he didn't want to interrupt them, he couldn't resist the delicious smells that were tickling his nose.

He pushed the door open and peeked into the room. Jonathan was sitting on a stool with his back to the door, his elbows resting on the kitchen island, a steaming cup in his hand. A petite black woman was standing on the other side of the counter, holding a coffee pot. She set the pot down on the stove.

A few curls of salt and pepper hair were escaping from beneath the woman's light blue turban. Her small frame supported a crisp blue gingham dress that was covered by a clean starched apron. Her dancing brown eyes sparkled when Jonathan spoke. Her warm smile was the first thing to greet Charlie as he let the door swing shut behind him.

"Good mornin', Missah Chahlie," she said softly. "I was hopin' we' have da chance to meet formly. I sees yo at meal tams, but I can't talk when I be servin'. Miss Rose don' like it." She wiped her hands on her apron then extended a small, brown hand to Charlie. "Mah name is Rachel. Jonathan's wife." Charlie liked her immediately. There was a familiar warmness about her. He took her hand and shook it gently.

"Nice to meet you, Rachel," he said sincerely. "And thank you for all the wonderful meals. You're a great cook."

Jonathan turned slightly in his seat. "Would ya like coffee, sah?" he asked politely.

Rachel blushed. "Aw'll get 'im 'is coffee, Jonathan!" she scolded. "Aw'll get 'im 'is brickfis, too, if 'e tell me what it is 'e wants." Before Charlie could answer, her dark brown eyes grew big with excitement.

"Ah know," she cried. "How 'bout some of mah delicious flapjacks, wid homemade buttah an' syrup? Ah'll fry ya up a big ol' slab a' bacon, too. Smith always did—"

Jonathan set his cup down with a thud and scowled at his wife. "Why you don' make a brickfis like dat fo me? Alls I gets is a bowl o' grits."

"Really," said Charlie, easing himself onto the empty stool beside Jonathan. "Don't go to any trouble, Rachel. I'd love a cup of coffee and a bowl of grits with some of your homemade butter on 'em, too. If you have any to spare?"

Rachel turned to her husband, who had quickly retreated to the back door where he was struggling with a pair of work gloves. "See what ya done did, Jonathan Holland? Ya scared da poor boy."

"No, really, he didn't," assured Charlie. "I'm anxious to get outside and do some explorin'. And besides, I have to save room for whatever you'll be makin' for lunch, don't I?"

Rachel dipped her head and smiled sheepishly. "Well, okay, Missah Chahlie, but ah'll pack ya sumpin' to snack on whilt yer explorin'."

"Great," said Charlie, grinning. "And Rachel—"

She looked up at him with wide, curious eyes.

"Please just call me Charlie. I'm no one's master or mister. Just Charlie." He glanced at Jonathan. "That goes for you, too. Just Charlie."

Rachel smiled. Reaching across the island, she patted his hand. "Yessuh. . . . I mean, Chahlie."

"Ah'll go 'n get yo' hoss ready, Chahlie," murmured Jonathan. "I don' think I be wanted here no mo, anyhow."

Rachel scowled again. "Not right now, ya ain't. Now skit ol' man." She walked around the island toward her husband, her hands flicking like a broom, sweeping him out onto the stoop. He waited until she got close enough, then gave her a quick peck on the cheek and disappeared into the sunny morning.

Turning back to Charlie, Rachel chuckled softly. "I love 'im dearly, but sometam I think I just have a big ol' child on my hands. I may be small, but he oughtta know bettah than to give me a hard tam, cuz ah'll tell 'im how da cow ate da cabbage, if ya know what I mean."

Charlie swallowed the laughter that was bubbling up from his throat. She was a small woman, but he wouldn't want to be on the receiving end of her vengence.

She poured him a steaming cup of coffee, then pulled a large bowl and wooden spoon from underneath the island. "Now, how 'bout dem flapjacks?"

After a hearty breakfast, Charlie took Star for a morning ride across the ranch. The more of the six hundred acres he saw, the more beautiful it became. Its rolling green hills, tall, full trees, and cold, clear waterways were easy on a man's eyes. He felt a tinge of sadness thinking about it belonging to someone else soon. If he didn't have the farm back in Pueblo, he might be tempted to stay here himself. Star loved it too. He could tell by the way the horse ran through the meadows and rested under the oaks that this was a good place, a safe place. But Pueblo was home. Where they belonged.

As Charlie patted Star's neck, Ryan's words from the night before came back to him. "Why would Ryan think this belonged to him?" he whispered. "Who is Ryan anyway? I better hold off talking to the family about selling until I know what's going on."

Star just nickered softly in reply.

Jonathan was sitting comfortably in a hay stack, pulling food from a picnic basket when Charlie and Star walked into the barn. Charlie had eaten a passel of Rachel's flapjacks for breakfast that morning, but it was nigh on two o'clock and he was famished. He put Star in his stall, wiped him down and fed him, then joined up with Jonathan, flipping a bucket over for a stool. Rubbing his hands together, he stretched his neck in anticipation and visually searched the basket as Jonathan pulled back the folds of the napkin that covered the wonderful contents inside.

"Hold on, Chahlie," said Jonathan, chuckling. "I be gettin' to da goodies as fast as I can."

"Not fast enough. I'm starving," said Charlie with a grin, tucking a napkin into his shirt.

"Here ya go," said Jonathan, pointing. "Take dat dere plate and fill it up wid some o' dat potato salad and git started. Den ya won' be slobberin' down my neck no mo'."

"Mind if I pray?" asked Charlie.

Jonathan looked over at him with wide eyes. "'Course not," he said, although he sounded slightly miffed.

Charlie asked a quick blessing. Once he uttered "Amen," he dug into the potato salad like a prospector after gold. What he took would tide him over until Jonathan finished unwrapping the delicious leftovers that Rachel had packed for them.

"Goodness," mumbled Charlie, wiping cream sauce from his mouth. "Is this how she fixes lunch every day?"

"Oh, no." Jonathan snickered. "Only cuz yer here. She took a likin' to ya right off."

Charlie nodded as he chewed. "I like her, too."

Jonathan looked at Charlie sideways. He looked like he was about to speak, but then stopped himself; he took a bite of ham instead.

Charlie reached for a chicken leg. "Ryan is a lucky man to own this place," he said, biting into the juicy meat. To himself he thought, *Good chicken, but not quite as good as Dixie's.*

Jonathan threw Charlie a wary look, but didn't say anything. For a second, Charlie thought Jonathan had read his mind and was about to defend Rachel's chicken. Then he realized Jonathan's look was in response to his comment about Ryan being a lucky man.

"I wonder if he'd be interested in selling it?" Charlie mused between bites. "I wouldn't mind livin' here."

Jonathan shook his head. "He won' sell."

"You don't think so?" Charlie glanced at him. "I imagine he would if the price was right."

Jonathan shook his head again. "Naw, not dis one. He been hankerin' to get his hands on dis piece o' land foe some tam now. He won give it up now dat he got it."

Charlie laid his plate aside and slowly pulled the napkin from his shirt. Now he was getting somewhere, but he didn't want to scare Jonathan.

"Was it a recent purchase for him?"

Jonathan chuckled and wiped his face with his napkin. "Naw, he didn't buy it, dat fer sure."

"Oh, then it must've been an inheritance. I guess I should offer my sympathy to the family."

Jonathan rounded on Charlie. Panic spread over his normally friendly face. "No, Chahlie. Ya can't say nuttin' to Missah Ryan. He'll kill me if ya do."

Jonathan had broken out into a sweat. The terror in the man's eyes was real. "I won't say a word," Charlie said, reaching over and laying a hand on Jonathan's shoulder. "I promise. But tell me what's wrong."

Jonathan threw a quick look at the barn doors. Charlie stared at the doors with curiosity. Had Jonathan seen someone? Charlie wasn't sure until Jonathan swiftly gathered the plates and shoved them into the basket, paying no mind to spills.

Charlie dropped from the bucket onto the hay-strewn floor, landing on his knees in front of the distraught man. He grabbed Jonathan's arm. "It'll be all right, Jonathan," he whispered. "But you've got to tell me what's going on here."

Jonathan shook his head so hard sweat flew off and hit Charlie in the face. "No, sah," he murmured. "I already done sayd too much."

"Jonathan, you're shaking."

"Yes, sah. Dat's what I does when I's scared."

Charlie looked around the barn. "What are you scared of, Jonathan?"

Jonathan threw the last item into the basket and got to his feet, groaning a little as his aged knees quivered beneath his weight. Reaching down, he grabbed the handles of the basket and whispered, "Sah, I don' mean to be rude, but I's got to get back to work."

"Can we talk some more tonight, when I come out to take care of Star?"

"We best not," said Jonathan, walking toward the doors. "I best just keep workin'."

"But—"

Jonathan had turned his face towards the outdoors. "It was nice meetin' ya, Missah Smif," he said loudly. "I be tellin' Rachel 'bout yo' braggin' on her chicken." He turned and disappeared, leaving Charlie alone in the barn.

Charlie got to his feet. Frustrated, he ran his fingers through his hair. Something was going on at the Smith ranch, something dark and sinister. Judging by Jonathan's behavior, it could even be downright life-threatening. He was going to find out what it was.

23

LATER THAT NIGHT, AFTER EXPLORING THE acreage on the other side of the river, Charlie hung the key on the board in the kitchen, sat down on a kitchen stool, and stripped his muddy boots from his feet. Not only did he not want to awaken anyone, he didn't want anyone to know he was back in the house. Maybe he'd learn something. He'd missed dinner, but Rachel's lunch had sustained him through the day.

He sat in a chair in the corner of the living room. *I'll sit here for hours, if that's what it takes.* Sniffing the wings of the chair, the lingering scent of Aunt Rose's pungent perfume hit him square in the face. *Well, maybe*, he thought. The last thing he wanted was to get sick, but he didn't want to leave either. He was still wondering about whatever he'd heard several nights before and wanted to find out who was calling his name.

In time he got used to the odor coming from the chair. His eyes adjusted to the dark room, too. He could make out shapes—knick-knacks and books on shelves, a picture, a porcelain treasure. Nothing had color or dimension; everything was flat and black, white, or gray. And there was no sound, except the morose ticking of the grandfather clock, which eventually began to lull Charlie to sleep. But it was while he was in that lull, in the world between awake and asleep, that the whispers floated to his ears.

"Chahlie," came the frail call. "Are you there? Help me, Chahlie. Please help me."

His eyes flew open and he was up, out of the chair in an instant; listening, trying to follow a voice that was as traceable as the wind. It was so soft, so low, that many times, he lost the direction from which it was coming. Sometimes it sounded like it was coming from the opposite corner of the large room, other times from under the grand staircase, or from the bookcases that lined the far wall. Every now and then, it even seemed to come from somewhere behind the grand fireplace. Through his search, he figured out that the voice was confined only to the living room, because upon his leaving the area, it disappeared completely.

He was feeling his way along the wall that ran beneath the stairs when he spotted something white on the floor, almost hidden by the grandfather clock. Leaning down, he touched it and found it was cloth. He picked it up and felt it; lace on the outer rim, soft cotton fabric in the center, with some sort of embroidery in a corner. Aunt Rose's handkerchief? Just then, other voices floated over the banister towards him. He was sure it was Ryan and the man called Lonnie. He quickly stuffed the handkerchief into his pocket and squatted behind the large chair.

"Maybe he just wants Rachel to shine 'em up a bit."

"Or maybe he took them off so he could hide somewhere and poke his nose into our business," retorted Ryan. "Light a lamp and have a look around."

"I don't think—"

"No, you don't," said Ryan, getting angrier by the second. "Have you already forgotten what happened to Jonathan this afternoon?"

"No, I haven't forgotten," mumbled Lonnie.

"Then I suggest you do as I say."

"Yes, sir."

Fortunately for Charlie, Lonnie didn't obey orders right away. Grumbling under his breath, he opened the front door and stepped out onto the porch. Grabbing one of the oil lamps that hung on either side of the massive door, he fumbled for something in his pockets. Charlie assumed he was looking for a match. Ryan had walked back toward the kitchen, apparently looking for something as well. With both of the men preoccupied, he knew this would be his only chance to steal through the darkness and up the stairs. He'd have to leave his boots in the kitchen, but should anyone ask in the morning, he'd say he took them off because he didn't want to track mud through the house, which was part of the truth.

Charlie peered over the chair. Lonnie was standing on the porch, his back to the window, smoking a cigarette. Charlie took advantage of the moment and bounded up the stairs, stepping over the loose boards that would give him away. When he got to his room, he closed the door to a crack and listened. He didn't have to wait long.

Lonnie came in from the porch and started to search the living room. Blasts of light bounced up the stairs as he passed the staircase below, swinging the lamp around in search of Charlie. Charlie exhaled slowly. Had he decided to stay hidden behind the chair, he would have been found, and that would've meant trouble. But he was safe, for now.

He stripped down to his long johns and climbed into bed. It had been a long day.

He wasn't sure if it was a sound or a flash of light, but something had awakened him. Yet, when he opened his eyes, he was alone and in total darkness. He sat up and looked around. Nothing looked different, but he was sure Ryan had been there. He just wasn't sure why. Maybe it was to confirm that he was in his bed and not hiding somewhere spying on him and Lonnie. Or maybe he was looking for something.

It was then he remembered the lace handkerchief he'd stuffed into his pocket earlier. Quickly, he scrambled out of bed and grabbed his jeans. Cramming his fingers into the pocket, he felt around for the lace trim. With rising curiosity, he pulled the delicate piece of fabric out and laid it on his knee.

It was old, yellowed with age; but the hand crocheted lace and elegantly embroidered initials looked as fine as they were the day the piece was finished. The letters were in old English, but he could make them out. There was an E on the left, an A on the right, and in the middle, a large S. He ran his thumb across the letters and wondered who E.A.S. was, and how she had come to own this handkerchief, apparently so many years ago.

Charlie put the handkerchief back in his pocket, flopped onto the bed and stretched out. Thoughts of his family ran through his mind. He didn't know much about Aunt Rose, other than that she was flamboyant and theatrical. She boasted that her dresses came from the best designers in Paris, yet somehow she lacked elegance. Her makeup, at her age, looked ridiculous.

He didn't even know how she was related to him. In their conversations around the dinner table, there had been no mention of an uncle. And Charlie didn't want to ask. He wanted to listen. But still, he found it strange that a man was never mentioned—after all, this man would have been the Smith whence this family came. Where was he?

Cousin Ralph had owned the land on the other side of

the Missouri River, so who had owned this ranch? Who had been the master of this house? Grandpa hadn't talked much about his relatives here in Missouri, so he'd have to ask Ryan or Rose sooner or later.

Then there were Jonathan and Rachel. Charlie sat bolt upright. *Have you forgotten what happened to Jonathan this afternoon already?* Ryan had used it to threaten Lonnie earlier. Charlie jumped out of bed and threw on his clothes. He was outside and running to the small house before he realized he'd forgotten his gun, but it was too late now. He'd have to use other measures should trouble come his way.

Running past the barn, Charlie saw Jonathan's and Rachel's house. It was after midnight, but golden light flowed from the windows onto the grass outside. Someone was awake. He tapped on the door. After several minutes, a small voice called out. "Who be deah?"

"It's Charlie, Rachel. Can I come in?"

Inside, the bolt moved and the door creaked as Rachel pulled it open just enough to look up at him. She didn't welcome him in as he thought she would. Instead, she stood in the splinter of space and stared up at him, her eyes red and swollen. "Go way, Missah Smif. Ya got no busniss heah."

"Rachel, I need to see Jonathan."

"No, sah," she said, setting her jaw. "Jonathan ain't well enuf to see ya, so go away."

She started to close the door, but Charlie stopped it with the toe of his boot. "I'm not going anywhere until I see Jonathan, so you might as well let me in," he said sternly. "I know he's been hurt, and I want to know what happened! I promise I won't let anything else hurt him, Rachel."

"No," she snapped. "I ain't lettin' no one in."

In Green Pastures

"Rachel." A weak, yet firm voice came from within the house. "That be enuf. Dis weren't Chahlie's fault. Let 'im in."

Angrily, Rachel pulled her robe tighter to her chest. She glared up at Charlie through the puddles that had collected in her eyes. She mumbled something then nodded shortly. "Come on in den," she said. "But make dis short. Jonathan be very tired." She stepped aside and pulled the door open so Charlie could enter.

The house's one room was as neat as a pin. It was furnished simply, yet comfortably, with handmade doilies hanging over the two chairs that took up one corner of the room. A small table and two chairs served as their dining room, and a wood burning stove and a couple of cabinets comprised Rachel's personal kitchen. Across from the kitchen was their bed, and upon it lay Jonathan.

Looking over at the wounded man, Charlie wasn't prepared for what he saw. Jonathan was lying on his stomach and he hadn't just been hit, he'd been beaten with a whip, or a belt. His back was raw, bloodied, and in places cut to the bone. It looked as if Rachel had tried to apply balm to the open wounds, but more than that would be needed to make Jonathan whole again. Time mostly. Weeks, even. Yet, most likely, Jonathan didn't have weeks. Ryan might expect him to be up and working tomorrow morning, or this could happen again. It could even happen to Rachel.

He walked quietly to the bed. "Jonathan," he said as calmly as he could. "Are you all right?"

The man's eyes opened to slits. He squinted in pain. "I be fine, Chahlie. Be up in a few hours to get to work."

"I don't think so," answered Charlie. "I don't think you're gonna be able to move for a while."

"Got no choice, Chahlie. I gots to work."

"Well, we'll let the Lord take care of the details," Charlie said with a forced smile. "I just have to persuade you that He'll take care of this, too."

Jonathan glanced up at Charlie then closed his eyes. "What d' ya mean?"

"I'm asking you to trust me, Jonathan, to tell me everything. Why did this happen? If things were really right around here, if there were nothin' to hide, you wouldn't be layin' here like this. Please tell me, Jonathan. Tell me everything."

Rachel stepped over to the bed. "No, sah." She bristled. "Jonathan ain't gonna get hisself in no mo trouble. He ain't young no mo and I—"

"Woman, I surely can't look at Chahlie and tell 'im everthin' be fine, now can I?" Jonathan sighed.

"No, but ya don' have to be da one to—"

"Hush now!" Jonathan grimaced in pain.

Rachel turned sharply away from the bed and marched over to the stove. Throwing open its door, she shoved the poker into the fire and banged the iron walls. Slamming the stove door shut, she dropped a pot of water onto one of the burners, then stood in front of the stove with her arms folded tightly across her chest. Charlie knew she was accustomed to getting her way; but this time Jonathan wasn't going to bend.

Charlie swung a chair out from under the table and sat down beside the bed. Leaning forward, he rested his elbows on his knees. "I'm listenin', Jonathan. Start when you're ready."

Jonathan took a deep breath and closed his eyes. "This is deepah den ya think it be, Chahlie," he warned. "I din wanna say nuttin' earlier cause ya might not be ready fo' what ya gonna heah."

"I'm ready now. Go on."

"Ya have to promise me dat when ah'm done, ya won' go an do nuttin' dumb."

"Dumb?" asked Charlie. "Like what?"

"Like go hurt Missah Ryan."

"I'm not gonna go out and kill Ryan, Jonathan," said Charlie impatiently.

Jonathan held up a hand. "Chahlie. Ya just might afta ya heah what ah'm 'bout ta tell ya."

"Let me be the judge of that."

"Okay." Jonathan closed his eyes. "Here ya go." He sat up a little and took a long drink of water. He wiped his mouth with the back of his hand, then settled back down.

"Rachel an' me, we been 'round a long time. Back when Missah Ralph first started to come into his money. He bought me an da missus so we could stay a family. Lots a slave families was broke up back den, but Missah Ralph, he knowd me an Rachel needed ta be together, so he buyed us bofe. He pay us fo our work, too. He was a good man. He din have no slaves in da fields, won have it. Hired folks to work his fields and build his house. Den when da house was done, he let me and Rachel work in da house. She always don de cookin'. Missah Ralph sho' did love her cookin'!"

Jonathan paused, then continued with an effort. "We met yo' pappy when he come out heah from da West. A fine young man he was, too."

"Yep, he sho' was," murmured Rachel.

Charlie sat up. "You knew my pa?"

"Sho' did," she answered quietly. "He come out heah and

went on to school. Become a fine 'ttorney, too. Smart man. You're like 'im."

Charlie shifted in his chair. "Thank you, Rachel. I appreciate that. Grandpa often told me how smart my pa was. He didn't cotton to raisin' cows much, so he came back here to go to school. I didn't realize he'd built himself a law business though."

Jonathan nodded. "He met yo' mammie shortly afta comin' out heah, and it weren't long till they was married. A couple o' years afta dat, ya was born."

Rachel leaned her head back and smiled. "I member dat day like it was yesterday," she said. "I hepped bring ya into dis world. Yo' mammy sent word to the house fo' me to come help."

Charlie spun around in his seat and searched her face.

"That's why it felt like I'd known you all my life when I first met you."

"Because ya have," Rachel said, chuckling.

"Anyhow," continued Jonathan, "what none of us knowd was Ralph had him a chile wid a saloon girl 'bout da same tam yo' pappy was born. We din' even know 'bout 'im till he walked into yo' pappy's office one day lookin' ta make a deal wid 'im."

"A deal?" asked Charlie. "What kind of deal?"

"A bad one," answered Jonathan. "He figured since he be Ralph's son, he should be gettin' some of Ralph's money, and his ranch, too."

Charlie sat up in his chair. "You mean Ryan is Ralph's son?"

Jonathan opened his dark, puffy eyes as wide as he could. He nodded his head. "Yessuh," he whispered. "Miss Rose and

Missah Ralph never married, though. Missah Ralph din' tell no one he had a boy. He took care of da two of dem, money-wise, but he never made a family of 'em."

Charlie frowned. "But when Ralph died, he said he didn't have any family to leave an inheritance. He left his estate to my grandfather. And that included the six hundred acres on the other side of the river."

"Da's right," said Jonathan, nodding. "Ralph had been takin' care of 'em both, Missah Ryan and Miss Rose, but he din' want nuttin' ta do wid any of 'em afta yo' pappy died."

"So apparently, Ryan didn't get to make that deal with my pa?"

"No," Rachel said sadly. "Yo pappy was too good. He wouldn't rob Ralph to satisfy Ryan. Nuttin' was ever legally given to Ryan, not his house or land either. It'd be youm, now, I reckon." Rachel paused, then continued. "An we so sorry 'bout yo' pappy, Chahlie. He din' deserve to die dat way."

"Yeah," agreed Charlie. "Grandpa said it was a terrible accident, but he never did tell me what happened."

Jonathan lifted his head. His dark eyes searched for Rachel's. When their eyes met, Charlie thought he saw a look of confusion mixed with dread.

"What?" he asked anxiously.

Jonathan avoided the young man's gaze, laying his head back down on the bed and closing his eyes. "Nuttin'," he said wearily. "I just had some pain, dat's all."

"Well, I'll let you get some rest," said Charlie. "I better get some too. Got chores to do in a few hours."

"What chores?" asked Jonathan.

Charlie grabbed his hat. "Yours," he said, tugging it onto

his head. "And no arguing about it, either. I was raised on a farm, so I can handle everything you do around here."

Rachel followed him to the door. "Beside da regular stuff, he has a schedule of comin's and goin's that he wrote out and put up in da barn. It helps him to know when to saddle da hosses or have feed ready when they come in. You'll fine it."

Charlie leaned down and kissed her cheek. "And what about you?" he asked quietly. "Who will relieve you?"

Pulling her robe tighter around her thin shoulders, she smiled. "I be fine, Chahlie. I'm stronger dan I look." Casting down her eyes, she mumbled, "Ah'm sorry for bein' mean to ya earlier. I just get so scared."

"I understand, Rachel," he assured her. "No need to apologize."

Rachel looked up and smiled. "Thank you. . . . Now, off ta bed wid ya!"

Charlie stepped off of the stoop as Rachel closed the door behind him. Looking up at the midnight sky, he yawned. "Storm comin'," he murmured.

24

SITTING UP, CHARLIE RUBBED HIS EYES. THE cobwebs in his head cleared as he shook himself awake. Through the window shone sunlight—something that hadn't awakened him in a long time. He swung his feet to the floor and waited. All was quiet. No one seemed to be stirring in the house.

"Jonathan!" he said, remembering.

He jumped up and yanked on his clothes, praying his over sleeping hadn't caused the wrath of Ryan to fall again on Jonathan. But he was afraid it was too late. It was eight o'clock in the morning, much later than he normally slept.

He ran down the stairs, through the hall, and into the kitchen.

Rachel, standing at the stove, looked worried. "Ya awlright, Chahlie?" she asked. "Ya sure was in bed fo a long tam."

"I'm fine, Rachel. Is Jonathan in bed? He didn't try to get up and do anything this morning, did he?"

Rachel took him by the elbow and led him over to a stool. "Let me get ya a cup o' coffee," she said calmly. "Ya be worried 'bout nuttin'."

"Just tell me about Jonathan."

Rachel turned from the cabinet and smiled. "Jonathan be fine, Chahlie. He's sleepin' right now. Dere be no need fo 'im to get outta bed fo da tam bein'." Turning back to the cupboard she pulled out a cup and finished preparing Charlie's coffee. "Early dis monin', dere was a cowboy sittin' on da stoop.

Tolt me dat Missah Ryan brought 'im on just dis monin' to do chores. Whadevah need be done." Her smile lit up the room.

Charlie sipped on his coffee. "Really?" he asked skeptically. "Did you get his name?"

"Yep. Millah. Um, I believe he sayd his first name be Isaac, but I knows he sayd his last name be Millah. Yep, das it. Isaac Millah."

Charlie jumped to his feet. His eyes were as round as saucers. "Where would he be now, Rachel?"

Rachel stared. "In da barn, I reckon. Why? Is everthin' awlright?"

Charlie's eyes gleamed. "It will be," he said happily. "It surely will be."

Inside the barn, he found pristine stalls and tack—its silver details twinkling in the sunlight—hanging on walls in perfect order. Everything was just as he was used to seeing it. Jonathan kept everything clean and organized. But Charlie was surprised to see Star saddled and waiting for him. "What are you doin' here, boy?" he asked the horse, grabbing an apple from a rusty bucket. "Were we supposed to go somewhere this mornin'?"

"I thought you needed to take a ride into town," a voice spoke from behind him, sounding familiar.

Charlie spun on his heels and came face-to-face with Isaac Miller, the scout from the cattle drive he had ridden on last summer. "Miller!" he exclaimed, clasping his hand. "Am I glad to see you!"

"And I you, Charlie," he replied with a wide grin. "Been a while."

"Sure has," said Charlie, hanging his thumbs in his belt loops. "So, what's goin' on?"

"I'm here on a mission. I can't tell you about it now, other than that you need to get on your horse and ride into town. When you get there, send a message to the Pinkerton Agency in Chicago. Get Peterson out here as soon as possible."

Charlie frowned. "Peterson? You mean Sergeant Peterson?"

"That'd be the one."

"Why? What do I need Peterson for?"

Miller walked over to Star and pulled the reins from the post. "Proof," he said grimly. "There's more going on here than you think. Peterson knows how to gather proof. You remember he's a private investigator for the Pinkerton Agency in Chicago. Tell him to do his work in town first and not to come out here unless he has to."

"Okay," said Charlie slowly. "But what do I ask him to investigate?"

Miller handed him the reins. "He knows what to look for. I've already told him. He's just been waiting for a message from you telling him when it's time to come down here. It's time."

Charlie stared into his friends eyes. "I don't understand," he said softly. "What's going on? Why can't you do it? What's it got to do with me?"

"In time," came another familiar voice. Turning round, Charlie saw Jess, the mountain man who had come to his rescue so many years ago.

"Jess," he whispered.

"Do as Miller says, Charlie," said the big man. He gently laid a massive hand on Charlie's shoulder. "Everything will be fine, I promise."

Charlie searched his friend's face. Peace flooded over him. Without another word, he mounted Star and they dashed out of the barn. Saint Charles was eight miles away. Right then, it felt like an eternity.

"Here's your reply," said the post office clerk, handing a yellow slip to Charlie. He scanned the message. Its words were few and direct.

"Got message (Stop). Will arrive by train in two days (Stop). 4:00 p.m. Have more information for you (Stop). Peterson."

Charlie folded the note and put it in his jacket. "Lord," he prayed. "I don't know what's going on, but you do. I don't know what information Peterson has, or what he's suppose to look for when he gets here, but I'll trust you."

"Sir?" asked the clerk.

Charlie looked up and smiled. "Sorry. Just thinkin' out loud."

"Yes, sir. Can I help you with anything else?"

Charlie shook his head. "Naw," he answered. "That'll do. How much do I owe you?"

"Three dollars, sir."

Charlie reached into his pocket and pulled out his money clip. "On second thought," he said. "I would like to send two other telegrams, if you don't mind."

The clerk grabbed a pencil and a tablet. "Not at all, sir," he said, licking the lead tip of the pencil. "How would you like the first to read?"

"This one's for Phillip LeFaye and it should say . . ." Charlie paused and carefully pulled the pencil from the clerk's fingers. "Would you mind if I write them out?" he asked, retrieving the tablet too.

"Not at all, sir. Just make sure the message is legible."

In Green Pastures

Charlie scrawled out a couple of sentences for each telegraph then passed the paper and pencil back to the clerk. "There," he said cheerfully. "That should do."

"Do you want a reply?" asked the clerk.

"Don't expect one from either," said Charlie.

Charlie paid the clerk then stepped out onto the boardwalk and looked up and down the street. Saint Charles was bigger than Pueblo, but not as big as Denver. With Miller on the ranch, Jonathan and Rachel were in fine hands, so he decided to explore a bit.

A couple blocks away, a train whistle blew. Horses pulled wagons and carriages up and down the streets. Children ran down the boardwalks and peeked into store windows. In the center of town lay the town square. The largest building around the grassy park was the courthouse, or county seat. Charlie thought of the University of Denver where he was supposed to start classes in the fall.

He sat on a park bench and watched folks bustle around the square. Eyeing the brick building, he made a mental note to send a telegram to the university to cancel his enrollment. Grandpa wouldn't have liked the idea, but he had too many other things to take care of right now. And moving to Denver wasn't one of them.

A chorus of laughter rose up behind him. One sound in particular ascended above the rest. Like a southern sonnet, it was music to his ears. *Surely not*, he thought, turning on the bench to look. Several handsomely dressed women were walking up the boardwalk toward him. He searched their faces. Then he caught a glimpse of a head of silver hair with just a few blonde streaks flowing through it. The woman laughed again and he had no doubt then that it was Dixie.

He had to look twice before realizing the beautiful girl next to Dixie was Rebecca. The only thing he recognized about her was her laugh. Her blonde hair, no longer in pigtails, had been curled and fashionably piled underneath a feathered hat. Her full and flowing dress in no way resembled the ginghams and pinafores he had seen her wear at the restaurant.

Standing slowly, he turned and faced the ladies as they came closer. He didn't know if he should address Dixie and Rebecca, not wanting to embarrass them in front of the other ladies, but he sure didn't want to miss talking to them either. To his relief, Dixie saw him.

"Charlie!" she exclaimed. "Charlie Smith?"

Rebecca spun around from the display window she'd been examining. Her bright eyes searched the street.

Dixie gathered her skirt, stepped off the boardwalk, and sailed over to the park bench. For Charlie, seeing her smile was like coming home. She threw her arms around his neck, and he hugged her back. He felt foolish to even think he could embarrass this woman in public.

Stepping back, she took him by the shoulders and looked up into his face. "My dear boy, what on earth are you doing in Saint Charles of all places?"

Rebecca quietly stepped up beside her grandmother. Charlie had watched her approach and for some reason, he couldn't move his mouth to speak. He swallowed hard and cleared his throat. "Hello, Miss Dixie." Then he nodded at Rebecca. "Hello, Rebecca."

Rebecca didn't lower her eyes, but fixed them on Charlie. "Hello, Charlie," she said smiling. "What are you doing in Saint Charles?"

In Green Pastures

"I'm here on business," he said quickly. "What are you two doing here?"

"We're here to attend the suffrage convention," answered Rebecca proudly. "I'm too young to demonstrate yet, not quite eighteen, but Grandma said I should attend anyway, just to listen and learn."

Dixie took his hand. "It's so exciting, Charlie," she whispered. "Miss Susan Anthony is going to speak here tonight. We can hardly wait."

"Hmm," murmured Charlie. "Sounds grand."

"It is," replied Dixie. "If women will be allowed to vote in the future, she's the one who will make it happen. And of course, we women should have the right to vote. This is our country too, and we should have a say in who governs us."

Rebecca took Dixie's elbow. "It's all right, Grandma," she soothed. "Don't get yourself all worked up. Colorado isn't even a state yet. We'll just be ready when Congress decides it should be."

Dixie patted at her hair. "You're right, Katy," she said with a pleasant smile.

Katy?

Dixie added, "Won't you join us for lunch, Charlie? There's so much to talk about, besides women's suffrage."

He glanced at Rebecca. "I'd love to," he replied. Rebecca cast her eyes downward and she blushed slightly.

"Good," said Dixie. She slid her arm through his and started up the boardwalk. Rebecca followed along behind them. "Where to?"

A few minutes later, the three were settled around a small table inside a quaint restaurant. It felt odd being in their company again, especially here.

"So," began Dixie, spreading her napkin across her lap, "what business brought you here?"

"Just some family matters," replied Charlie. "Before Grandpa passed away, I found out I had kin out this way, so I thought I'd come out and meet them."

"Wonderful," said Dixie cheerfully. "I think it's absolutely wonderful that we should run into you here."

"You do? Why?"

"Yes," she said. "I've wanted to ask you something for quite a while, but preferred to do so in person."

Charlie squirmed in his chair.

"You see, right after Stuart died, the bank sent word that the mortgage on my restaurant had been paid in full and quite a bit of cash had been deposited into my bank account." She raised her water glass to her lips. "Any idea how that came about?" She took a sip.

Charlie stared at the floor. *Lord, help me.* He wasn't accustomed to lying, but he didn't want to go into the whole story about Ralph's generosity, Grandpa's request that he help Dixie, or how all of this was connected to his visit to Saint Charles. Some things he had to keep to himself. He raised his head and looked Dixie in the eye. "You know, Dixie, Grandpa use to say to leave the little details to the Lord. I can't answer your question, but God knows. And in time, if He wills it, you'll know too."

Dixie smiled, but she didn't seem satisfied with the answer. "Okay," she said softly. "I'll settle for that explanation, for now."

Charlie straightened his napkin. *Thank you, Lord.*

"Would you care for some tea, ma'am?" asked the server.

"I'm fine with water," said Dixie. "How about you, Katy?"

Rebecca shook her head. "No, thank you. Water's fine."

Charlie glanced at Rebecca. "I've heard you called Becky before, but never Katy. Did you change your name since I saw you last?"

Rebecca giggled. "No," she said, throwing a quick look at Dixie. "That's what my grandpa used to call me. My full name is Rebecca Kathleen."

"And every now and again, I call her Katy, too," said Dixie. "It suits her."

Rebecca's eyes sparkled. "And you may also, Charlie. If you like."

Their eyes met and he froze. Her eyes were the same color blue as he remembered them to be, but everything else about her seemed so different. So grown up. "What did you mean outside, when you said you weren't quite eighteen yet?" he asked softly. "You'd just turned twelve when I met you last year."

Dixie set her water glass down on the table. "If you two will excuse me, I need to find a powder room."

Rebecca watched her grandmother slip from her chair and walk away before she turned to Charlie. "I'm glad you asked," she replied. "Do you remember my grandma asking you to stop by to see us before you left Denver? She said there was something I wanted to share with you."

Charlie nodded.

"Well, that is what I wanted to tell you. I'm not going on thirteen, Charlie. I'm going on seventeen."

Charlie looked confused. "Then why in the world…"

"You have to understand where I came from, Charlie," she interrupted. "My world was so much different than yours. In the South, during the war, union soldiers barged into our homes and took over our lives. We owned nothing, not even our identities."

Charlie tried to comprehend what she was saying. She continued, "Not all of the commanders were gentlemen. They confiscated our farms for their headquarters, our horses for their soldiers, our . . . our . . ." Rebecca turned her eyes to the floor and blushed. "Well," she whispered, "some men committed the most heinous crimes against womenfolk. And it was worse if there were no men or boys in the home."

Charlie reached over and touched her hand. "I'm sorry, Becky. I had no idea. . . ."

Rebecca's eyes met Charlie's again. "Oh, I'm all right," she said softly. "I was just a child then, but Grandma saw neighbor friends…" She turned away again.

"Listen, Becky, you don't have to explain—"

"No, I want to. I need to so you'll know the truth." She sighed and went on. "Finally someone thought of dressing her older daughters like children, to make them look younger than they actually were, in hopes that the soldiers wouldn't take advantage of them. So if one could, one acted, dressed, and claimed to be much younger than she actually was in order to protect herself.

"After Lincoln's assassination, matters got worse. There was very little reformation, but in fact, several formations in the south. Formations of various groups such as the …, um, oh what are they called again? The men that wear the hoods. You know the Klu . . . um . . ."

"You mean the Ku Klux Klan."

Rebecca shuddered. "That's the name." She grew quiet for a moment, but then sat up and continued. "Since they organized, things got much worse. With our men gone, Grandma and I were on our own. Grandma got tired of sleeping with one eye open and a loaded rifle, so she picked up and moved us to Denver. As far from the south as we could get, but once we got there, we still didn't know what to expect. We didn't know how women were treated, or if it was safe to be—"

"You're safe with me."

"I know that now," stated Rebecca. "Besides my grandpa and pa, you and your grandpa were the kindest men I'd ever met, but I didn't know that when I first met you. Why, for all I knew, the four of you sitting at that table were nothing but lonely soldiers, looking for the attention of a woman. So, until we knew how life was going to be for us in Denver, Grandma had me revert back to our war days. I didn't mean to deceive you, but you understand don't you?"

Charlie searched her face. "I do," he answered. "And I'm glad you told me. Knowing the truth sure clears some things up for me."

"It does?"

"Yeah." He paused. "Rebecca, how long are you going to be in town?"

"A week. Why?"

"May I call on you in the next couple of days?"

Her eyes danced when she smiled. "Of course."

"I hear the Saint Louis Symphony will be playing at the theatre here in town on Thursday evening. Would you like to go hear them with me?"

"I'd love to. We're staying at the Saint Charles Inn."

The swishing of Dixie's dress reached their ears before she arrived at the table. "So," she said breathlessly, "what did I miss?"

"Nothing much." Rebecca smiled at her grandmother.

The server stepped up to the table with their lunch. The conversation moved on to other matters.

At the hotel door, Rebecca took Charlie's arm and looked up into his eyes. There was that heavy feeling in his chest again, the one that made it hard to breathe.

"By the way, thank you for the ribbons. I have one in my hair right now." She turned her head and pointed to the pale blue bow planted above the curls on the back of her head. "I noticed there was two of each color. I don't wear pigtails any longer, but I'll find use for the extras. I might even put them on our Christmas tree."

Charlie looked into her blue eyes and smiled. "Whose Christmas tree?" he asked softly.

"Ours. Mine and, and . . ." Her face turned a beautiful rosy shade of pink.

Charlie looked down into her eyes and smiled. "Good night . . . Katy."

"Good night, Charlie," she whispered. "I'll see you Thursday evening."

25

SUNSHINE FILTERED THROUGH ANCIENT oak branches as Charlie swung into the lane that led up to the Smith mansion. It was late, but he didn't care. Seeing Dixie and Rebecca had filled him with an unusual calm, but had also been exciting. His thoughts drifted from them to one of the telegrams he'd sent out that morning. He wondered what she would do when she received it.

He worried. *What if she thinks it's stupid? What if she just throws it away?* After all, the message didn't say anything they hadn't already talked about. Just an inquiry to her health and that he hoped to see her again soon. He squirmed in the saddle. He felt so dimwitted when it came to girls.

"Chahlie!" The voice crackled like a bolt of lightning. Rachel burst through the front door of the house and bounded down the porch stairs. She ran so hard, she had to hold on to her turban to keep it on her head.

Charlie pulled Star to a stop and slid from the saddle. "I'm here, Rachel," he called. "What is it?"

It took a second for her to catch her breath, but she was able to speak "It's Missah Ryan," she said, almost choking. "He be angry when he find out ya went to town widout tellin' 'im."

He wrapped an arm around her shaking shoulders and led her towards the house. "That's all? Take a breath, Rachel."

"No," said Rachel, shaking her head fiercely. "Ya don' undastan, Chahlie. When Missah Ryan gets mad, it be like he goes crazy."

"Is that what happened to Jonathan yesterday? Ryan got mad at him and went crazy?"

Rachel tightened her jaw.

"Well?"

"I can't," she whispered. "If he finds out I talked to ya, he whip me too, den dere won' be nobody to take care o' Jonathan."

Charlie stopped abruptly. "You mean Ryan beat Jonathan just because he talked to me in the barn that afternoon?"

"Please, Chahlie," she said as she wearily climbed the stairs to the house. "I can't say no mo'. Jus' be careful."

Charlie said a silent prayer, asking the Lord to calm him down before he ran into Ryan.

He wasn't sure what to expect. If nothing else, he knew one thing for certain: There'd be lively conversation at the dinner table tonight.

"Charlie, would you mind passing me the cornbread?" asked Aunt Rose.

"Certainly, Aunt Rose," said Charlie.

"I understand you went to town today."

Charlie glanced at Ryan, who had stopped chewing.

Turning back to Aunt Rose, he answered, "Yes, ma'am. I did. Nice town."

"And what was your business theah?" she said, slicing at the ham rather vigorously.

"Well, I—"

"Mother," said Ryan. "I don't believe that is any of *our* business."

"Why not?" she asked boldly, batting her eyelashes. "We're family here. We hold no secrets from each other."

Ryan looked at Charlie inquiringly.

Charlie almost rolled his eyes, but restrained himself. He knew there were more secrets in this house than in Dixie's chicken recipe, but he'd play along.

"It's all right, cousin," he said, stirring his iced tea. "I went to send a couple of telegrams to some friends back home. They'll panic if they don't hear from me once in a while. And then," he paused for just a second, long enough to get their curiosity stirred. "And then I explored some—you know, checked out the mercantile, ate lunch, that sort of stuff."

Aunt Rose dabbed with a napkin at her mouth. "Well, you should have told us you were going," she said pettishly. "Ryan could've gone with you, or provided you an escort."

"Escort?" exclaimed Charlie. "I don't need an escort. I'm quite capable of—"

"You are a Smith," interrupted Aunt Rose. "And the whole state knows we have money. I don't know much about the West, Chahlie, but here we have highwaymen, robbahs, who will try to get your money one way or the other, even if they have to kidnap you to get it."

Charlie was about to protest, when Ryan spoke up. "Mother is right. These parts look friendly enough, but we have our outlaws too. You need to let me know whenever you plan to leave the ranch for your own safety."

Charlie couldn't believe his ears. Was he going to be held prisoner in this old house? He was certain they just wanted to keep tabs on his whereabouts. *Do I look like a fool?* he wondered.

"I appreciate your interest in my well-being, Aunt Rose," he replied politely. "But really, I can take care of myself. And I don't want to be a bother to anyone just because I might get a hankerin' to go into town."

Ryan shifted his weight and laid his fork down on his plate. "Listen Charlie," he said firmly. "You won't be a nuisance. In fact, I insist that you tell me your plans when you leave the premises so I can escort you myself. I will be at your disposal, no matter the time or day."

"And if I don't?"

Aunt Rose gasped and dropped her fork. As it clanked around on her plate, she dabbed her face with her handkerchief.

"I don't mean to be rude, Aunt Rose; but really, I can't accept this. I was raised in the Territory. You know—Indians, rattlesnakes, bad guys. I can handle whatever may come my way."

Aunt Rose stood up with a jolt. Her robust thighs hit the table so hard, the crystal candlesticks rocked to and fro, almost falling over into the cooked carrots and green salad. "Well, I nevah . . ." she said with a huff. "You'd put our entire family in jeopardy because you considah yourself such a 'man'? Ryan, take me to my room. I feel faint." She turned toward the stairs.

"Hope you get to feelin' better soon, Aunt Rose," he called after her. Ryan glared at him, but kept his mouth shut. Pushing away from the dinner table, Charlie knew he'd crossed over an invisible line. There'd be no more talk of him being family now.

26

MOONLIGHT LAID A MILKY, WHITE PATH straight to Rachel's and Jonathan's house. It was another late night, but it had been almost a week since Charlie had checked on Jonathan. Knocking softly, he put his face close to the door. "It's me, Rachel. Its Charlie."

The door squeaked open a crack. The woman's dark eyes peered at him. "Ya 'lone?" she whispered.

"Yes, I'm alone."

Stepping back, she opened the door wide enough for him to enter. "Din' want nobody else tryin' to come in." Her eyes briefly searched the darkness behind him.

Charlie hurried to Jonathan's side as Rachel bolted the door.

"How're ya doin', Jonathan?" he whispered.

"Betta. Rachel's a good nuhse."

"He been up some," said Rachel, setting the coffee pot on the stove. "Walked hissef to the outhouse," she offered proudly.

"Good." Charlie nodded. "Things are bein' taken care of around here, so you concentrate on gettin' better."

Jonathan nodded slightly. "Need ta work, though," he muttered. "No work, no pay."

Charlie leaned in close to his friend. "Jonathan," he whispered. "Please don't worry about things like that. God will provide. He always does."

Jonathan closed his eyes and sighed heavily. "Yo' right, Chahlie. God'll take care of us."

Charlie got up. "Get some rest, both of you."

"Don' want no coffee, Chahlie?" asked Rachel.

"No, thank you," he replied. "I've got to make sure I don't put you two in harm's way again. I know Ryan will be watching every move I make now, so I better go."

"I talk to ya at brickfas in da mornin'," whispered Rachel.

Charlie nodded and went to the door. Placing his hand on the handle, he turned and gave Rachel a kiss on the forehead. "Let me know whatever Ryan says or does," he said quietly.

Rachel looked up and nodded. Her face was changed. The fear that had dimmed her eyes for so long was gone. It had been replaced with something else. Walking back to the house, he figured out what he'd seen on Rachel's face. It was hope. Surely that was something she hadn't felt in a long time.

Without a sound he shut the kitchen door and stepped noiselessly across the floor. When he reached the swinging door that led to the hallway, he heard voices coming from the direction of the foyer. He inched his way into the hallway so he could hear what they were saying.

"Take him to the hunter's shack on the other side of the river."

"You mean Ra- . . . um, that ol' house over by Whistler's Holler?"

"Yeah, you know of any other hunter's shack close by?"

"Um, no boss, just that one, but it's twenty miles away."

"Is that a problem?"

"Uh, no problem."

"Didn't think so. I don't want him anywhere near this house, so tie him up and take him up there. Make sure those ropes are good 'n tight too. We can't risk him gettin' away."

"When do you want me to do this, boss?"

"The earlier, the better."

"Tomorrow?"

"Find the right time and place. Remember, no one can see you or hear him, or we're both dead men. Kidnapping is a federal offense, and we'll hang if we get caught."

"Won't get caught, boss. I've done this before."

"Good. Now get outta here."

"Tomorrow it is, then. I'll be gone for a few days, totin' him all the way to Whistler's Holler."

"I know, now get!"

"Yes, sir."

Charlie pressed his body into a dark doorway and watched as Lonnie clomped past him. He waited until he heard the back door slam shut. Ryan had already gone up to his room. The creaky stairs had given him away. Charlie slipped into the living room and plunked down into Aunt Rose's chair. He spoke softly to himself, "Guess I'm gonna get kidnapped tomorrow. Better make sure my gun's loaded and ready . . . Don't want to—"

"Chahlie," came a tiny, desperate cry. "Chahlie, help me."

Charlie raised himself up from the chair. He closed his eyes and concentrated on listening. "Where are you?" he whispered. "*Who* are you?"

"I'm right here, boy. . . . I'm scared. I've been here for so long. I don't know if I can—"

"Can what?"

No response. The voice was gone.

He scanned the dark room in frustration. "Lord," he pleaded softly. "Help me get through one thing at a time, okay? Everyone seems to be in danger around here." He watched for the owner of the voice a while, but saw no one. Finally he crept back up to his room, careful to skip each creaky stair. He had a few things to put in order before he got kidnapped the next day.

Rachel slid a cup of coffee over to him as he pulled a stool out from the kitchen island and sat down to breakfast. "How's Jonathan?" he asked, blowing on the hot brew.

She hesitated a moment then smiled weakly. "He be fine," she mumbled.

Charlie set the cup down and focused on her face. She was tired. The sparkling eyes he had seen the night before were now dull and lifeless. Her cheeks were sunken and sallow. He reached over and took her hand. "Rachel," he whispered. "What is it?"

The woman looked over the counter at him. Her eyes quickly filled with tears. "It'd be his back, Chahlie. It be swollen awful bad. He can't hardly move, an he be burnin' wid fevah. Po' man."

"That happened mighty fast, didn't it?" asked Charlie. "He seemed fine last night."

"I know," she murmured. "He din tell me he was a' hurtin' till early dis mornin'."

"How bad are the wounds?"

Rachel lowered her eyes. "His back be infected real bad. Ah'm thinkin' he could die, with the fevah and all."

"I'll go check on him."

She pulled her apron up to her face and wiped her eyes. "I 'preciate dat, Chahlie. I be doin' what I can, but it ain't enuf."

He gulped down his coffee and handed the cup back to her. "Don't worry, Rachel. Keep prayin', but don't worry. Jonathan'll be fine."

Rachel nodded. "Okay."

The sun seemed to be struggling to get above the horizon. A few dark clouds still hung low to the earth, refusing to retreat. Charlie doubted if they'd run from a pale sun. Rain was coming.

He opened the cabin door slowly. Peeking inside, he saw Jonathan's limp body lying across the bed. He couldn't tell if the man was asleep or just trying to stifle the pain.

Closing the door quietly, he approached the bed. "Jonathan," he whispered. "You awake?"

"I am," came the feeble reply. "Jus' barely alive."

Charlie felt Jonathan's forehead. "You're burnin' up, man."

Jonathan shuddered. "Like ice."

"Mind if I take a look at your back?"

Jonathan took a deep breath and held it for a few seconds. Exhaling slowly, he rolled over to his side, just enough for Charlie to see his bare back. The stench hit Charlie square in the face and almost knocked him off his feet. Jonathan's back was a mass of rotting, puss-oozing flesh.

Charlie shook his head. "Jonathan, I'm gonna have to open these wounds and drain the infection."

"I know," he groaned. "Do what ya can, but I don' want Rachel in here when ya do it."

"How 'bout right now," said Charlie. "We shouldn't wait any longer."

"Awlright. What I need t' do?"

"Carefully roll over onto your stomach and relax," replied Charlie. "It won't take long, but it's gonna hurt."

"Can't hurt worse than it do now." Jonathan rolled over while Charlie pushed the blankets down around his legs.

"You rest now, while I put water on to boil. Then I'll go get some garlic, whiskey, and red peppers from the kitchen."

"Gahlic, whiskey, and red peppahs? Ya fixin' to make supper, too?"

Charlie chuckled. "No, my friend, it's for your back. It's an old Indian remedy my grandpa taught me. The red pepper will help ease the pain when I drain these wounds. It'll burn at first, when I rub it on your back, but after a while, you shouldn't feel much of anything. I'll use the whiskey to clean the wounds once I get the puss out. I have to warn you though—it's gonna burn like fire when I pour that stuff on those gashes. But I guarantee, when I'm done they'll be clean. As for the garlic, it'll keep infection from comin' back. Rachel will have to clean the garlic mud out once a day, but that's not hard to do. "

Jonathan caught his breath and shuddered in pain. "Like I say'd afore, ya jus' do what evah ya have ta do. I'll manage."

Charlie put a pan of water on the stove. "I'll be right back, Jonathan," he said from the doorway. "I'm going to beg those things from Rachel, and then we'll get started."

"Uh huh."

On the way back to the house, Charlie paused at the barn doors and scanned the stalls before going in. "Miller," he shouted. "Miller, you in here?"

Lonnie stepped out from behind a wall. He'd already palmed his gun and it was pointed at Charlie's chest. "No, he's not. But that's okay, 'cause you're leavin' anyway."

He didn't expect to see Lonnie. He'd forgotten about the kidnapping and had let his guard down. "Listen, Lonnie," he began.

"No, you listen, Mr. Smith. You and me are gonna take a ride. The horses are ready, you're here, and I see no reason why we can't be on our way."

"But Jonathan needs my help. I've got to—"

"Rachel will take care of him," said Lonnie impatiently. "You're coming with me, and now."

"But he could die."

"So?" replied Lonnie. "Mr. Ryan can replace him. In fact, that Miller fella is doing a great job, so old Jonathan won't be missed."

Charlie turned red with anger. "Why, you can't—"

Lonnie cocked his pistol. "Hold it right there, mister, or you'll get it right in the heart," he warned.

Charlie froze, seething with fury.

"I can and I am," Lonnie added. "Get on your horse!"

Charlie reluctantly climbed up onto Star. He was anxious to get back to Jonathan, but he had to be careful. He couldn't do much for his friend as a dead man. Lonnie made him lead as they left the barn. "Lord, take care of Jonathan," he whispered.

He wasn't sure where they were going, but after studying the sky, he decided it wasn't the kidnapping that bothered him the most. It was the storm that was brewing on the horizon.

27

LIGHTNING CRACKED OPEN THE GRAY SKY and hit the ground in a deafening explosion.

Star jumped and tried to bolt, but Charlie held him steady. Watching the swirling clouds, Charlie talked softly and patted the horse's neck, but he couldn't help but frown. The crystal blue sky had become an ugly green mass.

The clouds had turned from pillows of fluff into a sinister, churning brew. Thin, green fingers jutted out of the darkness and pointed downward, toward the earth, as if they wanted to escape the swirling frenzy, only to be pulled back up and thrown into the twisted dance again. Charlie had never seen the sky look so strange. And worse, whatever was coming was coming fast.

"Lord, help us," he prayed. "Please protect us. I'm not sure what's headin' this way, but it doesn't look good."

"What?" yelled Lonnie over the drumming of thunder.

"Nothin'," shouted Charlie. "We need to find shelter. That storm looks deadly."

"We'll find shelter soon enough. Just keep movin'."

Thunder grumbled above their heads. Lightning cracked, releasing a torrent of hail. Charlie pulled Star up under a tree and watched as the ice balls ripped through the landscape and bounced across the ground. He didn't like the accommodations, but it was better than being out in the open.

Lonnie drew up beside him. "Ever see anything like this before?" yelled Charlie.

"Yep," shouted Lonnie. "It ain't good, either."

"Why—what is it?"

"Right now, just a bad storm; but by the look of those clouds, the way they're movin', it could turn into a twister."

"Twister?" hollered Charlie, fighting Star to stay still. "What'll we do?"

Lonnie seemed to think for a minute. "Listen," he barked. "There's an old soddie, a dugout in the side of a hill, about a half mile from here. I'll have to lead the way—but don't you run! The worse thing you could do is run and get caught out here. If that mess turns into a twister, which it could any minute now, you'd never live to tell about it."

"Don't worry," yelled Charlie. "I'll be right behind you."

"Ready then?"

Charlie nodded.

"Let's go," shouted Lonnie. They turned their horses, darted out from under the tree, and raced across the prairie.

Halfway to the dugout, the hail stopped. An eerie calm surrounded them. The sky still swirled, but there was no noise. Leaves and fallen branches dotted the landscape as far as Charlie could see. He was grateful the hail had stopped and wondered if the worst was over, but within seconds he realized he'd eased up too soon. Behind him, a deafening roar erupted from the stillness.

Lonnie swung his horse into the face of a small hill and disappeared. Charlie didn't have time to figure it out, he just followed.

In the dark retreat, he sat still until his eyes adjusted to the darkness. "Is this a cave?" he asked, breathlessly.

Lonnie jumped from his horse and dug around in a saddle bag. "No," he replied, lighting a candle. "It's a dugout. Indians used them when they migrated. Sometimes the early settlers used them as temporary homes during the winter months while they passed through on their way west."

"It's big," said Charlie, looking around.

"And safe," said Lonnie. "Hear that?"

Charlie heard it. The roaring noise was getting closer. Thunder boomed across the sky. "Tornado?" he asked.

Lonnie latched what was left of a rickety door. "Better get the horses settled in," he said. "Once this thing passes, we'll need to collect some firewood, if there's any left."

Charlie took off Star's saddle and bridle and picketed him to a small patch of grass that he found deep within the dugout. Amazingly, the horse seemed to forget all about the storm and started to eat. Lonnie's horse edged his way over and joined him.

The ground shook under their feet. Wind wailed past the door of their haven and clumps of dirt fell from the ceiling. Something thumped against the door. Then another. Charlie followed Lonnie's example and sat down against an inner wall. They curled their bodies into tight balls and covered their heads with their arms. None too soon either. The world outside the dugout was soon swallowed by the roaring monster.

The horses stopped eating. Holding their heads high, they rolled their ears forward and started to prance about anxiously. Charlie tried to talk to Star, but his words were lost in the rushing wind. He wanted to jump up and calm him, but decided to stay hunkered next to Lonnie. No telling what was going to happen. Seconds turned into minutes.

The twister seemed to camp right on top of them. The hill shook violently. All sorts of things banged against the door, or what was left of it. They could hear trees cracking beneath the power of the wind. It seemed to grab the very air they breathed and wrench it from their lungs.

Then, as quickly as the tornado had ravaged the prairie, it was gone. They slowly raised their heads and listened. When they thought it safe, they carefully made their way out of the dugout and out onto the hillside. From there they watched a giant, swirling finger slide across the landscape, cutting a wide swathe through the prairie. Charlie was amazed at the power of the storm; it was plucking cottonwoods from the ground as easily as he would pick a wildflower. He wasn't sure, but he thought he saw a cow fly through the air.

"Incredible." He sighed.

Lonnie looked around. "Well, looks like we'll be campin' here for the night. Go get firewood. Don't stray too far, though. Some of these trees are pulled up or broken, they just haven't fallen yet."

"Why can't we just go back to the house?" asked Charlie. "I don't know why Ryan wanted you to bring me out here, but it's—"

Lonnie rounded on Charlie. "You heard our plan?"

"Yep," answered Charlie. "And it's ridiculous. What's the purpose? I mean, folks are gonna notice I'm gone, and what will Ryan tell them? They're sure to suspect him, and you, when you turn up missing."

Lonnie looked around nervously. "Just help me pick up some of these branches. We aren't gonna go back because, well, for one reason, you don't go traipsing out and about right after a tornado. Gotta give nature time to heal itself. The other we'll talk about later."

Charlie opened his mouth to protest, but his words were cut off by the creaking of a tree. Just a few yards away, a large cottonwood slammed to the earth.

He looked at Lonnie with round eyes. "Okay. You're the boss."

When the storm rolled out, it had taken the late summer's warmth with it, leaving a chilly night in its wake. The fire inside the dugout was comfortable, and thankfully, Lonnie had enough foresight to pack some food.

Charlie huddled against the sod wall, a warm bowl of stew held close to his chest. "Mind if we talk about the purpose of this adventure, now?" he asked, raising the spoon to his mouth and blowing on it.

Lonnie was already chomping away. "When I'm good and ready," he snorted.

Charlie snickered and blew on another spoonful. "Listen, Lonnie. I know you're not as tough as you want me to think you are, so why don't we just sit here, enjoy our supper, and talk like two men."

"Why you little whipper-snapper! I could shoot you right now and not think twice about it."

"Really? Then why were you so concerned about me runnin' and gettin' killed by that twister? Sure, you warned me not to run—because of what that twister could've done to me, not because I'm your prisoner."

"I coulda cared less about you gettin' hurt in that storm," scoffed Lonnie. "You'd 'a been stupid to try. I'm more scared of Ryan—"

"I know," Charlie said.

"That's not what I meant," replied Lonnie. "I ain't afraid of him. He's tough an' all, but—"

In Green Pastures

"Then why do you want to be like him? He's a ruthless outlaw, but that isn't in you."

"You don't know me," Lonnie replied tersely. "Why I could—"

Charlie tossed his bowl down on the earthen floor. "Then do it!" he said impatiently. "Shoot me."

Lonnie tossed his bowl aside and whipped out his pistol. "I just might," he said, grinning. "But then I couldn't torture you into signing away your legal rights, and Ryan would have my hide."

Charlie nodded. "I see. Ryan wants what cousin Ralph left to us. That's why you were in Colorado a few months back . . . to kill Grandpa so he wouldn't inherit Ralph's fortune."

"Now you're gettin' the picture," Lonnie replied, a wicked smile sliding across his face.

Charlie closed his eyes. It took everything he had to keep from jumping up and beating the man. "How do you know Trevor Cassidy?" he asked.

"Trevor Cassidy?" Lonnie picked his bowl up and raked a spoonful of food into his mouth, frowning. "Oh, you mean Big T."

Charlie nodded.

"He was my boss, temporarily. I wanted to blend in when I was in Denver, so I asked Big T to hire me on as a cowpuncher. I couldn't believe my luck when I heard him fussin' about you one night. Now, he was drunk, but still, he was awful mean towards you. And when I told him that I could take care of you and that old man, he jumped at the chance to let someone else do his dirty work. Later on, he let me know that ol' Smith didn't die, but had recovered from my bushwhackin'. Needless to say, he wasn't happy about that, but I promised him and

Ryan too, that I'd take care of you when the time was right."

Charlie raised his eyebrows. "And then I come out here and fall right into your hands."

"Yep."

"So, what's your take? How much of my inheritance has Ryan promised you?"

Lonnie shifted his weight. He glanced nervously around the bunker. "Well, he promised he'd give me a stake, once the job was done. He didn't mention a specific amount, but he said he'd set me up."

"And you trust him? What if he lets you do all the dirty work and then decides to take you out of the picture? More for him, ya know."

Lonnie glared at Charlie. "Ryan wouldn't do that. Took me in when no one else would. He's the best boss I've ever had."

"He's a mean, selfish, gun-totin' outlaw, Lonnie. Why, he'd kill you without thinking twice about it. Threatens you all the time, doesn't he? He only took you in 'cause he needed a gopher and you were willing to take on the role."

Lonnie frowned. He got up and walked out of the dugout. Charlie followed him. "Listen, Lonnie. I know someone who will treat you better than a brother. He'll take care of you without asking you to rob or steal for him. He'll provide for you, and give you your fair share of all he owns. More, actually."

Lonnie lit a cigarette and blew a ring of smoke out into the darkness. "That hombre don't live in these parts," he said quietly. "If he does, he don't hire much."

"He does live in these parts," stated Charlie. "And he takes in folks all the time."

Lonnie flicked ashes from the cigarette. "Who is he, then? I been in these parts goin' on thirty years and I've never heard of a boss like that around here. If I had, I'd a' checked him out a long time ago."

Charlie smiled. "I can introduce you to him right now."

Lonnie straightened up and threw a quizzical look at Charlie. "What in the world are you talkin' about?"

Charlie pulled a small, worn Bible from his hip pocket and stepped closer to the man. "Come on in by the fire, so we can see the words better."

"Now wait a minute." Lonnie groaned and waved Charlie off. "If I'd a knowed you were talkin' about God, I'd—"

"Why?" interrupted Charlie. "Does it make a difference that He isn't flesh and blood now? He's real nonetheless, and loves you more than any human boss ever could. He definitely cares more for you than Ryan does."

Lonnie blinked hard. "I don't know," he said slowly. "It's been a long time since I've even given God a second thought. My ma used to take us to church all the time. She was a good Christian woman. I was just a bad egg." He kicked at the dirt and took another pull on his cigarette.

"You're right about Ryan, though," he continued. "He is one mean bugger. I do take care of the dirty work, but I've seen him shoot . . . Well, never mind. I never left him 'cause I didn't know where else to go."

"Anywhere would be better," murmured Charlie.

Lonnie threw him an angry look. "That's easy for you to say," he snorted. "You've always had a home, someone to love you and take care of you. I've been on the streets since I was fifteen. I've always been an outsider—a gopher, as you call it."

"You can have a home now," urged Charlie.

"Listen, I just can't go bargin' in and act like me and God have been best friends after all these years. I've done some pretty bad stuff. I wouldn't even know where to start lookin' for him or what to say if I found him. And I'd still need a job."

Charlie had been watching the man as he talked. "Mind if I tell you a story?"

"Suit yerself. But let's get the horses inside first. It's gettin' a bit nippy out here."

Charlie agreed and left to retrieve Star from the prairie. Jess came up along side of him. "Nice job at holding your temper back in the dugout," he said. "I know it took a lot of inner strength to keep from pummeling that man after finding out he's the one who almost killed your grandpa last fall."

"I wanted to," admitted Charlie. "But it wouldn't have done any good. Lonnie doesn't need a whippin', he needs the Lord."

"Good boy," said Jess.

Charlie got Star into the dugout and rubbed him down with handfuls of prairie grass. He pulled the saddle blanket back up over the horse's withers, just to make him feel a little more comfortable in the strange place. He then sat down by the fire across from Lonnie.

"Now," said Charlie. "I was about to tell you a story. From what I understand, you think you wouldn't know how to approach God if He was standing right in front of you, right?"

Lonnie leaned back and rested an elbow on his saddle. "That'd be about right."

Charlie leaned back onto his saddle, too. "Well, back in 1835, there was this young lady named Charlotte Elliott. She was visiting some friends over in London when, one night, these friends invited their preacher over for supper. While they were eating, the preacher looked over at her and out of the blue said, 'Miss Elliott, I hope you're a Christian?' Well, Miss Elliott didn't like this question at all. She didn't think her spiritual welfare was any of his business and told him so. He, being an English gentleman, apologized for offending her, but said he just liked to say a word for the Lord whenever he got the chance and that he hoped she too, would someday come to Christ."

Lonnie pulled a small tin out of his vest pocket and rolled another cigarette. Charlie went on with the story.

"Well sir, three weeks later, the preacher and Miss Elliott met at their friend's house again, and you know what Miss Elliott told that preacher?"

Lonnie looked up, his eyes wide. "What?"

"She told that preacher that ever since they met, when he told her that he hoped she would come to Christ, she'd been looking for Him. She wanted to meet Jesus, but she didn't know how she was supposed to approach Him."

Lonnie stared at Charlie. He'd forgotten to lick the paper and was spilling shredded tobacco all over his lap. "See, that's what I'm talking about," he murmured. "I wouldn't know either."

"Then I'll tell you what that preacher told her," said Charlie, the reflection of the camp fire gleaming in his eyes. "He told her to go to Him just as she was."

"Just as she was?" repeated Lonnie. "What's that mean?"

Charlie smiled. "To go to Jesus just as she was. It didn't matter what she'd done or not done in the past; what guilt she'd been carrying, or secrets that she thought no one knew. Jesus wanted her to come to Him just as she was. So, she did. She went to Him, right then and there, in the middle of her friend's living room, just as she was. And she found out that

He loved her, no matter what. A little while later, she wrote this song."

Charlie sat up and cleared his throat. In a strong baritone, he sang:

Just as I am, without one plea,
But that Thy blood was shed for me,
And that Thou bidd'st me, come to Thee,
Oh Lamb of God, I come! I come!
Just as I am, and waiting not,
To rid my soul of one dark blot,
And to Thee, whose blood can cleanse each spot,
Oh Lamb of God, I come! I come!
Just as I am, Thou wilt receive,
Wilt welcome, pardon, cleanse, relieve,
Because Thy promise I believe,
O Lamb of God, I come! I come!

Lonnie's head fell into the crook of his elbow. The fire crackled softly and once in a while, Lonnie sniffled. Charlie let him be for a few minutes, praying that the Holy Spirit would speak to his heart. Finally, Lonnie lifted his tear-stained face and searched Charlie's.

"That's all?" he whispered. "That's all I have to do, is be willin' to come to Him just like I am and He'll take me?"

"That's all," replied Charlie. He reached over and placed a hand on the man's quivering shoulder.

"I didn't think anyone wanted me," Lonnie sniffled. "No one but Ryan."

"And he only took you in to use you. He doesn't love you," replied Charlie. "God will take you just as you are, and love you forever."

In Green Pastures

In the damp sod of a forgotten dugout, Charlie watched a lost sinner kneel before God. No pomp and circumstance. No fancy prayer. Just a lonely old man seeking forgiveness, and acceptance. As Lonnie prayed, Charlie imagined his tears melting into the rich soil beneath their knees and mixing with those of folks who had used this bunker before them; perhaps a young pioneer mother crying out in the agony of childbirth; or the exhausted survivor of an Indian raid, shedding tears of anguish; or maybe a weary sojourner who found refuge here from a harsh winter storm. *Lonnie was such a traveler once,* thought Charlie. He was lost and alone, running from the snares of sin, seeking a refuge. Life's tempests had tossed him aside, but here in this dugout, he found the love his heart had so desperately craved.

On the edge of a storm, in a far off green pasture, Lonnie found all that he needed, all that he ever wanted, in Christ.

28

THE TWO MEN REINED IN THEIR HORSES ON a hill top. "We'll be back at the house in about an hour," said Lonnie. "Ryan isn't gonna like the change in plans."

"Let me worry about Ryan," replied Charlie. "How far is town?"

"About five miles that way. Why?"

"I've got to go into town for a couple of things, and I think I'll have a talk with the sheriff while I'm there. Just to be on the safe side. Stay here; I'll be back as soon as I can."

"Ryan really isn't gonna like that. What should I say if he sees me?"

"Tell him the truth. Tell him I'll be back any moment and he can talk to me."

Lonnie nodded. They turned and headed in opposite directions.

Charlie told the sheriff all that he'd witnessed at the ranch, including the results of Jonathan's beating. The sheriff took notes and agreed to come out to the ranch to check on things as soon as he could. Charlie didn't like the thought of what might happen before the law could get out there.

Leaving the jailhouse, Charlie stepped out onto the boardwalk and heard the shrill whistle of a train off in the distance. "Peterson," he whispered.

At the depot he anxiously watched passengers leaving the train, not knowing if he'd recognize the soldier who had traveled with him last summer. Peterson was a southerner, a lanky, wiry haired soldier at the time of the cattle drive.

In fact, it was Peterson who recognized Charlie first.

"Wow," said Charlie, shaking Peterson's hand. "You sure have changed." Peterson looked urbane in a suit and tie.

"What?" he said. "You mean I don't look like a dust covered, half drowned, buffalo soldier?"

Charlie laughed. "And you don't sound like one either."

"Well, you do." Peterson grinned, looking Charlie over. "A mite taller, but still covered in dirt and mud. Where've you been?"

Charlie looked down at his muddy boots, embarrassed. "I've been, um, distracted and didn't have time to clean up before I came into town. Sorry."

"Doesn't bother me if it doesn't bother you." Peterson chuckled. "We can still talk."

They left the train station and found the same restaurant where he had eaten lunch with Dixie and Rebecca a few days before. At Peterson's request, they were seated at a private table. Peterson got right down to Pinkerton business.

"I've been doing some investigating and have found some interesting things about your cousin, Ryan Smith. First, he's not legally your cousin." Charlie's eyebrows lifted as he lowered his coffee cup down to the table. "Ralph Smith never legally married Rose Gaitlin," added Peterson.

"But Ryan is Ralph's son. So married or not, Ryan would still be my—"

"If Ryan were Ralph's son," interjected Peterson. "But he isn't. He is Rose's son from a previous marriage. She used her son to blackmail Ralph."

Charlie sat upright. "Blackmail Ralph? How can you

blackmail someone with a story like that?"

"Easily. Ralph was an executive of the railroad. He'd worked hard through the years to earn and keep an honest reputation. Rose could've destroyed that in a matter of minutes just by claiming that Ryan was Ralph's son and Ralph had refused to take care of his own."

"This whole thing's built on fraud and lies. Poor Ralph."

"Yes, indeed," muttered Peterson. "But only circumstantially. He was very wealthy. And at first, it was just Rose who wanted his money. But the older Ryan got, the greedier he became. When Ralph died, Ryan wanted everything; but you and your grandfather, my friend, stood in his way."

Charlie looked up at Peterson, a hint of understanding in his eyes. "So that's why Ralph claimed he had no family in his will. Because he didn't."

"Exactly. Your grandfather was all he had."

Charlie lowered his eyes. "So Ralph got trapped in Rose's blackmailing scheme, didn't he?"

Peterson shook his head. "Not really. He took care of Rose and Ryan because he wanted to, not because he had to. He knew Ryan wasn't his, but he figured the little boy needed a man in his life. Ralph was a good man and treated Rose with respect. He decided to care for them because he could, and no one else would."

"But his reputation?"

"That didn't bother Ralph. He knew that the rumor mill would take care of itself. And it did. What Ralph didn't count on was how cold blooded Ryan would grow up to be. It seems none of Ralph's Christian ways rubbed off on Ryan." Peterson shook his head. "He took a lot from those two over the years, but finally Ralph had enough. After . . . well, after a while, he wouldn't have anything to do with either of them. He changed his will, leaving everything to his real family—your grandfather."

Charlie pulled a pocket watch from his vest. "Are you going to be around for a couple of days?" He glanced at the his watch.

"No, not really," answered Peterson. "I'm going out to the ranch to talk to Miller, then I've got to head back to Chicago for a briefing. Seems the governor of this fair state wants to put a few Pinkerton men on the tail of the James gang. I'd like to get a piece of that action if I can."

Charlie smiled, but didn't say anything.

"If you have any other questions about this situation, Miller will be able to answer them for you. He'll also share all the other interesting tidbits I was able to dig up."

Charlie desperately wanted to continue this conversation, but he knew a young lady over at the Saint Charles Inn was waiting for him. He'd have to talk to Miller later.

Rebecca was sitting alone in the hotel parlor. Her eyes sparkled when she saw Charlie come through the door, but as he approached her, the sparkle melted.

"I'm sorry, Rebecca. I know I look a mess. I've been off the ranch for awhile and haven't had the chance to get back there and clean up."

"Oh, it's all right," she said softly. "I thought you'd been hurt or something."

Charlie chuckled. "No, I was caught in a bad storm, but nothing to worry about."

Rebecca stood to her feet and picked up her silk bag. "Well, shall we go then?" she said with a smile.

Charlie's eyes rounded. "Go? Heavens, Becky, I can't let you be seen in public with me lookin' like this!"

"There's nothing wrong with the way you look, Charlie Smith. It's just a few smudges of dirt here and there. And besides, if I don't mind, then why should you?"

"Out of respect, Miss. I can't—"

"Then we'll sit outside," she interrupted. "I've been looking forward to this since you asked me a couple of days ago and I'm not going to let you back out now. If you refuse to go into the theatre with me, then I'll just have to sit outside with you."

"But—"

"No buts!"

"Fine," said Charlie with a grin. "Outside it is."

The couple found a bench in the town square across the street from the theatre. Several other couples were sitting on benches or blankets, all dressed up in their finest. Charlie felt grimy. He kept wiping the palm of his hands across his knees. He glanced at Rebecca out of the corner of his eye. She looked lovely in her summer gingham and lace, which made him feel even dirtier.

The doors of the theatre were open, and at 5:30 sharp, music began to float out to the square. Charlie forgot how filthy he was as sonnets flooded the air ... the most beautiful sounds he'd ever heard. One piece was a polka that made him tap his mud laden boot.

Rebecca raised her twinkling eyes to his. "Pardon me for being forward, but would you like to dance?" she whispered in his ear.

Charlie stopped tapping. The warmth of her breath on his neck sent chills down his spine. "Um, no, not really."

"You don't have to stop tapping your foot." She smiled. "I was just wondering."

Charlie smiled back awkwardly. "I was absent from school the day they taught dancing."

Rebecca laughed. "I could teach you."

Charlie looked around the park. "Out here?"

"Why not? The horses won't tell on you."

Charlie looked into her eyes. "Maybe next time," he said slowly. "I might take you up on your offer if I was dressed for the occasion, but I won't embarrass you on two counts."

They listened to the music a while longer, but finally Charlie excused himself. It was getting late and he still had to travel several miles back to the ranch. And he had no idea what he'd have to contend with once he got there.

They walked back towards the hotel in silence for a minute, but then Charlie boldly took Rebecca's hand and wrapped her arm in his. "Thank you for a lovely evening," he said. "I enjoyed every minute of it."

"Thank you for following through with it," she said happily. "You could've backed out once you got here, but you didn't, and I appreciate that."

At the hotel doors, Rebecca stood on her tiptoes and kissed his cheek.

Charlie looked down into her blue eyes. "I wouldn't have missed this evening for the world."

Her smile made her eyes dance. "Good night, Charlie."

He felt her arm leave his and he watched her go back into the hotel.

29

CHARLIE RODE PAST THE HOUSE AND UP THE lane where Miller and Lonnie waited at the barn doors. Relief spread across Lonnie's face.

"Wondered where you were," said Miller. "Things okay?"

Charlie swung his leg over and slid off the saddle. He glanced at Lonnie. "Couldn't be better," he said with a smile. "You tell 'im, Lonnie?"

Miller looked at Lonnie. "Tell me what?"

Lonnie shoved his hands into his pockets. "Charlie here shared a story with me, and explained how to come to God."

"Oh?" Miller took the reins from Charlie. "How's that?"

"Just as I am," replied Lonnie with certainty.

Miller smiled at the two of them. "Yep, that's how."

"You a Christian, Miller?" asked Lonnie.

Charlie chuckled. "He is! Very much so."

Miller nodded to Lonnie then led the horse to the barn.

"Well, now that I know you're back safe and sound, I think I'll call it a day. Haven't seen Ryan, but then again, he doesn't know I'm back, so he isn't lookin' for me." Lonnie sighed heavily. "So, I'll see you in the morning, that is, if Ryan doesn't see me first."

Charlie took his arm. "God is much bigger than Ryan, Lonnie. Don't worry about him. And, not that it's worth much, but I'm here, and so is Miller." Lonnie nodded. "You give a shout if you need us."

"I will. . . . Oh, I've got a question, Charlie."

"Yeah?"

"Why weren't you wearin' your gun yesterday? You knew I was gonna kidnap you. Why didn't you strap on iron?"

"I did." Charlie chuckled. "You just didn't see it."

Lonnie glanced at Charlie's waist. "Where? I don't see your gun belt."

"Guns don't have to be worn around the hips, Lonnie." In one fluid motion, Charlie extended his arm, and with a slight jerk, caught a small pistol in the palm of his hand. Before Lonnie knew what had happened, Charlie had it cocked, and pointed at his chest.

"What in tarnation?" The stunned man's eyes darted from Charlie's face to the gun and back. "You could've killed me any time," he gasped.

"I could've. But I don't pull iron unless I plan to use it."

Lonnie swallowed. "You're a good man, Charlie Smith."

"So are you, Lonnie."

Lonnie came close and inspected the tiny gun. "Where'd you get this thing?" he asked nervously.

"In town, when I first got here. The shopkeep said they're popular with the riverboat gamblers, but more and more folks are buyin' 'em to use . . . well, for emergencies."

"Coulda had my hide nailed to the wall," said Lonnie.

Pushing the derringer back up under his sleeve, Charlie looked toward the Hollands' cabin. "I better check on Jonathan," he said. "I hope he's okay."

"Well, I'm gonna go get a bite to eat and then turn in for the night. I doubt the Hollands would wanna see me, after what I did to Jonathan. I'll see you in the mornin'."

The two men went their separate ways. As Charlie approached the cabin, he heard laughter coming from inside.

He knocked lightly.

"C'mon in," called Rachel.

He opened the door and stepped into the room. To his surprise, Jonathan, Rachel, and Jess were sitting around the small table, drinking coffee.

Jess turned to Charlie and winked. Jonathan got up and gave him a hug. "Thank ya fer yo' help."

Charlie rocked back on his heels. "But I wasn't able to help. Lonnie . . . had an errand, and I—"

"But ya told me what ya were gonna do with de herbs, and I told Rachel. She fixed me right up, thanks to yo'."

"Den Missah Jess here rapped on our door dis mornin' and Jonathan been fine ever since," added Rachel.

"Thank you, Jess," said Charlie reverently.

"My pleasure," he answered, standing to his feet and hiking up his britches. "I'll let you folks catch up now."

"You don't have to leave 'cause I'm here," said Charlie.

"I'm not," assured Jess. "I've got some work to do, but I'll be around. You know that, Charlie."

Charlie nodded. "Yeah, I know."

On his way out Jess turned. "Oh, and before I forget, I brought some things for you. Left them in the barn with Miller. You might need them before too long."

"Okay," stammered Charlie, wondering what Jess had brought him. The big man closed the door and Rachel slid a steaming mug under Charlie's nose. He relaxed in a chair. He wasn't sure why, but he was happy to be back.

Next morning, Charlie had just sat down on a kitchen stool, ready to indulge in a strong, hot cup of coffee, when Ryan came bursting through the swinging door.

"Where's Lonnie?" he growled.

Rachel shrunk back against the cabinets, holding onto the edge of the counter to steady herself.

Charlie shrugged his shoulders. "Don't know," he said. "I haven't seen him since last night."

"Find 'im!" ordered Ryan.

Charlie took a long sip from his cup. Then putting it down, he looked up at Ryan. "I don't take orders from you, Ryan. You might be able to bully others around here, but not me. If you want Lonnie, you go find him."

Ryan's face turned crimson. Hatred glittered in his eyes. "We'll talk about this later," he said, gritting his teeth.

"No, I don't believe we will," said Charlie.

Ryan stomped across the kitchen to the back door. "And Ryan," added Charlie. "When you do find him, you better not harm him in any way, understand?"

Ryan swore and took a step forward, but Charlie was up before the older man could take another. "No need to mess up the kitchen, Ryan," he said icily. "But if you really want to take a swing at me, we could step outside."

Ryan hadn't expected this. He stepped back. "Later!"

"Whenever," answered Charlie.

Ryan spun on his heels and stormed out the back door.

Rachel pulled herself from the corner and slowly sat down on the other stool, holding her head in her shaking hands. "You all right?" Charlie asked.

"I can't believe ya talked to Missah Ryan like dat and he didn do nuttin' 'bout it," she said in a trembling voice. She slid her hands part way down her face, revealing her eyes, but still covering her mouth. "I just can't believe it."

Charlie laughed. "He's a smart man, Rachel."

Rachel gathered her apron and wiped her face. "Ya sure have whupped things up 'round here, Chahlie."

"How's Jonathan this morning?"

"Oh, he be just fine," she replied with a slight smile. Standing, she made sure her legs would hold her before she went back around the island to the stove. It wasn't long before she started to hum and flutter around the kitchen.

Charlie watched her flit from one cupboard to the next. "Rachel, may I ask you a strange question?"

"Sho," she replied, half interested.

"Is this house haunted?"

Rachel stopped where she stood. Slowly, she turned around. "Ya mean, do dis house have spirits?"

"Yeah. Is it haunted?"

Rachel stepped up to the island and leaned over toward Charlie. "Why?" she whispered. Her dark eyes filled with worry again. "Did ya see one?"

"Well, no, not actually. I mean, my first night here, I saw one of those gargoyle things looking at me through the living room window, but that was just Lonnie trying to scare me. But since then, I have heard something—or someone—that I've not been able to figure out."

Rachel started coughing so hard Charlie had to get up and slap her on the back. When she finally regained her composure, she tried to change the subject. "Dere ain't no spirits heah, Chahlie. Now, why don' ya go fine Missah Millah or Jonathan and hep them wi' the chores."

Charlie sat back down and picked up his cup. He wasn't going anywhere. "What do you know, Rachel?"

"Nuttin'." She flitted about the kitchen again.

"Rachel!"

She grabbed the counter to steady herself. "Yessuh?"

The fear in her eyes broke his heart. *These poor people*, he thought. *Pushed and bullied by Ryan for so long; they're scared out of their minds.* "I'm sorry, Rachel," he whispered. "I didn't mean to scare you." After being strong for so long, she now buried her face in Charlie's shoulder and whimpered.

"I'll figure things out myself. Don't you worry your lovely head about it. Now, I'll leave you to your kitchen. I need to go see Miller." He left her, no longer flitting, but slowly pulling bowls and spices out of the cupboards.

Out at the barn door he yelled, "Miller! You in here?"

"Yep," answered the familiar voice, "in the tack room."

In the tack room Charlie found the scout sitting on a hay bale with a big brown saddle straddling one knee and a towel draped over the other. With an oily rag he was polishing that saddle like there was no tomorrow. Without looking up, he asked, "How can I help you?"

"I saw Jess yesterday and he said he put some stuff in here for me. Would you know where he put it?"

"Yep." Looking the saddle over carefully, Miller spat on it and started rubbing again. "Last stall on the left."

"Thanks." Charlie left Miller to his chore.

Jess was right. It was just stuff. Rummaging through the crate Charlie found two old iron griddles, a worn out bear pelt, a few dried buffalo patties, some rope, and an old blanket. "What in the world?" he grumbled. Stepping out of the stall, Charlie called down the hall, "Miller, did Jess say what I'm supposed to do with this?"

"Not to me," Miller called back. "Said you'd know."

Charlie grimaced. "I've no idea." He packed it all back in the box. "Guess I'll figure it out."

On his way out, Charlie stopped at the tack room. "Think we could find a few minutes sometime to talk about what Peterson reported to you?"

Miller didn't look up. The tip of his tongue stuck out as he worked on the saddle. "Uh huh."

"Good. I'll check back later."

Angry voices grew louder as Charlie got closer to the bunkhouse. He stopped and listened.

"I don't care if Mary herself came and shook your hand," yelled Ryan. "You owe me. You'd be jobless and penniless, if not for me. I found you drunk and worthless and made something out of you, so don't sit there and tell me you can't do your job anymore. You owe me!"

"No need to call names," growled Lonnie. "Yeah, you made somethin' outta me all right. You made me into a lyin' thief. Why, practically a murderer too. But you know what? God didn't care about none of that. And I'm not like that anymore, Ryan. Once He took me in, He cleaned me up."

"I don't believe this," hollered Ryan. "You, goin' and gettin' religion. You of all people—"

"—needed it," finished Lonnie. "Yeah, me of all people needed to find, not religion, but Christ." Charlie heard shuffling and then footsteps coming toward the door.

"This will be the last task I'll ever ask you to do," Ryan said more quietly. "And it isn't going to hurt him, just scare him. Make sure when he goes out to take care of his horse tonight that he sees a ghost. I want him scared so bad he'll tear off this ranch and won't look back. He'll give it up if he doesn't want to live here, and I want him convinced that he doesn't want to live here. Understand?"

"But—"

"I'll not take no for an answer. I'll pay you handsomely for your troubles, and I promise, it'll be the last time I ask you to do anything for me."

Charlie ducked behind a tree just as the door swung open and Ryan stepped out onto the porch. He looked back into the dark bunkhouse. "You just make sure you scare 'im," said Ryan, "I'll take care of the rest."

Charlie stayed hidden until Ryan disappeared up the path to the main house. "What was that all about?" he asked as he walked through the door of the bunkhouse.

Lonnie was pacing. "You sure got a way of findin' things out," he said, shaking his head. Picking up his cigarette tin, he stared at it for a moment then set it back down on the table. "I'm supposed to scare the livin' daylights outta you tonight. Make you leave this place and never come back."

Charlie laughed. "How are you plannin' on doin' that?"

"Haven't figured that out yet." Lonnie grinned. "I might just draw you a picture of me when I was a young'n. Teeth missin', hair standin' straight on end. Believe me, that would scare anyone." The two men howled with laughter.

Charlie tried to catch his breath. "I don't know if Ryan would be convinced that I was scared if I was laughing."

"How 'bout if I throw a sheet over myself and climb up and down the stairs. Would you think it was a ghost?"

Charlie laughed again. "No," he said gulping in air. "I'd probably think you got caught up in the laundry."

"I give up," Lonnie said chuckling. "You got any ideas?"

Charlie stopped laughing. He glanced at Lonnie and smiled slyly. "As a matter of fact, I do. Here, grab a seat. This is what we're gonna do. . . ."

30

THE MOON GLEAMED THROUGH BRANCHES of the quivering oaks, casting eerie shadows across the lawn. Charlie had started a fire with some bark chips and the buffalo patties from Jess's box. Thick smoke swirled up into the inky sky. Lonnie helped him get ready behind the barn. "Sure am glad Jess let you in on what we were s'pose to do with all this," Lonnie said, eyeing the empty box. "I wouldn't 'a guessed in a million years what to use the griddles for."

Charlie nodded and threw the bear pelt over his shoulders. "Now, you go get Ryan," he said in a hushed voice. "I'll stay by the fire and get started."

"You'll be all right? Ryan's apt to get really mad."

"It's okay. We're just turnin' the tables on him. We'll catch him at somethin'. Go on now and get 'im."

Lonnie left and Charlie could hear him yelling something about a monster out by the barn. Charlie began making his own sounds—chanting the song he learned from the old Ute Indian, Nakima, at Grandpa's grave. He chuckled a little to himself realizing he probably sounded like a "screaming cat" but he let loose and really got into the wild-sounding chant. Then he also started the dance of the Bear. His voice, along with the smoke from the fire, soared upward. His feet stamped across the hard ground, as he bellowed out words in Cherokee.

He heard the two men bounding down the porch stairs. "I swear to Pete," Lonnie yelled. "I've never seen nothin' like it in all my days. I was out here tryin' to think of a ploy to scare

Smith, when this thing appeared outta nowhere."

Peeking from beneath the bear head, Charlie could see that Ryan was in a rotten mood. His face was red, even in the moonlight. He walked with deadly determination, the belt of his house robe flapping behind him as he stomped toward the fire.

"You better be sure it's a monster, Lonnie," he fussed. "'Cause I'll have your—" Ryan stopped in his tracks. "What in the . . . ?" The rest of his question floated on the breeze.

Lonnie's eyes widened with mock astonishment.

Ryan looked dazed. He just stood there and stared, as if not sure what to make of the dancing bear in front of him. Then, "Kill it," he hissed.

"What?"

Ryan's face, glowering in the campfire, held an evil smile. His lip was pulled back, exposing his teeth. His eyes reflected the flames. "Kill it, or I'll kill you," he snarled.

"Now wait a minute, boss. That there is—"

Ryan pulled a gun from his pocket and shot Lonnie in the chest. Before Charlie could react, Ryan shot him too. Both men fell.

Ryan's red eyes bulged. "Serves you right," he yelled. "You both deserved it."

At that moment Jess stepped out from the shadows, covered Ryan with a blanket and pinned him. The captive struggled and fought. "What's going on here?" he yelled. His muffled words fell back into his face.

"Quiet," said Jess calmly. "You'll survive. You're just going to spend the night in the barn with me. We'll have a nice long talk, and in the morning the sheriff will come and get you."

"Who are you?" Ryan cried. "Why are you doing this?"

"First question, my name is Jess. Second question, because you're a bad man, but I hope that changes in the course of the night."

Ryan stumbled. Jess picked him up and slung him over his shoulder. "Soon as we get to the barn," Jess told him, "I'll unwrap you. In the meantime, be still."

Miller ran to Lonnie. He was out cold. Charlie, wrapped inside the bear pelt, moaned. "Mmmm. Where am I?"

"Right where you landed," snorted Miller. He untangled Charlie from the hide and helped him up. "Now you know what all the stuff in the box was for," he said with a snicker. "Don't question ol' Jess. He knows what he's about."

Charlie rubbed his chest. It was already sore. He unbuttoned his shirt and untied the griddle that had been strapped to his chest. Holding it under the lantern, he found the bullet imbedded deep in the iron. "This old griddle saved my life," he whispered. "Let's hope it did the same for Lonnie."

Lonnie rolled over in the dirt and rubbed his head. "Good grief. I feel like I've been kicked by an elephant. Just can't figure out if it kicked me in the head or in the chest."

"Probably both," said Miller, offering a hand to help him up. "Your head hit the ground pretty hard when you fell."

"Mmm," moaned Lonnie. Standing, he rubbed the lump that was forming on the back of his head. "Shouldn't be broke though," he mumbled. "Too hard." His clumsy fingers had trouble untying the rope around his chest and his griddle slipped and fell, landing on his foot. "Dern!" he yelped, hopping around the yard. "I better get to bed before I kill myself!"

"Will you be all right for the night?" asked Miller, choking on a laugh.

"Yeah, I'll be all right," answered Lonnie. "I'll say good night now if you don't mind."

"Go on," said Charlie. "We'll meet up with the sheriff in the morning."

Miller and Charlie watched Lonnie limp across the yard toward the bunkhouse. "You go on too," said Charlie. "I'll be turnin' in soon myself, after I clean up here. I just hope Aunt Rose isn't wandering around the house lookin' for Ryan."

Miller grunted and picked up the bear hide. "You go," he said quietly. "I'll clean up here."

"No, thanks," said Charlie. "I'll clean this stuff up. Got the box right here."

Miller stamped out the fire while Charlie gathered the remainder of the items he used for the bear dance. Looking at the stuff piled in the box, he smiled. *Jess always knows*, he thought. The only thing missing was the old blanket. He'd collect that from Ryan in the morning, before they met with the sheriff.

The house was dark. Apparently, the ruckus outside hadn't awakened Aunt Rose. Charlie slipped inside the kitchen and took his boots off just as he did every night. He tiptoed down the hallway, hoping he'd make it up to his room without stirring up any more excitement; but just as he rounded the banister to go up the stairs, a movement in the living room caught his eye. Slowly, he turned his head. To his surprise, standing in front of the large picture window, was a tiny, old woman, dressed in a white, flowing gown.

Her long, silver hair lay softly on her fragile shoulders. Her face was pleasant but she looked scared. Her eyes were dark and her lips were thin, almost invisible. Charlie stood frozen to the first step, afraid to blink. The old woman, her translucent skin bathed in the moonlight, brought a boney finger to her lips. She then slowly pointed at the wall across from where she stood. Charlie's eyes followed her finger.

A boot slipped from his hand and hit the stair with a thud, then rolled to the wooden floor below. He watched it fall, as if in slow motion, but snatched it up quickly. He cast a quick glance up the stairs to make sure Aunt Rose wasn't stirring then looked back at the window. The old woman was gone.

He had taken his eyes off of her for only a second. Where could she have gone in that time? *Wait a minute*, he thought. *Ryan. How did Ryan do that? How did he produce something that looked so real? Reflections through the windows? Moonlight?* He walked over to the window and looked out.

She had pointed at the clock. Was she trying to tell him something about time? Time to leave? He scanned the room, hoping to see something he'd never noticed before, but there was nothing. No mirrors. No angled lamps. Nothing out of the ordinary. *Good job, Ryan. If I hadn't known of your plan to scare me silly, I may have run away and never looked back. She sure looked real.*

Charlie grabbed his boots and ran up the steps, hitting every squeaky board in the staircase.

31

CHARLIE RUBBED HIS BRUISED CHEST AS HE sat down in the kitchen. He was disappointed to see nothing on the stove; Rachel was nowhere in sight. He waited a while, drumming his fingers against the countertop. Several minutes passed, and still no Rachel. He got up and went outside. Off toward the barn, a small group of people were chatting excitedly. In the middle of them was Rachel. No one noticed Charlie approaching.

"He wanted me to kill Charlie," Lonnie was saying. "He ended up shooting both me and him. I can show you the bruise from the bullet." Lonnie began unbuttoning his shirt.

"That won't be necessary," said the sheriff. "I believe you. Good thing you two tied those griddles around your chests or you'd both be dead right now." The group made various sounds of agreement.

"Is anyone willing to press charges?" asked the sheriff.

No one said anything, but then Jonathan stepped up. "I will," he said firmly. "Dat man be a mean soul and need to be punished for his crimes. I'll put my mark on dat paper."

"Good. Deputy, please retrieve the prisoner from the barn. And Mr. Holland, if you'll just make your mark on this line, I'll start the process when I get back to town."

As he handed the paper to Jonathan, the sheriff saw Charlie. Apparently finished with the niceties, he offered no "good morning" or "hello," but said in a businesslike manner, "We might need your testimony at the trial, too, Mr. Smith."

Charlie nodded. "Just let me know when and where."

"It'll probably be next week. I'll check with the judge when I get back to town."

"I'll be there."

The deputy came out of the barn with a very tired, very angry Ryan in tow. His hair was disheveled, his face was covered in stubble, and his hands tied behind his back. He threw a look of pure hatred at the small group outside the barn before allowing the deputy to help him up onto his horse.

"Another one of my deputies will be out soon to gather up Miss Rose," said the lawman.

Rachel gasped and covered her mouth. "Not Miss Rose," she whispered. "She'll die in da jail."

"Miss Rose is as much a part of this as Mr. Ryan is," replied the sheriff.

"What about me?" Lonnie piped up. "I worked for Mr.—uh, for Ryan."

"No one here has charged you with anything, Lonnie," said the deputy. "Unless Mr. Smith wants to press charges for kidnapping?"

"Or Jonathan for da whuppin' dat he—" said Rachel.

"No, Rachel," Jonathan said, laying his hand on his wife's arm. "Missah Lonnie only done what Missah Ryan told 'im to do. I hold nuttin' agin him."

Lonnie stepped up to the Hollands. "I'm sorry for what I done," he said, taking his hat off and slowly turning it in his hands. "I hope the two of you can forgive me."

Rachel looked up into the cowhand's face, her dark eyes brimming with tears. "Jus as the good Lawd forgiven us, we forgive yo'," she whispered.

"How 'bout you, Mr. Smith?" asked the sheriff.

Everyone looked back at Charlie. "Well, let me see," he teased. The group started a noisy protest before he had a chance to defend himself. Smiling, he shook his head and firmly said, "No, sir. No charges. But with that one," he pointed to Ryan, "you can use the Judgment Tree."

Ryan went pale. "No," he shouted. "Not the tree!"

"Be quiet, Ryan!" demanded the sheriff. "We don't do things like that around here. You'll have a judge and a jury; the whole shebang.... Although," he added thoughtfully, "it would be easier if we could just take care of business...."

The group could hear Ryan whining all the way down the oak lined lane.

Rachel turned to the men. "Ready for some brikfas?" she asked pleasantly.

"You bet," said Miller. Charlie, Jonathan, and Lonnie didn't have to be asked twice either. They followed Rachel into the house and made themselves comfortable in her large, spotless kitchen.

Rachel had given the men their coffee and was pulling out utensils when the swinging door flew open. Aunt Rose burst into the kitchen, her robe billowing behind her. Her grey hair was short and unruly, not the long, soft curls she usually wore. She had no make-up, and her large eyes were seething with anger.

"What is the meaning of this?" she shouted. "Where is my son?"

Miller pushed his chair back and stood up. "He's gone into town, Rose. We're not sure when or if he'll be coming back."

"I saw him being hauled away by the sheriff," she said, her face turning darker with each word. "What have you worthless people done to him?"

"We've done nothin' but tell the truth, Miss Rose," said Lonnie. "You need to get ready for your own trip into town."

"Me?" she fumed. "What are you talking about, you drunken fool?"

Miller placed a hand on her portly shoulder. "Calm down," he said gently but firmly. Immediately her demeanor changed. "Now, sit down," he said, "and we'll tell you what's going on."

Rose obeyed without a word, blinking back tears as she looked up at Miller's face.

The scout sat down next to her. "Now, this is what happened...." Miller told her everything, starting with her blackmailing Ralph so many years ago. "He wasn't Ralph's baby was he, Rose?" asked Miller low and gentle.

"No," she admitted. "Ryan was ... someone else's." She started to cry and her voice intensified. "My husband left me with a newborn baby! I had nowhere to go but the saloon. I didn't know how to cook or sew. I had no choice.

"No one's talking about what you thought you had to do to survive, Rose," assured Miller. "They just don't understand how Ralph came into the picture."

Rose sniffled and blew her nose. "Ralph came into the saloon a few times to eat and meet with some other men. I met him there. He never drank or smoked, or ..." she lowered her eyes. "... or asked for my company. He had a reputation of being a good, honest man, and he had lots of money. I knew he'd take care of us." Her eyes darted around the room. "With him, I wouldn't have to work the line anymore and the women of this god-forsaken town would finally give me some respect. But most importantly, Ryan would be raised properly, with an education and all."

"You two never wed, though, did you?"

The woman's head drooped. "No," she said quietly. "Ralph knew Ryan wasn't his."

"So you are not Mrs. Smith?"

Rose hesitated a moment. "No," she admitted. "But Ralph never married. He swore he'd take care of us."

"Maybe because he feared your threat to ruin his reputation if he didn't," said Miller.

Although none of this was a surprise, Charlie hung on every word.

Rose began to cry again. "He stayed until . . ." she glanced at Charlie then broke into sobs. "He let us stay in the house, but he left and moved into town. He said he'd given all he was going to give to a family that wasn't his."

"Unbeknownst to you until just a year or so ago, when Ralph did leave, he immediately went into town and changed his will, didn't he?"

Rose nodded. "Yes. I got a letter from the attorney after Ralph died telling me of the changes. I didn't know what to do."

Lonnie turned to Charlie. "That's when Ryan sent me out west to take care of your grandpa, Charlie. I didn't know any better then. I'm sorry—"

Charlie held up a hand. "It's all right, Lonnie. Good things have come from both bad situations. God took care of everything."

Miller continued, filling Rose in on how they found out about Ryan's plan to have Charlie kidnapped and forced to turn over his estate. And when that plan didn't work, how he wanted to scare Charlie and then kill him when he was fleeing, and later Lonnie, just to be rid of him.

Lonnie jolted upright. "How'd you figure that out?" he

asked. "I didn't even know about that."

Miller grinned. "I have my ways, Lonnie." Facing Rose again, the scout explained where Ryan was and what charges were being held against him. "Kidnapping alone is a federal offense, punishable by hanging," said Miller. "But he also has murder, attempted murder, and a list of other crimes held against him."

"S . . . s . . . so why do I have to go in to town?" stammered Rose.

"Because you are an accessory to the crimes, Rose," he answered. "You knew what he was doing, but didn't stop him. In fact, sometimes you even helped him. Your punishment may not be as severe as what he'll get, but you will be tried and sentenced."

Rose buried her face in her hands. "I didn't mean to," she cried. "He would've killed me if I didn't do what he said."

Lonnie nodded slightly. "He probably would've," he said softly. "He's a bad hombre. I know I tried never to cross him."

"But there is one more thing that only you are accountable for," said Miller.

Rose lifted her head and looked at him with angry eyes. "And what is that? Haven't I gone through enough?"

Rachel squirmed in her seat. "Ah think I have to go to da outhouse. I be back."

"Sit, Rachel," Miller said firmly. "No one leaves until this is over."

Rachel sat back down. Jonathan patted her shoulder.

"What about Mrs. Worthington?" asked Miller.

Every drop of blood seemed to drain from Rose's round face. She glared at Rachel. "You told, didn't you? I knew I couldn't trust you. How dare you come into my home and—"

"She didn't say a word to anyone," interjected Miller. "We found out on our own."

"Who's Mrs. Worthington?" asked Charlie.

Miller looked unsure of how to answer the question at first, but eventually found his voice. "Well," he started. "Worthington was your mother's maiden name. Mrs. Worthington would be your maternal grandmother."

Charlie slowly got to his feet. "My grandmother? What does she have to do with my grandmother?" he asked, glaring at Rose.

Miller's answer was interrupted by a loud knock at the door. Jonathan shuffled over and answered it.

"Deputy Reynolds here to collect Mrs. Smith."

"C'mon in," said Jonathan, opening the door wide enough to let the deputy into the kitchen. "We just havin' a family meetin', dat's all."

Miller looked deep into Rose's eyes. "It's not too late for your soul, ma'am," he whispered.

Rose didn't respond, but got up and walked tall and straight towards the hallway. "I need to get dressed and collect a few things," she said.

"I help ya, ma'am," offered Rachel.

"No," snapped the old woman. "I need no help. And with men at every door, I can't escape now, can I? Allow me a few minutes of privacy."

"Yes, ma'am," said Rachel, sitting back down.

Rose left the kitchen with Deputy Reynolds on her heels.

"Now," said Charlie. "What about my grandmother?"

Miller stood up and started pacing. "Let me see," he mumbled. "Where to start?"

"The beginning!" said Charlie anxiously.

"It won't be easy for you."

"Just tell me the truth, that's all I ask," said Charlie.

Miller paced again. "Okay, Jonathan, go ahead."

Jonathan took Rachel's hand. "Well, I reckon I don' know how ta say it, but . . ."

Charlie edged closer to the black man. "Go on," he said. "I'm listenin'."

"Yo pappy din' die in no accident, Chahlie. He was kilt. Kilt by Ryan."

Lonnie squirmed in his seat. Clearing his throat, he looked nervously around the room. "It's the truth, Charlie. I saw 'im do it."

Charlie looked from Lonnie to Jonathan and stared until the room started to spin. He sat down heavily on his stool. "Ryan did what?" he mumbled.

"He murdered yo' pappy," Jonathan said again. "Shot 'im in cold blood one night when he be leavin' his office. Shot in da back, too. Din' even know—"

"Dat's enough, Jonathan," whispered Rachel.

Charlie didn't hear her. He was too busy trying to breathe. His heart was beating in his ears. He put his face in his hands, but the room was spinning so badly, he couldn't tell if he was even looking in the right direction.

There was Rachel—*Bless her*—helping him sit down. She told him he looked sick. He said no, he didn't feel . . . Then he threw up in the bucket that Rachel had thrust under his chin. Grabbing it, he stumbled to the door and out onto the stoop.

The breeze soothed his damp skin until his teeth started to chatter. Rachel threw a blanket around his shoulders and tried to get him back into the house, but he refused. He needed to be outside. He needed to find true north. Jess told him years ago that God's throne sat in the north and the North Star was a good reference point when wanting to kneel before the throne and speak to the Father. If there was ever a time he needed to seek God out for a face-to-face, it was now.

Lord, for almost sixteen years, I've been told that my pa died in an accident, but now I've been told it was murder. And the man that did it has been sleeping less than thirty feet away from me for the last two months.

Charlie stumbled further out into the yard and fell to his knees. He earnestly tried to pray, needing to feel God's embrace and assurance, but found he could not. He wanted to ask for forgiveness for the hatred that was boiling in his blood against the man who ended his pa's life, but he couldn't utter a word. And worse, he couldn't ask forgiveness for the anger he was feeling toward his grandfather for not telling him the truth about his pa's death in the first place. He could only lift his arms to the sky and let his heart cry out to the Lord, hoping that what he felt, what he wanted to say, was being carried to God's throne on angels' wings.

32

CHARLIE COLLAPSED IN THE GRASS, LYING there listening to the breath rush in and out of his chest. Sweat slid down the side of his face and dripped into the grass. A cool breeze swept over him. He listened as it played through the branches of the giant oaks. He rolled onto his back and opened his eyes; the trees swayed in a comforting, rocking motion.

"You'll be all right," whispered Jess.

Charlie turned. There was the mountain man lying close by, his big hands behind his head—gazing into the heavens.

"Let the Lord's peace flow over you," he said tenderly. "Just as if you were lyin' in a green pasture beside a cool stream."

"But Grandpa . . . lied to me. He said—"

"He wanted to protect you."

"I'm not protected now, am I?"

"Yes, you are."

"But why didn't Grandpa tell me the truth? We didn't keep secrets from each other."

"Because he knew this news would've scarred you for life. He knew there was a strong possibility of you growing up with a hate streak in your heart. Your only goal in life would've been to hunt down the man who killed your pa, and your life would've been wasted on revenge. But things have worked out, haven't they? There's no need to hate a man for the rest of your life, because you know God is going to deal with him. You don't have to."

"But—"

"'Vengeance is mine, says the Lord.'"

Charlie felt his body relax in the grass. He closed his eyes and imagined he was lying in the middle of a green pasture, its soft grass cool and comforting. Beside him, water flowed in a stream, ready to fill his cupped hand and quench his thirsty soul. Jess was right. God was in control. He still believed that.

He got up and strolled back to the kitchen. Although weak and exhausted, he was determined to hear Miller out.

"Go on," he said, resuming his seat. "Let's finish this." Rachel passed him a cup of coffee then left the room.

Miller picked up where Jonathan left off. "Ryan asked your father to be his attorney, but he refused. So Ryan killed him."

"Why'd he refuse?" asked Charlie feebly.

"Ryan needed legal protection because he double crossed some businessmen," continued Miller. "Once your pa realized what was going on, he refused to represent Ryan, and Ryan, figuring Theo knew too much, shot him to make sure he couldn't use what he knew against him."

"But isn't there some kind of agreement between attorney and client so's the information is kept secret?" asked Lonnie.

"Yes, there is," said Miller, "but because Theo refused to be Ryan's lawyer, there was no attorney/client relationship." Miller looked around the room. "We all know Ryan didn't trust anyone, but he thought Theo would at least fall for the 'we're family' plea. When he didn't, Ryan thought the only way out was to kill him."

Charlie set his cup down on the counter and brought his hands to his face.

"Your father was a very honorable man, Charlie," said Miller. "You have much to be proud of."

"I just wish I could've known him better."

Mysterious Ways

"You will someday," said Miller.

Charlie glanced at his friend and gave a weak smile.

"But let me continue," said Miller. "There's more."

Charlie picked up the coffee and took a gulp. "Go on," he said, wrapping his fingers around the cup.

"After your father was killed, your grandparents took you to Colorado to live with them, so you'd be safe. They tried to get your ma to come too. She planned to join you, but wanted to stay close to her ma for a while. Or that's what she wanted everyone to believe."

Charlie's head came up. His brows knit in confusion. "But that's impossible. My ma was already dead by then. She died giving birth to me three years before."

Miller looked at Charlie with compassion. "She did die in child birth, but not yours."

"What?" Charlie yelled, jumping to his feet. The stool clattered to the floor. He grabbed the counter. "I can't believe this! You're telling me my ma was alive when I went to live with my grandparents, and that she had another baby?"

Miller nodded. "I am."

Then Charlie remembered the dates on his mother's headstone. He thought the inscription had been a mistake, but apparently, it wasn't. She was alive for two more years after Charlie went away. "But why?" he mumbled aloud.

"After killing your pa, Ryan forced your ma to marry him."

"Forced her?"

"By threatening to kill all her family, including you, if she didn't marry him. That's when your grandparents came out here to get you. Your grandfather had heard that Anne was in some sort of trouble, so he hoped to take both of you away, but she wouldn't hear of it. She allowed him to take you, to make sure you were safe, but she stayed behind for fear of Ryan. Your grandparents didn't understand. They even blamed her for the death of your pa, thinking her selfish and uncaring. Now we know she stayed here to protect you, her parents, and everyone else she loved. She was led to believe he'd kill you all. We don't know whether Ryan would've followed through with his threat, but he had her scared enough to believe it."

"But to have a child with him," shuddered Lonnie. "He was pure evil to do that to a woman, wasn't he?"

Charlie wanted to get on Star and take off. It was this kind of stuff, not silly ghosts, that made him want to leave this place and never look back. But he felt too weak to stand.

"Ya doin' awright, Chahlie?" asked Jonathan. "Yo' awfully pale lookin'."

Charlie forced a smile. "Am I?" He looked at Miller and cleared his throat. "So, what you're telling me is, I have a sibling out there somewhere?" Miller and Jonathan nodded.

"Do you know where he or she is?" he asked, trying to remain calm.

"You have a half sister," said Miller.

Charlie swallowed hard and whispered, "I have a sister?"

"Yessuh," said Jonathan proudly.

Charlie squeezed his eyes, trying to soothe the dull ache that was growing behind them. "Where is she?"

"We're not sure yet," said Miller. "Peterson's working on that." Charlie had forgotten about Peterson. "And," continued Miller, "you have a living grandmother."

Charlie rounded on Miller. "I do?"

"Mrs. Worthington," replied Miller. "Your mother's mother. She's here."

"Where?" asked Charlie, looking around anxiously.

"Right here," said Rachel, pushing a wheel chair into the kitchen. In it sat a frail old woman. Her silver hair flowed gently down her shoulders, her green eyes danced with joy, and her face, although wrinkled with age, had a soft glow. It was the woman Charlie had seen in the living room the night before. She was real. He knelt in front of her and all he could say was, "Grandma?"

"Chahlie." She said his name in a weak, Southern drawl, then lifted a thin hand and caressed his cheek.

He recognized her voice immediately. "It was you calling for me in the night, wasn't it?"

She nodded. "Yes, it was I. I wanted you to find me, but I was afraid to tell you where I was hidden because of Ryan. For my own safety, Rachel hid me and has been taking care of me, but if I had to stay in that room much longer, I don't know what I would have done."

Charlie glanced up at Rachel. "What room?"

"The one under the staircase. It can be quite cozy, but—"

"How long have you been kept under there?"

"Months!" she replied. "See, we wanted Ryan to believe I was gone. Whether that meant dead or out East, it didn't matter. I just had to be gone or he'd have killed me."

"Why?" Charlie asked wearily.

"For his own selfish pleasure and ego. Rose wanted this house, and he was determined to get it, one way or the other."

"I don't know how much more I can take, Grandma. Why would Ryan want to kill you for this house?"

"Because Rose wanted it. No other reason."

Charlie looked confused. "But Rose said Ralph let her and Ryan live here, even after he moved into town."

The old lady chuckled. "This isn't the house that Ralph let

Rose live in. This isn't Ralph's house, it's mine. But Rose didn't want Ralph's house after he died. She had no money to buy something grander, so she thought she'd take mine. Ralph's is on the other side of the river. Ryan called it a hunter's shack."

"You mean that's where Ralph lived?" said Lonnie, totally amazed at what he was hearing.

"Yes, it was," answered the old woman. "He had all that money, but hardly spent any of it on himself. The debts he owed when he died were because of Rose, Ryan, and their bad business deals. When he died and these outlaws couldn't get his money to build themselves a mansion, they plotted to get rid of me and take over my ranch. They led my friends and folks in town to believe I sold it to them and left, or died. I'm not sure which story he spread around."

The old woman dabbed her forehead with her hanky. "Rachel hid me in my own home. She took the best care of me she could. But she was afraid that Ryan would find out, so I was banished from communicating with anyone." She squeezed Charlie's hand. "Until you came. You gave me hope."

"Rachel caught you talking to me one night, didn't she?" he asked, looking up at Rachel and smiling.

His grandmother smiled back. "She did, and gave me a good razzing for it too. But I knew she only did it because of her love for me." Rachel beamed from behind the wheelchair.

Charlie had been watching his grandmother finger her hanky when he remembered the one in his pocket. Carefully retrieving it, he asked, "Grandma, do you know whose this is?"

Mrs. Worthington took the old handkerchief and studied it. A light of recognition filled her eyes, and then tears.

"It was your mother's," she said softly. "E.A.S. was your mother. She preferred to go by her middle name, Anne, but her full name was Emily Anne Worthington. Then Smith when she married your father," she said looking up at Charlie. "My mother, her grandmother, made this for her as a wedding gift. Anne tucked it in the sleeve of her wedding dress when she walked down the aisle. How did you come by it, Chahlie?"

"I found it one night beside the grandfather clock. I didn't know how it got there, but I held on to it."

Mrs. Worthington handed it back to Charlie. "I don't know how it got there either, but keep it as a treasure. Something that once belonged to your mother."

"Grandma, the other night, when I saw you in the living room, what were you pointing at?"

"To the room under the stairs," she said wearily. "I was trying to tell you where I was hiding, but I was afraid to do or say too much because I knew Rose was still in the house. I saw Ryan leave with Lonnie, but Rose could've been just as deadly if she'd found me."

The old woman sighed heavily. "I'm very tired. Would you mind if I go lie down for a while?"

"Heavens no," replied Miller.

"Grandma," whispered Charlie.

"Nana," she corrected him. "That's what you called me before they took you away to Colorado. You were only three and couldn't quite pronounce 'grandma'."

Charlie leaned over and kissed her cheek. "Stay with me for a while, Nana," he whispered in her ear. "Sleep peacefully, but don't leave me yet."

She stared into his dark brown eyes and a tear formed in hers. "I promise I'll wake up. We have years to catch up on."

33

CHARLIE WHEELED HIS GRANDMOTHER TO the porch so they could watch the rising sun.

"I can walk," she fussed.

"I know," he said with a smile, "but I want you to be as comfortable as possible."

She turned her face eastward. "We always did have beautiful sunrises," she whispered, barely audible. "I'm so glad I get to see one again, before I go home to be with the Lord."

"But, Nana," said Charlie. "You don't know when—"

"It's close, Charlie," she said softly. "And that's all right. Because, it could be, the next time I see the sun rising, I will be in a new and glorious place." She turned her faded green eyes to Charlie and smiled faintly. "That's exciting, isn't it? To think, that just beyond that giant fireball in the sky, lies a new and glorious place. And I'm ready, Chahlie."

He knelt at her side and gently took her weathered hands in his. "Now that I've found you, I don't want to let you go, but if the Lord takes you home sometime soon, will you do me a favor, Nana? Will you tell our Lord that I love Him? I mean, tell him face-to-face. And then when you're done, will you find my Grandma Smith and both of my grandfathers and tell them I love them, too, and miss all of them terribly. And then my ma and pa, and—"

Nana chuckled softly. "Your list is going to keep me busy for most of eternity," she teased. "But I'll start the process until you join us, whenever that will be."

Charlie leaned over and kissed her soft, translucent cheek. "Thank you, Nana." She smiled warmly and patted his hand. A cool breeze skipped across the porch and she shuddered.

"It's getting colder." He tucked the blanket around her knees. "Would you like to go in now?"

"Yes. But I've one more piece of business to settle with you before we have breakfast. Please take me to the parlor."

He wheeled her into the house and over to the fireplace. Without moving, Nana pulled a palm-sized portrait from beneath her blanket. "I want you to have this, Chahlie," she said softly. "It isn't much, but it's all I have of her."

He leaned forward and reached for the picture. "What is it, Nana?" Taking it from her trembling fingers, he stopped smiling. Although the edges were worn from years of Nana's caresses, and a few ripples made by time ran across the image, he recognized the beautiful face and the bright, dancing eyes. He looked at his grandmother. A million questions ran through his head, each reflected on his face.

"I know her," he whispered.

"Of course you do, sweet boy. That's your mother. That picture is all I have of Emily Anne Worthington Smith."

"My mother?" he breathed, looking back down at the portrait. "How can that be? She is so young."

Nana sighed. "Yes. She was very young when she died. But she was beautiful wasn't she?"

Charlie went to the fireplace and rested his elbow on the mantle. He stared at the face in the picture. Then he looked back at this woman he barely knew, who claimed to be his grandmother. "Nana? Why didn't—"

"Chahlie, let me start over. That is a picture of your mother. I hid it from Ryan all these years because I knew he would take it from me if he got his hands on it. I didn't send it to you because I wasn't sure how your Grandpa Smith would feel, him faulting her for Teddy's death and all."

"I can't believe this is my mother," he said looking down at the picture. "She's so, so . . ."

"Lovely," said Nana. "We had that picture taken just before she died giving birth to your sister."

Her words pierced him like an arrow. He stumbled to the sofa and eased himself onto the arm before sliding down onto the cushions.

"My sister?" his voice cracked as he spoke. Then barely audibly he said, "*She's* my sister."

"Chahlie?" asked Nana. "You look terrible."

"Do I?"

"Didn't Mr. Miller tell you of your sister?"

"He did. But I had no idea that she looked—"

"Maybe we should continue this conversation later."

Remembering how she had just talked about death when they were on the porch, Charlie lifted his eyes and shook his head. "No, I want to hear more. Please, Nana!"

"Rachel!" the old woman called. "Rachel!"

Rachel rushed in, wiping her hands on her apron.

"Ma'am? What is it?"

The old woman pointed at Charlie.

"Why, he look like he just saw a ghost."

Charlie opened one eye and looked up at Rachel. The room stopped spinning. His heart was back in his chest. His ears returned to normal, and he heard himself laughing. "A ghost," he said. "I look like I've seen a ghost. Well, I'll be, if that isn't what I've seen." He took Rachel's head in both hands and kissed her forehead.

"Guess what, Rachel?" he said, grinning. "I have a sister."

"Well, course ya do. I was dere when she was born, same as yo'. Matter o' fact, since I was yo' mammie's nursemaid, I was da first to hold ya both."

Charlie went back to the sofa. "You delivered her, too?"

"Yep," said Rachel, proudly.

"Charlie, you still look sick. I think we've talked enough," said Nana. "Would you mind wheeling me into the dining room, Rachel?"

Rachel grabbed the back of the wheelchair.

"One more question before you leave, Nana," pleaded Charlie.

The old lady held up a withered hand, signaling for Rachel to stop. "Just one more." She smiled.

"Where is my sister?" he asked.

"That I can't tell you. When your mother died, the only thing the family believed we could do was place the baby up for adoption secretly. We certainly weren't going to leave her for Ryan to raise."

Rachel anxiously shifted her weight from one foot to the other. "'Member how mad he got when he find out 'bout dat? Why he ain't nevah been dat mad afore nor since."

Mrs. Worthington lifted a frail hand to her shoulder and patted Rachel's strong fingers. "It wasn't because we gave his child away, Rachel," she said strongly. "It was because we butted into his business. He probably could've made a bundle for her on the black market, but we interfered."

Rachel visibly shuddered. "Evil man," she whispered.

"Do you know the name of the family that adopted her?" Charlie leaned forward, waiting for an answer.

Nana eyed the young man curiously then sighed heavily.

"I'm afraid finding her will be impossible, Chahlie. It would cost far too much money, and heaven only knows where she is. Why, only God—"

"I apologize if I'm bein' rude, Nana, but the name? Do you remember the name?"

His grandmother dabbed her lips with her kerchief then looked up at the anxious young man. "I don't remember their names. He was studying at the University of Virginia. She was a foreigner, or taught a foreign language. I can't remember. They were a nice young couple. It was rather sad that she couldn't have children of her own, but they were willing to adopt. They fell in love with our baby girl the first time they saw her, but who wouldn't?" The old woman started trembling, raising her handkerchief to her lips. "They took our little girl and left. To Georgia, or maybe back to Virginia. I don't know."

Charlie slumped down into the sofa and rubbed his hands over his face. "I have a sister," he murmured. But Nana didn't hear. Rachel had already started to wheel her to the dining room.

34

THE TRIALS FOR ROSE AND RYAN GAITLIN were typical of those held for folks who were suspected of being guilty as charged. Ryan took his sentence for the murder of Charlie's pa the hardest. But then he would. It meant his life was over.

It had been almost sixteen years since Ryan killed Theodore Smith and he truly thought he'd gotten away with the crime. However, he learned in court that there was no statute of limitations for murder; no matter how many years went by, if one is caught, one will be tried. Because of Lonnie's eye-witness testimony, Ryan was found guilty of first degree murder and sentenced to hang. The other charges—including attempted murder, kidnapping, fraud, and extortion—weighed heavily with the jury, but once the judgment for murder was passed down, his case was all but closed.

The court didn't see fit to use the Judgment Tree. The judge ruled that the historic landmark was too old and he didn't want it damaged during the execution. So, the townsmen spent a hundred dollars and built a new gallows.

Rose cried during her trial, either because she was upset at being caught or because Ryan had laid the blame on her. Regardless, the judge and jury were unmoved. She was found to be an accomplice to many of Ryan's crimes, with the exception of the murder of Theodore Smith. Ryan alone stood guilty on that charge.

Several times during her trial she had pleaded with the

jury that what she'd done was for the sake of her child. But she found no sympathy. The judge, in fact, scolded her for dishonoring motherhood by using it as part of her defense. She was sentenced to life in the woman's prison in Saint Louis.

Nana, however, had found a new reason to live. With the arrival of Charlie, she changed her mind about giving up on this life so quickly. There was the possibility that he could find his sister; Nana's granddaughter. The thought of holding both her grandchildren in her arms before the good Lord called her home put a sparkle in her eye and hope in her heart.

Charlie was making plans to have Nana, Jonathan, Rachel, and Lonnie come to Denver for Thanksgiving. President Lincoln had declared a specific day in November as the national day of Thanksgiving, but Charlie and Grandpa had never observed it. Grandpa said he was thankful for God's blessings every day, and Charlie agreed then, but now he wanted to celebrate, to make new traditions with his remaining family. He hoped to have a special gift for Nana upon her arrival too.

On his trip back to Colorado, he read a newspaper article entitled, "Former Soldier Hanged on the Gallows." It saddened him to read of the trial and execution of Kerry McQueen. He read how Kansas City was in an uproar over losing the opportunity to try him for a murder he'd committed in their town before he enlisted in the army years before. He was tried in San Antonio first, and once they got ahold of him, the Texas court wouldn't let him go. He was executed within the week of that trial convening.

The last paragraph of the article related how, when McQueen was asked if he had any last words, he raised a defiant fist to the heavens and cursed God and his dad.

When he read it, Charlie hung his head and wept.

35

CHARLIE SLID OFF HIS HORSE AND THREW the reins over the hitching post in front of the Tuttles' cabin. Before he had got to the door, Wilbur stepped from around the side of the house and greeted him with a wide grin. "Hey Charlie. When did you get back?"

Charlie slapped him on the shoulder. "Just yesterday. Thought I'd drop by to see how things are goin'. I'm gonna be havin' some family in from the East for Thanksgiving and wanted to invite you to join us."

"That's sounds great, but I'll be headin' to my brother's house to see Ma and Pa. I think I'll be livin' with 'em."

"Really? What made you decide that?"

Wilbur looked down at his leg. "Can't do what needs to be done around here anymore." He sighed.

"Umm."

Wilbur jerked his head for Charlie to follow him around back. "Who's out East?" he asked. Charlie noticed he was limping.

"Folks I met over the summer," Charlie answered, thrusting his hands into his pockets. "My maternal grandmother, Jonathan and Rachel Holland, a man by the name of Lonnie Weaver, and, oh, a sister I never knew I had."

Wilbur stopped. "A sister?"

"It's a long story," said Charlie. "Why don't you come over for supper tonight and I'll tell you all about it. LeFaye wants to hear the details again, too."

Wilbur sat down on a log and grabbed his polishing rag. He swung a saddle onto his lap and spit on it. Round and round he rubbed the spittle into the old saddle, slowly bringing the worn leather back to life.

"Anything I can help you with here?" asked Charlie, looking at the pieces of tack strewn around the yard.

Wilbur shook his head. "Naw, just keepin' myself busy while I make plans of my own."

Charlie sat down in the grass in front of Wilbur and pulled on a dandelion. "Plans?"

Wilbur glanced at him then rubbed the saddle again. "Funniest thing. After you and LeFaye brought me home from Pueblo awhile back, I tried to keep my head on straight. I started workin' hard, doin' what I could around here to make honest money, but it never seemed to be enough. I wasn't able to make the payments on Pa's bank loan."

Charlie looked up. "Bank loan?"

Wilbur kept working. "Yep, don't know if you knew, but they had to mortgage the property to pay for Mary Lou's schoolin'. When she died, they gave back what they hadn't spent, but they still owed for what they had used, which was plenty. It isn't cheap gettin' a girl ready to go to school, then gettin' her there and settled. There's room and board, and books. Well, then Pa fell sick and couldn't work. I was doin' what I could, workin' at the post office and some other odd jobs, but it wore on me somethin' fierce."

Charlie nodded. "Yeah, I remember."

"Anyway," continued Wilbur. "I ended up on the wrong side of the law."

Charlie wrestled another dandelion.

"I thought I was tough enough to be an outlaw. Since

honest work didn't seem to pay, I went and joined up with this gang. The leader told me I'd be able to pay the loan off after my first holdup." Wilbur stopped shining the saddle. "Can you imagine? He told me it would be that easy, and I believed 'im."

Charlie stared back at Wilbur, unsure what to say. Finally, he asked, "Who was the leader?"

Wilbur blinked, then went back to working on the saddle. "Tom—"

"Howard," finished Charlie. "Also known as Jesse James."

Wilbur looked up, but avoided Charlie's eyes. "I was desperate, Charlie," he said softly. "I didn't know where to turn. Pa made sure no one knew of our debts. He didn't want charity from anyone and I felt the weight of tryin' to take care of everything on my shoulders."

"Grandpa used to say that charity is love, and we all should accept what is given in love."

Wilbur sat motionless. "You knew it was me the night of the train robbery, didn't you?"

"I suspected it, when I saw the hoof prints beside the tracks after the gang rode out. Your horse's back left hoof leaves a little deeper print than the other three, due to his bum left leg. Besides, I thought I saw you take the seat up ahead of me in the car, but I never saw your face." Charlie looked at Wilbur's leg. "Frank said the new guy hurt his leg real bad. Seein' you now walk with a limp just about sums it up."

Wilbur nodded. "Yeah. Broke it in two places jumpin' off the train. Doc says it'll be lame the rest of my life. I'll be able to work some on a farm, but not alone, so I'm gonna sell and move up to my brother's place with Ma and Pa."

"I'll hate to see you leave."

"Me too. Will you take the farm, Charlie?"

Charlie scanned the property. "In a heartbeat. How much do you want for it?"

"From you, not a dime."

"What? You've got to get somethin' for it."

"You've done enough. I've been to the bank, Charlie. I went in to plead my case to the bank manager, but he told me everything had been paid in full. I know it was you who did it." Wilbur shook his head. "There I was, ready to do a bad thing that would change my whole life, when my debt had already been paid."

"You need to learn to trust God, Wilbur. He'll always provide for you."

"You angry with me for ridin' with the James gang?"

Charlie stared off in the distance for a moment. "No, not angry," he finally replied. "But sorry. I'm sorry that you didn't feel like you could talk to me right from the beginning. And I feel like after all these years, I let you down. I'm sorry, Wilbur."

"Me, too," Wilbur mumbled. "But you didn't let me down, Charlie. You've always been there for me. It's like you say, I just need to learn to trust."

Charlie didn't say anything, but walked over to the cabin and looked in the window.

"By the way, I doubt if you know it, but Jesse actually saved both of our lives that night," said Wilbur.

"How do you reckon?"

"For me, he told me to go home. He didn't want me ridin' with 'im no more. Said I'd be a drag on the gang; and he reckoned I'd be safe enough. Neither the law nor the newspapers would be interested in a kid who only rode with him once and had nothin' to show for it but a busted up leg."

"Well, that was a mercy," Charlie exclaimed.

Wilbur went on. "With you, Frank was serious about shootin' you on the train. When he hit 'three', he was ready to pull the trigger, but it was Jesse who shot first, at Frank! He missed him on purpose, of course, but he did it so Frank would miss you."

"I wonder why he did that?"

"'Cause he liked you. You shoulda heard him and ol' Frank go at it back at camp. It got worse, too, when Frank learned that all they got out of the robbery was two necklaces and a couple silk purses."

Charlie grinned. "That was it?"

Wilbur nodded. "Jesse told us it wasn't meant to be a real robbery, just a test. It was his first attempt at robbin' a train and he just wanted to see how smoothly things would go. Of course, he didn't tell us that until it was over."

"What did he conclude?"

Wilbur shrugged. "Oh, he'll do it again. The world hasn't seen the last of Jesse James."

Charlie turned from the cabin. "Well, let me know when you're ready to draw up the papers for the farm. Right now, I'd best be goin'."

Wilbur set the saddle on the ground. "There is one other thing. While I was goin' through my stupid stage, I was awfully mean to you, and, well, I'm sorry."

"No need, Wilbur."

"Charlie, please. I need to get this out."

Charlie sat back down in the grass. "Okay. I'm listening."

"I was so angry back then." Wilbur rested his head in his hands. "I was angry at my sister for running out in front of a horse and gettin' herself killed. I mean, she was raised on a farm, for Pete's sake. She'd been around horses all her life." Wilbur slowed down. "And then I was angry at Pa for gettin' sick, and both Ma and Pa for leavin', and then at myself for resenting it all. I had a heap of 'poor me' goin' on."

Charlie nodded. "I know what that's like."

"But I was mostly angry at you."

Charlie looked up. "Me?"

Wilbur nodded. "Yeah, don't ask me why, 'cause I really don't know. I guess because it seems that whenever anything bad happens in your life, you know how to handle it. You pray and get answers to your prayers. You always seem to have peace when the world around you is fallin' apart."

"Oh, Wilbur," whispered Charlie. "If you only knew. There've been so many times I didn't have peace. And sometimes I feel like my prayers don't get above my head."

"But you can pray," insisted Wilbur. "You believe God listens and cares. I don't have that, and I want it. We went to church together all our lives and I've heard the same sermons you've heard, but I don't have what you have." Wilbur shook his head. "How can I have that kind of faith?"

Charlie stared at his friend.

Pulling the worn Bible from his hip pocket, Charlie slid closer to his friend. "It's so simple, Wilbur. All you have to do is come to Him, just as you are."

Wilbur lowered his head. "Will you pray with me?"

"Of course I will."

Acknowledgments

I give my Lord and Savior first acknowledgment. It is through His strength and guidance that I can continue to face life's challenges. The completion of this book and the continuation of the *Mysterious Ways* series is another testament to His grace and goodness in my life.

I would like to thank two dear friends who literally carried me into my Western journey, Socks and Tuscan. It is because of these horses that I was able to live my dream of being a cowgirl. Socks, a tall, sway back sorrel, taught me that animals do think, and they do have minds of their own. And Tuscan, who showed me that, despite my errors, animals are patient and forgiving as well as great teachers (and that I won't always need a ladder to climb up onto a horse. Some are "just right.") Although our adventures never took us past the high pasture, they taught me so much. For that I will be forever grateful. (And to their owner and trainer, Latigo, I hope you find these books a blessing.)

I thank my family, immediate and extended. Their prayers, never ending enthusiasm, and encouragement are such wonderful blessings. A special thanks to my father-in-law, Lon Gallup, who has supplied me with some wonderful historical documentation, and to my grandsons, Blaine and Brian. I love looking at the world through your eyes.

I will always be grateful to my mother and deceased father, Roberta and Mahlon Westover. The lessons they taught me are invaluable. The faith, inner strength, and sheer determination they instilled in me are beyond price.

To Char Wixson and Mel Hilgenberg. Thank you for donating your eyes and time to critique this work. I appreciate every comment, question, and suggestion.

And a very special thanks to my readers, without whom these books would be useless dust collectors. Thank you for reading them and recommending them to others.

About the Author

Donna Westover Gallup is a poet and musician. She is currently an employee and a student at Colorado State University, where she is working on a Bachelor of Arts degree in creative writing. She holds a Bachelor of Science degree in Business/Pre-Law from Liberty University and an M.B.A. from the University of Phoenix. Donna is the mother of three grown daughters and the grandmother of two wonderful boys, with another grandbaby due in 2010. She lives in Fort Collins with her two boxers, Harley and Cheyenne.

In her free time, Donna enjoys riding horses, visiting friends, and exploring parts of Colorado as research for future books. Her desire is to convey God's love through her writing.

GAL   **Gallup, Donna Westover, 1958-**

L m w   **In green pastures.**

Enjoy all the adventures of Charlie in the
Mysterious Ways frontier novels:

White as Snow

Rock of Refuge

In Green Pastures

&

The Crimson River (forthcoming)

Available from online retailers,
through your local bookstore,
or at the publisher's website: www.cladach.com.